THE TRAVELER SERIES - 2

WATCHER

NOLA NASH

Black Rose Writing | Texas

©2023 by Nola Nash

All rights reserved. No part of this book may be reproduced, stored in a retrieval system or transmitted in any form or by any means without the prior written permission of the publishers, except by a reviewer who may quote brief passages in a review to be printed in a newspaper, magazine or journal.

The author grants the final approval for this literary material.

First printing

This is a work of fiction. Names, characters, businesses, places, events, and incidents are either the products of the author's imagination or used in a fictitious manner. Any resemblance to actual persons, living or dead, or actual events is purely coincidental.

ISBN: 978-1-68513-327-6
PUBLISHED BY BLACK ROSE WRITING
www.blackrosewriting.com

Printed in the United States of America
Suggested Retail Price (SRP) $20.95

Watcher is printed in Garamond Premier Pro

*As a planet-friendly publisher, Black Rose Writing does its best to eliminate unnecessary waste to reduce paper usage and energy costs, while never compromising the reading experience. As a result, the final word count vs. page count may not meet common expectations.

DEDICATION

Life is a journey.
I dedicate this book to all those who have helped show me the way.
You're like my GPS, but cooler.

WATCHER

It is not in the stars to hold our destiny but in ourselves.
—William Shakespeare

CHAPTER 1

Chaos reigned where Athena once held court. Turquoise shimmered in the heat of pyres burning at the base of the Parthenon. White clouds dulled in the black smoke that drifted toward an indifferent sky above the trembling city. Screams and shouts replaced the rich chants of the priests and faithful. Swords clanged and blood spurted onto the gleaming marble floors. Bodies fell where penitents once knelt at the feet of the goddess.

Shelby Starling's hand instinctively went to the dull ache in her chest, the spot where Apollo's arrow struck as she dropped into the cavern light. Numb, she stood between massive marble columns on the temple porch in the middle of the battle trying to make sense of it all. Gone was the shimmering stone temple and the smiling face of her boss Dina. No. Oracle Dina. And Apollo. Where was he in all of this? Had he just left her here to figure out how to save Athens on her own? Surrounded by fighting, Shelby felt separate from it all. Seeing it, feeling it, but not part of it. Like a memory.

Looking down, she realized her white robe from the temple had been tucked and bound around her waist and shoulders with gold cording into the typical Athenian dress. A gentle breeze fluttered the hem at her ankles and the fabric billowed slightly. As the air swirled, it pressed the cloth against her legs, and she could see sandals on her feet. Shelby pushed back a thin strand of dark hair that blew across her eyes. Where loose waves had been during her purification ceremony in the temple at Delphi, intricate loops and braids now clung tightly to each other. Across her forehead, and worked into the braids around her head, was a thin band, cold and metallic, as her fingers gently touched it. At her hip was a small dagger in a sheath threaded onto the gold cording along with a small pouch made of coarser cloth. Shelby's fingers ran over the outside of the pouch determining the shape of the contents, knowing instinctively that the midst of a battle wasn't the place to see what was inside. Flat and rectangular. A book. There was something else in it, too, but she couldn't tell what it was. It didn't matter. She didn't have time to figure it out.

"*Run!*" screamed a voice behind her bursting the bubble of warped space and time insulating her from the chaos.

Instead of following directions, Shelby spun around and nearly collided with a fleeing soldier barreling down the temple hallway. She dove to the ground before the Spartan sword taking the express to the Athenian hoplite's head made an unscheduled stop at hers.

"Damn it, Shelby! I said '*run*'!" the hoplite cursed as he turned on the Spartan. There was a sickening gurgle and thud from the Spartan soldier as his shield clanged to the ground next to his limp body.

Shelby's eyes flew from the temple floor she was laying on to the face standing over her. "Benny!" she breathed. Benito Moretti held one hand out to help her as she scrambled to her feet, a blood-soaked sword in his other. "*What are you doing?*"

"I have no idea."

From the look on his face, Shelby knew he truly meant that. Her stunned gaze wandered from the dripping sword tip to the pool of crimson oozing around the fallen Spartan. Shelby stepped back as the thick life of the soldier crept toward her feet. "Jesus," she cursed.

"Hasn't been born yet," Benny said, wiping the blade of his sword on the soldier's tunic. He picked up the dead Spartan's weapon that had skidded across the temple floor and handed it to Shelby. "You're going to need this." Unfastening the belt and sheath, he tossed it to her. "And this. Put it on. We've got to get you out of here."

Taking the sword, she stared at Benny who was clearly more in control of the situation than she was. "I'm no soldier. What am I supposed to do with this?"

"Stick the pointy end into anyone coming at you with another pointy end. So far, that's worked for me."

"Thanks," Shelby said meekly as the stupidity of her question sank in. Shaking hands fumbled at the belt before she finally got it in place around her waist.

"Come, bella," Benny said sliding his sword back into place and guiding her by the shoulder toward the rear of the Parthenon.

Still reeling, Shelby followed his lead blindly. "Where are we going?"

"Not sure. Maybe there's somewhere to get out of all this inside the temple. We need to get our bearings."

For the first time, Shelby saw the temple for what it really was, in all its vibrant glory. What had been an open space when she stood here in her own time was now closed overhead by an ornate roof. Rows of columns flanked marble walls creating smaller spaces within the massive structure. As small as she felt before, she felt even smaller in the splendor of the place. Small and afraid.

They raced down the long hallway and ducked into the cella that housed the massive golden statue of the goddess Athena. Heavy doors stood open, splintered in the middle where a battering ram had beaten through them. Inside, the bodies of slain Spartans littered the floor at the feet of the goddess. They, like Benny and Shelby, were trapped as soon as they went through the door. At least now there weren't hoplites waiting to ambush the Travelers.

"There's no way out!" Shelby cried as she spun around. They were surrounded by two stories of columns that rose just inside of a solid wall around the statue creating a narrow, but impenetrable walkway around the main chamber. The shattered doors lay at the only entrance.

"This way!" Benny said, grabbing her wrist and pulling her back through the doors and down the exterior hall once more.

"But -" Shelby started.

Benny shushed her, flattened his body against a massive column, and motioned her back into the shadows. She followed his example as a pair of Spartan soldiers raced down the hall between the rows of columns with swords drawn. "That was close," she whispered.

"Too close," Benny answered. "This might've been a bad idea."

"It's not like we know what a good idea around here looks like," she said. "Nice legs, by the way." In moments of fear and panic, people often focus on the ridiculous, and say ludicrous things. Shelby was no exception.

Benny's face went crimson as he looked down at his short soldier's tunic that left his calves bare and tended to kick up over his thighs as he ran. "Thanks," he grumbled. "Why couldn't destiny be some time with pants?"

More footsteps on the marble floor flattened both of them against the column once more. Several Athenian hoplites raced past in pursuit of the Spartans, swords drawn and shields rocking with each step. "Something tells me pants aren't the problem we need to focus on right now," Shelby said as she released the breath she was holding.

"Right. Come, bella," Benny said turning her around and heading back into the Athenian sunshine and combat. Once out on the huge porch of the temple, he pointed toward a stand of scrubby trees in the distance from the fighting. "Head down. Pointy end out," he tossed over his shoulder as he drew his own weapon.

"Got it," Shelby said too frightened to care about the sarcasm. She tugged the blade out of the long sheath and gripped the handle. Sweaty hands made it seem heavier than it really was. Her arm vibrated under the strain of holding the weight of it off the ground, and adrenaline was the only thing keeping her from dropping it completely.

Benny shielded her as they made a break across the rubble toward the trees, leaping over bodies too mangled to tell what side they started off on. Soldiers streaked in blood and sweat collided on all sides of them. Any semblance of organized ranks had fallen completely apart. The pair caught the eye of one of the Spartans who broke into a run with his sword held over his head, the blade glinting in the sunshine breaking through the smoke haze. Shelby instinctively gripped the hilt of her sword tighter having no idea if she could even use the thing. Benny planted his feet and braced for the attack as an Athenian soldier charged from behind, driving his sword between the Spartan's shoulder blades. Shelby's scream caught in the back of her throat along with the bile that lodged itself there. Drawing his blade back out, the hoplite gave a sharp nod to Benny, who returned the gesture in gratitude before grabbing Shelby's wrist and breaking into a sprint.

Once safely hidden among the trees and scrub brush, Benny and Shelby collapsed trying to catch their breath and still their trembling. Twisted branches and sparse leaves of the trees would have made weak cover except for the ragged bushes wrapping the trunk bases. Crouched in the golden dust, the pair were well hidden from the soldiers crashing together in a morbid dance of swords and shields along the edge of the Acropolis.

"You ok, bella?" Benny asked, holding her face in his hands.

Tears streamed down her face leaving muddy trails in the dust. "I can't do this, Benny. What was he thinking?"

"You know what Apollo was thinking. He told you. You have what you need to do this," Benny whispered and stroked her cheek. "We just have to figure out how."

Shelby nodded but was certain at this point that Benny and Apollo were both wrong. "You're doing a hell of a lot better at this save-the-world thing than I am."

"No, I'm not."

Shelby shook her dark head. Sunlight glinted off the golden band across her forehead. "I'm serious. When you first found me, you- you killed that Spartan. How-?" Looking at him now, Benny seemed a far cry from the snarky carefree guy she fell for in Rome. The man in front of her embodied an Athenian hoplite more than anything else. He was both familiar and foreign.

Benny leaned back against a tree trunk and closed his rich Roman eyes in thought. After a moment, he sighed. "Shelby, taking that soldier down wasn't me being more cut out for destiny than you. That was me doing what I was trained to do."

"That makes no sense. You're a *tour guide*."

Pushing a sweaty strand of dark hair away from his forehead, he said, "When I was small, we had almost nothing, living in a small flat in the center of the old town. Most times, I was running loose on the streets of Rome. Nonna raised me there, when we weren't eating pasta at Carmelita's in Toscolano, after my parents died. Car accident in France. They went away when I was six years old for an anniversary trip and never came back."

Shelby laid her head on his shoulder and wrapped her exhausted arms around his strong one. "I'm sorry, Benny."

He shook his head and shrugged. "I don't remember them much. Too young. When Nonna died a few years ago, that hurt most. She did what she could, but we barely got by. I worked my way through school but had no idea what I wanted to do with my life. One day, I joined the army until I could figure it out." Benny turned to look at her. "When that soldier raised his sword, the training kicked in and I just...reacted."

Shelby squeezed his arm a little tighter. "Tell me something, soldier."

"Mmm?"

"Are we going to live through this?"

A faint smile flickered on the edges of his mouth. "I don't see Apollo letting us off with this destiny thing just because we died, so, yeah, we'll live."

"What were we thinking doing this? This isn't our war. Are we insane?" She looked up at Benny, who looked down at her, but kept one eye out for rogue blades and arrows.

The corner of his lips curled as he rested a hand on the hilt of the sword at his hip. "Probably. No sane person jumps into a giant hole because a god told them to go save the world. By the way, when do you plan on doing that bit?"

"*Me?*" Shelby asked staring at him. "Oh, no you don't. You're on the hook with this shit, too, remember? I'm not the only Traveler here."

"Easy, bella, it was a joke." Benny twisted a strand of her hair around his finger. "I'd never make you do this alone." His words were soft and sincere as the adrenaline of their arrival began to wear off and the very real danger settled heavily on their shoulders. Apollo sent them here for a reason, but as usual, was less than clear about what they were supposed to do once they got to ancient Athens. "You'll know what to do when the time comes, bella. We'll figure it out." Pulling her to him, Benny kissed the corner of Shelby's mouth before wrapping his arms around her.

Shelby sank into him. Even in this strange time and place, his chest was comfortable and familiar. He even smelled the same. If she closed her eyes, she was back in the hotel in Paris lying next to him listening to his heart beat. But this wasn't Paris. It wasn't even the same century. Hell, it wasn't even the same era. "So, this is what BC looks like," she mumbled into his chest.

"Not sure I'm a fan just yet."

"Me either. So, now what?" Shelby asked.

Benny glanced over her shoulder at the fighting in the distance. "I don't think the two of us are going to take down the Spartan forces. There has to be something else we're supposed to do." Shelby sighed and leaned against the tree next to Benny moving the pouch around to the front of her hip. As she thought, her fingers absently tapped on the flat thing inside. "What's that?" he asked.

"Don't know," Shelby said remembering the pouch for the first time since she first noticed it in the Parthenon. "Had it when I got here. Feels like a book."

"You didn't open it?" Benny asked. His dark eyes stopped just short of glaring at her.

"There's been that whole battle thing distracting me," she snapped more than she meant to.

Benny glanced at the soldiers in the distance. "We've got a minute. If Apollo gave it to you, it might tell us what we're supposed to be doing." Once he worked the drawstrings loose, Benny pulled out a worn leather book. "It's-"

"Eli's journal," Shelby whispered as her hands began to sting. "But, why?"

"Was there something we missed?" Benny asked.

Shelby shrugged. "We never finished reading it. We figured out what was going on before we got to the end."

"Think, bella. Why would Apollo send us to 404 BC with a journal from the Victorian era?"

"How have I had it all this time and not had my hands burn like they are now?" Shelby volleyed rubbing her hands even though that never did any good.

Benny examined the coarse fabric pouch turning it over in his hands. "Maybe something to do with this. Let's find out." He picked up the journal by the corner using two fingers like the thing carried the plague and slipped it back into the pouch. "Well?"

"Better," Shelby answered spreading her fingers wide. No burning pins and needles.

"Looks like Apollo thought we needed it enough to give you a way to carry it with you."

"But, why? How can Eli help us here? And now? He was only barely helpful in our own time and place!" Shelby was struggling to keep her voice down in her frustration.

Shouts around them grew louder as part of the battle inched closer to where they hid. Benny peered through the trees to see what was going on. "I don't know what we're supposed to be doing, but we need to get out of here to figure it out.

Head for the city. There doesn't seem to be as much fighting down there. For now, the Athenians seem to be holding them up here."

Shelby glanced around and nodded as she quickly tied the pouch back onto the cording at her waist. Scrambling to her feet, she looked down the hill toward the gleaming Greek city below them. They couldn't go down by way of the processional path and any other way was treacherous. Open spaces meant being seen by soldiers, and covered spaces meant tedious picking through brush and low trees. "Anything could be in there," Shelby said as Benny pointed toward the overgrown hillside.

"Hopefully nothing with a pointy end."

CHAPTER 2

"Stick to the shadows," Benny said, letting her hand go at the edge of the city and sliding his sword back into its sheath.

Shelby gave up trying to wield her sword somewhere about halfway down the hillside after an unladylike sprawling fall in the loose dirt and brush. "I don't think anyone cares about us. They're too busy trying to save their own skins," Shelby said.

"And we're trying to save ours. Shadows."

"Right."

Even under a layer of destruction, Athens was a staggering masterpiece of architecture. Form and structure slow danced with art and poetry. Gleaming marble facades and polished statues cowered under a shroud of dust from the fighting on the hillside. Columns along the promenades of the massive stone structures provided intermittent cover for the fleeing pair where shadows were elusive. Avoiding the wide-open and abandoned agora market, Shelby and Benny stuck to alleys and back streets through the city as they raced for the walls in the distance. Parts of the city had escaped damage, but others were crumbling under the weight of the carnage. Some buildings had smoke rising out of their tiled roofs, set either by the Spartans ridding the city of Athenian excess, or by the Athenians taking what spoils they could away from the Spartans before they conquered the city. Either way, it was devastating to watch.

Rounding a corner of what appeared to be a public bath house, the pair ducked into an alcove before they could be seen by a small group of men, clearly wealthy by their dress, standing with a young Athenian soldier in heated conversation in the deep shadows between the close-set buildings. Benny jerked his head toward them, then pointed down a side street just ahead to avoid a possible confrontation. As they crept closer, Shelby's hands stung and tingled. Blue sparks jumped from the turquoise bracelet on her wrist to the small pouch on the cord around her waist. Someone was trying to get her attention, and it had something to do with those men.

"Stop," Shelby hissed at Benny.

"What? We've got to-"

"No, stop!" she insisted, thrusting her wrist under his nose, his eyes widened at the blue sparks dancing along the Egyptian bracelet.

"Seshat?"

Shelby nodded. If she had learned anything in all the mess that brought her to Athens, it was not to ignore the Egyptian goddess when she used the bracelet to get her attention. "It's got something to do with those men. And this," she said tugging at the pouch. Since her hands were already burning, she dug out the contents. Eli's journal didn't seem to trigger anything unusual to let her know Seshat meant that. Thrusting her hand inside once more, she pulled out a scrap of fabric. Sparks glowing bright blue with no heat jumped wildly from her bracelet and washed over the fabric as Shelby unrolled it. "I can't read this! It's in freaking Greek!"

"Let me see," Benny said. Shelby didn't know what good that was going to do since Benny was Roman, not Greek, but did as he asked. She put the paper in his open hand, and the sparks didn't follow. Instead, they spun around Shelby's wrist as Benny squinted at the word. "I've seen this before. It's a name. *Alcibiades.*"

"Who the hell is that?"

Benny shrugged. "Must've been somebody important if I've seen it before, but I can't remember why I know the name." He ran a hand through his hair as if he could pull the information from his memory. "Damn it. I *know* I know that name!"

Shelby leaned exasperated against the polished stone wall behind her as shouts and echoes from the fighting seemed to get farther away. Athens was pushing Sparta backwards, for the moment. "Leave it to those idiots to give me a clue I can't figure out."

"You might not want to go around calling gods 'idiots', bella."

"Then, they probably shouldn't *be* idiots. Don't they know history isn't my thing? I mean, isn't knowing stuff like that sort of their *job?*"

Benny handed the scrap of cloth back to her. "This isn't doing us any good. When did the bracelet start going nuts?"

"When I saw those men over there," Shelby answered cutting her eyes over at the group still arguing and looking furtively at the Acropolis above the city. Smoke rose from fires built in front of the massive temple where Sparta had officers posted directing the battle around them. The group of men seemed panicked about whatever was going on up there and were too distracted to notice the pair of Travelers watching them. Words floated over to them as the men argued. "Why can we understand them?" Shelby whispered.

"I guess it would've been hard for us to do whatever Apollo wanted us to do if he had to wait around on us to learn Greek."

"Think one of them is this Alcibiades guy?" Shelby asked, her eyes darting from the fabric in her hand to the cluster of bickering men.

"Maybe, but we can't exactly go up to them and ask, can we?"

Benny was right. They were ridiculously out of place even if they were dressed the part and could understand the language. Neither of them knew any more about ancient Athenian culture and customs than Apollo told them on their tour, which wasn't much. Until they had a better grip on the whole Greek thing, they didn't need to go waltzing into elite conversations. "No, we can't do that. I've got half a mind to walk my happy ass back to Delphi and tell Apollo where he can shove this piece of crap. But since I can't do that..." Shelby slapped Benny across the face, startling him and getting fleeting attention from the group of Athenians.

"What the hell was that for?" Benny snapped.

"Chase me but catch me close enough to hear them."

Shelby smacked him again and took off running. His arm shot out to grab hers and just missed as he tore after her down the street towards the group of men. The young hoplite soldier let his eyes wander over Shelby as she passed, and Benny shot him a warning look as he caught up to her. Seconds later, Benny had Shelby pinned against the wall kissing her just in earshot of the men, who lowered their voices some, but not enough. Shelby pretended to struggle against Benny's advances, but listened as the men ignored them and went back to their heated discussion.

"Lysander's army doesn't have the supplies to hold siege on the city for long," one older man said. Draped over his shoulder was a deep purple cloth with a hem intricately embroidered in silver thread. Even knowing little about the culture, the Travelers could tell these men were rich, which made them important.

"And we have even less!" a red-faced heavy-set man insisted. His simpler cloak was a similar shade to his face. "He's cut off the supplies from the outside, and these city walls have become our tomb!"

A tall thin man with a white beard in soft curls held up a hand to stop the bickering. His clothes were understated, elegant, in dove gray with delicate silver threads along the edges of the drape. There was no need for flashy fabrics and embellishments to mark him as the leader. Calm and control amid the chaos of battle and argument boiling around him. Maybe it was the stately way he held his frame that made him quietly impressive. "Dexios," he said addressing the soldier, "you've been quiet. What do you think?"

The young hoplite hesitated and rested a hand on the leather-wrapped hilt of his sword as though instinctively braced for conflict. He wore a short tunic and sandals like Benny, but on his wrists were wide leather bands laced shut to protect them from stray blades in close combat. From the scarring on the leather, his vulnerable veins beneath were lucky the bands were there. The soldier's eyes searched the ground buying a few seconds before he answered the elder Greek cautiously, "You know what I think."

"Now-" the red-faced man turned on him, "don't start that again!"

Once more, the man clearly in charge held up a hand to silence him. "It's too dangerous, Dexios. You know that's not an option."

Bolder, the young fighter stood up straight. "Then, don't ask me what I think we need to do. I've fought alongside him. I don't care what they say. If we're going to take Athens back, we need Alcibiades."

Benny, who was enjoying his role in the charade a bit more than he should have, froze at the name and looked at Shelby. Her eyes locked with his as her breath caught in her chest.

Fuming, the red-faced man sputtered protests at the soldier. "But- but- that's *treason!* If we bring him back here, we'll lose our heads!"

"Then don't. Let Lysander take them off for you instead." Glaring at the men in front of him, the soldier clearly had enough of the indecisive statesmen.

"Dexios," the tall man called as the young soldier turned to go.

Not looking back, Dexios answered, "No, father, there's work to be done. Talk yourself into your own capture. I said what I had to say." Determined strides took the soldier down the street with his shoulders firmly squared. Rounding the corner, out of his father's sightline, he stopped and sighed, muscular shoulders sagging under the weight of his defiance. Taking another deep breath, Dexios stood straighter, but his shoulders remained slumped and unsure as he continued on.

"Follow him," Shelby whispered putting her stinging palm flat on Benny's chest. Sparks swarmed like caffeinated ants along her fingertips. Benny knew full well what that meant. Grabbing her wrist, he continued the act of abducting her for the benefit of the group of men who had gone back to their bickering.

For a soldier trained with a heightened awareness of his surroundings, he was strangely oblivious to the pair following him. Dexios strode down the street consumed with his own thoughts. Walking on, his strides slowed, and fingers ran through his hair. Finally stopping at a small gurgling fountain, the soldier fell to his knees. Water scooped into his hands from the small marble basin and splashed onto his face, almost hid the tears from Shelby. Almost.

"Dexios?" she asked softly.

Startled, the soldier's hand flew to this sword and the blade rang as it slid out of the scabbard. Shelby's hands raised and Benny held his out and away from his own sword. "Please," Benny said gently, "we just want to talk to you."

"Who are you?" Dexios asked, still not lowering his sword, but not advancing on them either.

"That's a long story," Shelby said smiling. "We just want to ask you about someone. Alcibiades."

Slowly, the gleaming blade lowered, but his grip on it never wavered. "I don't know what you're talking about." It was a hollow lie, and a rehearsed one. If what they had overheard before was true, asking him about Alcibiades might not be as easy as they hoped. If it was treason to bring the man back to the city, being associated with him might not be something people were quick to admit.

"We aren't here to arrest you," Shelby said. "We need to find him, and you seemed to know where he is."

Dexios eyed Benny cautiously but seemed inclined to talk to Shelby. "Why? What do you want with a traitor?"

"Same thing you do. We need him to win a war." Shelby leveled her gaze at the young man and held her ground.

He seemed to study her face to see if she could be trusted. Athenian women weren't known to be as brazen as the Spartan women, but Shelby was clearly not Spartan. Dexios seemed to suspect there was something strange about the young woman in front of him but was too intrigued to walk away. "He's been condemned to die for his crimes against the gods and Athens. It won't be easy to get him back here." Dexios sighed and sheathed the sword, then glanced at the smoke rising above the buildings around them. "But we need him. He's the only one who can bring Athens to victory."

"Look," Benny began, "we need to find him, and, from the way things are going, we don't have much time. Do you know where he is?"

Dexios hesitated, sizing Benny up. "Who are you?"

Benny glanced at Shelby, who nodded. "My name is Benito, and this is Shelby."

"You're not Athenian," Dexios said taking a step backwards.

Shelby was losing patience and the stinging in her hands was getting painful. She'd had enough with diplomacy. "Alright, soldier boy, we're going to find Alcibiades with or without your help, but it would be a hell of a lot easier if you'd tell us where he is. If you won't, then fine, but we're done wasting what little time we have on your trust issues." Irritated, Shelby tossed the scrap of cloth on the ground. She took the stunned Benny by the hand and started to walk away with a toss of her head.

"What are you doing?" Benny whispered.

"Playing hard to get."

Seconds later, "Wait."

A satisfied smile flashed across Shelby's face quickly replaced by a scowl as she turned on the soldier. "Well?" she asked with flashing dark eyes, her defiance matching what Dexios dished out to his father.

For a moment, the soldier seemed disarmed by her reaction, but recovered his composure. "I can't believe I'm doing this," he said, pushing a hand through his close-cropped curls. "I'll help you."

"Really?" Shelby asked suspiciously. "Why the sudden change of heart?"

Dexios turned the scrap Shelby tossed on the ground over in the palm of his hand. On one side was the name *Alcibiades*. On the back, that Shelby and Benny hadn't noticed, was a silver bow and arrow. "This." He ran a finger across the gleaming image. "I don't know who you are or where you've come from, but I know who sent you."

Benny raised a dark eyebrow. "You do?"

Dexios nodded. "Apollo." Holding the fabric out to Shelby, he said softly, "I've seen this once before. It was years ago. My father took me to Delphi to seek the Pythia, the oracle, about my future. This," he said pointing to the bow and arrow, "was on her wrist. Shining silver. I was captivated by it. It seemed painted there, but at the same time like a part of her skin. It was as if the god himself had marked the Pythia as his."

Shelby's mind raced as she thought back to Dina and tried to remember a silver bow and arrow on her wrist but couldn't. Maybe Dexios had it wrong. Or maybe Dina's brand was elsewhere. There was no way to know if Dina was Dexios' Pythia or if that was before her time. Either way, this was Shelby's ticket to the hoplite's trust. "There are things I can't tell you, and things I can," she began as cryptic as the god that irritated her so much. "But I *will* tell you that you're more right than wrong."

Reverently, Dexios slid his sword out of its sheath and held it flat across his palms. Kneeling, he held the blade out in a gesture of fealty. "I'm honored to serve those that serve the gods."

Benny looked at Shelby and shrugged. Shelby knelt and laid her hand on the hilt. "We don't need you to serve us, Dexios, but we do need your help." Her lips parted in a warm smile as the young soldier raised his eyes to hers. With a nod, he smiled back at her and stood. "That's better," Shelby said. "We're in your world, Dex. Where do we go from here?

"Persia."

CHAPTER 3

"I may never be able to live up to my father's expectations, but it's nice to be able to use his influence once in a while," Dexios said pulling a couple of crates together in the storage hold of the small trade ship rocking in the port of Piraeus at the mouth of the Athenian Long Walls. Tugging a sack of something softer over for Shelby, he and Benny settled on the crates. Deep in the hold of the boat, they made themselves as comfortable as they could among the ship stores and mildew. At least they had been given a jug of wine and some bread. Shelby could handle just about anything with enough wine.

Shelby's stomach rolled with the waves as the boat lurched away from the dock and headed toward the open sea. "The captain didn't seem too excited about us stowing away. You sure he's on your father's side?"

Dexios nodded. "My father is the reason he has trade business in the city. Eneas may not be happy about having company, but he won't betray us. He's as salty as the sea, but he's not stupid. Sides change in this war with the tide, and he has business to do. Eneas stays as neutral as he can. We're taking a bigger risk with the Persians, especially since they aren't exactly on our side. The Persian leaders on the interior have sided with Lysander."

"Wait a minute," Benny scowled. "Let me get this straight. You're telling me that the same Persians who are harboring Alcibiades are on Sparta's side?" Dexios nodded. "And we're going to Persia after him."

"Yes," Dexios replied as if it all made perfect sense.

Shelby's forehead crinkled. "But Alcibiades is Athenian, not Spartan."

The corner of the young soldier's mouth curled in a mischievous grin. "Is he? Who knows with him? There was that ridiculous business with the vandalism of the gods' statues which earned him a death sentence from the Athenian leaders and sent him running to Sparta. He betrayed Athens to Sparta once already and may have stayed Spartan if he hadn't gotten the king's wife pregnant. Athens brought him back, then there was that whole mess he made at Samos and Notium that pretty much did his reputation in."

"What the hell are you babbling about?" Shelby asked.

"You really don't know?" Dexios asked. Benny shrugged and Shelby shook her head. "But you were the ones looking for him."

Benny said, "All we know is what was on that cloth. Beyond that, this is all new to us."

Dexios sighed. "What you heard in the city is right. He's a traitor. More than once. But he's also a brilliant military strategist."

"Then, how did he make a mess of whatever that place was?" Shelby asked.

"Samos. It wasn't really about Samos. He never could stay in the good graces of the city leaders, no matter how successful he was because most of his decisions were based on his own ambitions. He made as many enemies as friends and some of them implicated him in charges of blasphemy for mutilating the statues of Hermes. They said he and his cronies got shitfaced and knocked the phalluses off the statues."

Shelby put her hand over her mouth to stop the laugh from flying out, but quickly gave up. It was just too damn hysterical. All she could think of was the florist logo traipsing around with his man parts dangling out. "What the hell did they do that for? I mean, isn't it funnier to have a bunch of statues *with* those things than *without* them?"

"You'd think," Benny said stifling a laugh. "Knocking them off the statues is blasphemy?"

"Seems a little harsh," Shelby added, still giggling.

Dexios' confusion was splashed across his face. "But they were statues of a *god*. You wouldn't think it was funny if they took the manhood off a statue of Apollo."

Shelby snorted. "There are times when I've wanted to do that to more than his statue. Damned annoying for a god."

The soldier didn't seem interested in getting pulled into her sacrilege, so he got back to the biography. "Funny or not, the leaders took exception to it and pressed charges, ignoring the fact they didn't have much proof. His trial was deferred until after the battle in Sicily, even though Alcibiades wanted to defend his innocence before he left. While he was gone, the leaders condemned him to death and ordered him back to Athens. Well, he wasn't going to go running back to his own demise, so he snuck away to Sparta. They were happy to have him since he gave them information on how and when to beat the Athenians."

"Classy guy," Shelby said with a sneer.

Dexios shrugged and went on. "He was apparently pretty happy to be a Spartan and went along with their customs. Going around naked, eating that nasty black stuff. However, he got a little too comfortable, especially with the king's wife. Of course, the king ran him out of Sparta when he found out his wife had a baby when the king had been gone over ten months. So, Alcibiades fled to Persia and managed to weasel his way in with the leaders there. He advised the Persians to stay out of the battles and wait on both sides to wear themselves out, making them easy to defeat. Of course, he was also playing both sides of the fence with the Athenians. Mostly, he just wanted to return to Athens. Eventually, Athens realized they needed him, so they brought him back. He made quite an entrance on that chariot with some girl dressed as Athena. One thing Alcibiades has is style. The city leaders, my father among them, gave him his title of General back and put him in charge of one arm of the fleet."

Shelby's head was throbbing, and the rocking of the ship getting underway wasn't helping. She may have written promotional material for historical places, but history was not her thing. The more she tried to keep up, the more confused she got. Apollo thought Alcibiades was the man they needed, but she couldn't keep track of whose side the guy was on. "How did they know he wouldn't change sides again?" Shelby asked and took a bigger chug of her wine than she meant to.

"Who knows?" Dexios answered with a shake of his dark head. "At some point, I guess they thought it was worth the risk. With Lysander taking control, Athens needed a stronger military leader than they had without Alcibiades. The charges were dropped, and he was given command. I was with him at that point, and I'd never seen a general more charismatic and in control. It was amazing. Especially with the odd way he talks."

"Odd?" Benny asked.

"He has a lisp. It's strange. Most of the time a lisp is distracting, but his seems to make him more interesting to listen to."

"So, we're going after a traitor with a speech impediment. Sounds like just the guy to turn this whole disaster around." Shelby rolled her eyes and threw back the rest of her wine. Part of her was glad the wine was weaker than the Roman chianti she was used to so she could focus on the details, but the rest of her was wishing she could drink herself into blissful oblivion and forget all about Alcibiades and his turn-coat self.

Dex continued his story with a shrug. "There was some scuffling going on near Ionia, and Alcibiades went to go take care of that leaving some of the fleet in Samos. Sparta had ships nearby, but Alcibiades gave clear orders to Antiochus not to engage Lysander."

"Let me guess," Benny said. "Someone didn't follow orders."

"You got it. It was a disaster. Lysander took advantage of Alcibiades being away and the fleet was crushed at Notium. If I hadn't gone with Alcibiades..." Dexios trailed off pondering the fate his fellow soldiers and sailors faced at the hands of the Spartan military leader.

Shelby put a hand on his arm. "You didn't know, Dex. No one could have known what would happen."

Dexios smiled at her reassurance, but sadness simmered in his eyes. "True, but the uprising we were dealing with was nothing compared to the Spartan forces. I'm not even sure why we went. The Athenian leaders seemed to think the same way, because they were after Alcibiades' head at that point. They blamed him for the whole thing and stripped him of his position. Before they decided to do more than that, he ran for the hills. He tried to come back not long after, but his advice was ignored. Realizing he didn't hold as much influence anymore, he eventually made his way back to Persia."

"But if Persia is sympathetic to Sparta, why would he stay there?" Shelby asked impressed with herself for having remembered that part.

"I wish I could answer that one," Dexios said. "Maybe he doesn't realize how far into Lysander's pockets the Persians are, but that doesn't seem right. Maybe the Persians aren't as tight with Sparta as we think. Alcibiades usually has his finger on the pulse of all things political and military. Maybe he's changed sides again."

Shelby tapped her fingers on a crate next to her, then realized that was a dumb thing to do. Whatever was inside was leaking making the wood outside sticky and nasty. Wiping her fingertips on the sack she sat on, she said, "If we don't know whose side he's on, it makes it a lot more difficult to just waltz in there and say, 'Hey, Al, Athens needs you, hon.'"

Benny's brow knit as he thought. "We need something that will get us into his confidence. A gift or something. Some way to get close enough to him to know what's going on so we know how to convince him. What does Alcibiades like?"

Dexios looked at Shelby who was fidgeting with a knot on the cord around her middle. As she loosened it to retie it, the fabric of her layered dress shifted giving her an inadvertent plunging neckline before she could resituate it. Dex grinned. "I think we may have just the thing."

Shelby's eyes flew to the young hoplite's. "You've got to be kidding me."

CHAPTER 4

Dust hovered at their horses' flanks and gravel crunched under weary hooves as the Persian landscape yawned in front of them. The sun glared overhead washing the dirt road to a bright white that snaked through an endless sea of grass. Ahead, it undulated in rolling waves of green broken only by occasional islands of rock. Bored and exhausted, Shelby slouched in her saddle. Dexios rode ahead scouting for trouble, but so far, no one seemed to care about the band of travelers. Greeks with their own troubles paid no attention to them, except for Shelby, who seemed to confuse passersby. Her brazenness smacked more of Spartan women while her dress and hair pegged her as an Athenian who should have been at home meekly tending house. She was a mystery and therefore raised some eyebrows.

Outside the Greek port city the trade ship deposited them in, the countryside opened up to rolling land with little in the way of scenery and less in the way of people. The Persian governors, or satraps, seemed content to contain their energies to their palace walls rather than send troops roaming the expansive agrarian lands. Once in a while, the trio would come upon a small group of Persian travelers and the passing parties would eye one another cautiously as they gave each other wide berth.

As heat rippled off the road, Dexios spotted a lone traveler approaching from the bend half a mile ahead. For the moment, it was just a shimmering shadow, but it didn't take long for the horse and rider to cover the distance and come into focus. It was a soldier. A sword clanked at his side, but it wasn't drawn. The rider seemed more intent on speed and purpose than taking in the scenery. Shelby noticed

Dexios' hand slide to the hilt of his sword as his eyes narrowed. Benny followed suit, ready to defend Shelby. Dexios squinted hard, then his face relaxed into a grin. "I know him. It's alright. The gods must truly be on your side, Shelby." She and Benny had no idea what he was talking about, but it was enough for Benny to lower his hand from his sword and for Shelby to unclench her teeth.

Jabbing his horse in the side with his heels, Dexios lowered his head as the horse broke into a run toward the oncoming rider. "Selagus!" he called out.

The figure on the horse leaned forward, then raised an arm in salute. "Dexios?" The young man wore a hoplite's gear with his shield strapped to the side of his horse. The only difference was the longer metal guards on Selagus' forearms secured with leather straps where Dexios had the wide leather bands that wrapped his own wrists. Suntanned muscles from wielding the heavy shield and sword glistened with sweat in the Persian sun. Road dirt gathered on his sandals and calves as well as his horse's flanks. Selagus pulled his mount to a stop alongside his fellow soldier. "Gods, man, what are you doing all the way out here?"

"I could ask you the same thing, but I'm too glad to see you to care." Dexios laughed. Dust clouds churned then dissipated as Shelby and Benny brought their horses to a stop just behind Dexios. Shelby shifted in her saddle, more uncomfortable from the long ride than the newcomer's presence. "Selagus, this is Benito and Shelby. Some friends from outside Athens."

Benny and Shelby nodded in greeting but kept their mouths shut in case their accents raised questions about how far outside Athens Dexios meant. They had gotten enough side-eye glances in the port town to know that even though they could understand everyone, there was something different in the way they sounded to the locals. Sparks leaped on Shelby's wrist and her hands pricked with pain the nearer she got to the new soldier. Pulling some of the fabric from her dress loose, she draped it over her hand to hide the tiny blue flashes. Seshat was getting her attention about Selagus. Either she needed to be wary, or he could be useful somehow. Or both.

"Interesting names," Selagus said scanning the pair before deciding that as friends of Dexios he didn't need to be suspicious of them. "You're a long way from home. Does that mean what I'm afraid it means?"

Dexios nodded as Selagus' face fell. "Athens was in shambles when we left. Not sure she can rise from this."

Selagus' spine straightened as his military and Athenian pride kicked in. "She can rise from anything. Especially Spartans." He spat in the dirt accenting his feelings about the invaders. "Where're you headed now?"

Dexios looked at Shelby who nodded leaving it to Dex's judgement if the stranger could be trusted or not. "We need to see Alcibiades. Do you know where he is?"

"You can't be serious?" Selagus asked, surprised. "Do the city leaders know what you're up to? Does your *father*?"

Dexios shook his head. Selagus tried to hide a glare at Shelby and Benny as if they were to blame for corrupting his rule-following hoplite friend. "They asked me what I thought we needed to do, and I told them. Of course, they didn't want to hear it, so I left them and their swollen heads to Lysander."

"It's treason, you know. I'm already in up to my neck. There's no reason why you should be, too," Selagus cautioned. The look on his face made it very clear that he didn't completely trust his friend's silent companions, but his manners wouldn't let him say as much. Fellow travelers seemed to be fine with him, but with the mention of Alcibiades, Selagus seemed to waver on his first impression of Shelby and Benny. "If Athens has fallen, even *he* won't be able to resurrect her alone."

"I'm not entirely sure you're right about that," Dexios said. He stopped short of mentioning the divine nature of their mission to Selagus. Apparently, there was a limit to Dexios' trust in his old friend.

Selagus sighed. "There's no way I can talk you out of doing this?"

"None. Like you, we're in too deep to go back now."

"Alright." He dug into a pouch on his saddle and pulled out a folded tanned animal skin. Shelby's hands burned painfully as Seshat made her point about Selagus' usefulness. Unfolding it, he revealed a crudely drawn map. Roads snaked across it winding around small blobs and tiny peaks. "Follow this road here," Selagus instructed, his finger tracing one of the fading lines. "Then, once you pass the outcropping, take this road. By nightfall, you should make it to town. He's got a place on the edge of the city. For the most part, the people tolerate him so you shouldn't have too much trouble getting information. Keep your business to yourself on the way, though. Not everyone needs to know how to find him. And this doesn't go back to Athens with you," he said folding the map and handing it to Dexios. "Wouldn't want it falling into the wrong hands." he added with a fleeting glance at Benny and Shelby.

"What about you?" Dexios asked. "You going to be alright? What with the Persians siding with Sparta and Sparta getting the upper hand in Athens?"

Selagus laughed. "The Persians do what they want. Whatever suits their coffers best. They may side with Sparta now, but there's no way they would burn bridges with Athens. Just in case the Athenians prove financially useful someday. As long as that's a possibility, they won't go randomly hacking off Greek heads unless they have a damn good reason to. And I'm good at making sure they don't have one."

The soldiers said their farewells and Selagus rode swiftly on making up for time spent chatting on the roadside. As the thunder of hoofbeats faded, Shelby asked Dexios, "How much do you trust him?"

"Completely. I saved his life once. He owes me mine." With that, he nudged his horse ahead of the pair of Travelers.

"I'm not so sure I trust him as much as Dexios does," Benny said cautiously. "He may owe Dex his life, but he doesn't owe us anything."

Shelby nodded and glanced over her shoulder at the diminishing cloud of dust in Selagus' wake. "My thoughts exactly. I hope I'm wrong." Her stinging hands calmed some as she and Benny caught up with Dexios and moved further from Selagus. Shelby hoped that meant the hoplite had served his purpose and wasn't a lingering threat.

* * *

Whether Selagus was trustworthy or not, he at least made good on his directions. A bright half-moon eased over the horizon as their horses clattered from the dirt road onto paved stone. Buildings seemed to rise out of the slight slope of the ground directly behind a defensive wall that would have been laughable next to the mighty Long Walls of Athens. As they drew nearer, the city details came into focus. Formal stateliness of Greek influence infiltrated the more ornate embellishments of the Persian architecture giving the place a familiar, yet exotic feel. Columns spanned the fronts of ornate stone buildings with huge relief carvings on the exteriors. Gold leaf and vibrant paints gave elegant detail to the structures built into the rise of the hill. Once they were through the city gates, the intricacy of the city architecture came alive. Art adorned the walls and stood in open public areas. Clean paved roads wove through smaller, simpler homes and shops built around the larger public structures and elite homes. Rich smells of spices and roasting meats made Shelby's stomach rumble. Inhabitants in a mix of simple and colorful embroidered clothes eyed the newcomers, but none reacted to the Athenians trotting their horses down the middle of the street.

"Is it just me, or were you expecting more, I don't know, aggression?" Shelby asked.

Dexios scanned the people going about their business with only a passing interest in them. "Does seem odd that they aren't reacting to a group of Athenians, but then, maybe they've had to change sides so much they just don't give a damn unless they have cause to. Look at us," he said with a sweep of his hand. Their clothes and exposed skin were covered in dust from the road and little muddy trails where sweat beaded and ran in the heat of the day. "We're not exactly a force to be reckoned with."

"Unless the smell is as bad as I feel like it is. I could use a bath." Shelby stretched her back and neck that ached from hours in the saddle. "Then again, I'm not sure I can stand up once I get off this thing."

Dexios waved down an older portly man in finely embroidered clothes. He was hesitant to approach the filthy strangers and stood at a reasonable distance without appearing rude. "Something I can help you with, traveler?"

"We're in need of lodging and somewhere to get cleaned up. It's been a long hot journey from the coast," Dexios explained.

Looking them over and letting his eyes linger on the swords only momentarily, the man finally said, "You'll find both at the far side of the center of town. Stay on this road, and you'll get there."

Shelby smiled, the crusted dirt on her face creasing. "Thank you."

Benny grinned as he watched the man blush slightly as his eyes roved over Shelby. Even filthy she was sexy. The older man's defenses melted as he returned her smile. "My pleasure," the man answered, and Benny was pretty sure it was.

CHAPTER 5

Fires in braziers and torches in iron brackets on columns and entryways fended off the dark of the evening by the time the three road-worn travelers emerged from the inn having found a room and a small meal. People strolled along the paved roads taking advantage of the cooler night air for getting out and socializing. Exotic colors and intricate Persian embroidery swirled with the deep hues of the elegant Greek dresses and cloaks. Shelby always thought the Greeks only wore white when they weren't wandering around naked. Probably because the only exposure she had to Greek culture were statues and pottery at museums. In reality, the clothing, hair, and accessories of the ancients were bright and colorful. Sculptors and painters of the time seemed more focused on form and function than fashion. Or, maybe, like Egypt, the color had disappeared over time leaving only a shell of how vibrant the people really were. Up and down the street, colors splashed through the art and fashion with a sophisticated intricacy that spilled into the decadence of the food and culture. The night was a sensory spectacle under the stars as music played in the distance and laughter bubbled over the rooftops and around corners.

Feeling somewhat less stiff and in a better mood with food and a considerable amount of wine in her stomach, Shelby couldn't wait to soak in a hot bath to melt off the layers of dirt and sweat. "So, how does a girl get clean around here?" she asked Dexios.

"In Athens, you'd have to wait 'til morning when women are allowed in the bathhouses, but they may have different rules here."

"Morning? You can't bathe whenever you want?" she asked with one indignant hand on her hip. There was a lot about ancient life that wasn't going down easy with Shelby. The lack of deodorant, air conditioning, and mechanized transportation was bad enough, but not being able to bathe whenever she wanted could push her completely over the edge.

Dexios cleared his throat. "*I* can, but, well, *you* can't. Look, I don't know what women are like where you come from, but I get the feeling they're a lot more like the Spartans than Athenians." Shelby screwed up her face on the verge of insult. "Not- not that I'm saying that's bad," Dexios added quickly.

"Some great democracy," Shelby spat. "I'm going to take a bath." Only fairly certain there was no death penalty for rogue bathing, Shelby turned on her heel toward the bath house.

"Come on, Dex," Benny said with a sigh as he followed in her determined wake.

"Can't you stop her?" Dexios asked, his eyes pleading with the Roman.

Benny stopped and looked at the hoplite squarely. "Have you *met* Shelby? You weren't wrong with your Spartan thing. She'd tell Apollo where he could stick this mission. She'll take a bath if she damn well pleases, especially when she's halfway under the table with wine."

Dexios sighed and trudged behind Benny as Shelby continued her determined march to the bath house on the hill. Eyes followed her, but none of the town inhabitants made a move to approach or stop her progress, seeming to have a sense that she was not likely to be easily deterred from whatever it was she was planning to do. Shoulders set and the gold band in her dark hair gleaming in the torch light, she was formidable and feminine at the same time, despite the slight list to the left the wine had given her walk. Men stopped and stared, letting their eyes drift over her figure as she strode past them. Women set their lips firm next to their enthralled husbands but said nothing. Shelby, oblivious to it all, focused on her goal, wondered if the ancients had figured out bubble baths while they were coming up with all their other brilliant shit.

Pale stone walls rose up in front of them with pointed arches reaching above the Greek columns that formed the decorative facade of the bath house. Exterior walls were emblazoned with carved waves and fountains heralding the refreshing oasis in the middle of the landlocked Persian city. Large elaborately decorated wooden doors were set into the inner walls that formed the main structure but stood open to allow the cooling night air to filter through to the inside of the building. Completely ignoring the protests of the slaves at the entrance, Shelby strode through the doors into the sparkling marble room. Vaulted ceilings held up by arches perched atop columns gave the space an echoing cavernous feel. Details in vibrant color gathered in the corners of the arches and the tops of the columns bursting like a kaleidoscope in the ceiling arches high above. Torches burned in braziers on each of the columns washing the entire space in golden dancing light. Smaller columns with gilded engravings from top to bottom formed hallways around the room that led to smaller chambers on the perimeter of the main bathing space. A small man dressed in a long, embroidered tunic hurried over to where Shelby stopped for a moment considering her options among the small passages not knowing which one would get her to the bath she was desperately in search of.

"What are you doing?" the small older man asked her with his dark eyes wide. The question was abrupt, but not as much rude as surprised.

Shelby wheeled around to face him just as Benny and Dexios caught up with her and stood in the doorway to watch the drama unfold. In her inebriation, the room spun slightly, but she quickly pulled it back into focus. "Look at me," she said holding her hands out to show how filthy she was. "What do you *think* I'm doing? This is a bathhouse, isn't it?"

"Y-yes," the flustered man sputtered. "Bathhouse."

"Then, I intend to take a bath. Where's the water?" Shelby asked losing patience with the odd little man in her way. Wine had dulled the ache in her hands, and she was doing her damnedest to ignore the burn she could still feel. Whatever the Egyptian goddess wanted, it would have to wait until she was clean.

The Persian glanced at Benny and Dexios who just shrugged at him. Both were too amused to bail Shelby out on this one. "Inside," he said pointing over her shoulder to a door behind her. "But,-"

"Thank you," Shelby said cutting off his protest.

Dexios leaned over to Benny and asked, "Does she not know how these work?"

"I don't think she does," Benny said with his mouth curling into a devilish grin beneath twinkling rich Roman eyes. "Or she's too drunk to care. Either way, this should be fun." He leaned his shoulder against a column smirking at Shelby as she turned on her heel toward the door.

"But she hasn't had a sweat or an oil scrub, and that's the-" Dexios began.

"Shh." Benny hissed, cutting him off with a raised hand. "She didn't want to listen. Let her go. She won't get far." Benny crossed his arms on his chest and watched as Shelby strode through the opening.

Shelby pushed open the carved door and a wave of warm air washed over her. The rich smell of thick earthy herbs and bright mint was intoxicating and clean. Small but elaborately carved basins dotted the walls around the large, darkened room with embossed metal bowls set on the edges glinting in the firelight. Torches burned in the corners of the room, but the space was largely dark and relaxing. High in the walls, stars sparkled through openings along the ceiling. During the day, long sunbeams would have illuminated the space, but at night, it was dim and cozy. The feeling was so much like a candlelight bath back home that she began to instinctively relax even with the relentless sting in her hands. Stone tiles around the large basin were rough under her feet as she pulled her sandals off and set them on the floor beside the stone ramp that led up to the raised edge of the pool. The whole structure resembled a vast garden fountain with its center pedestal and statue of leaping dolphins. Wide steps descended from the rim into the dark still water. Firelight glinted off tiny ripples as she stood with her feet in the water on the first step. It was warm and silky on her ankles as she began unwinding the cord holding the white dress in its Athenian arrangement.

The pouch with Elijah Faircloth's diary was deposited with her sandals far enough away from the water's edge to keep the book from getting wet. Shelby and Benny trusted Dexios not to betray them but weren't ready to show him the journal just yet, which meant they hadn't had a chance to read the end of it either. The last thing she needed was to get the thing wet and smear the ink before they could see what was in it that Apollo thought was so important.

With a contented sigh, she tossed the fabric of her dress aside and eased into the huge basin. In the doorway, Benny and Dexios leaned on the columns watching her brazenly descend into the men's bath. Benny was thoroughly enjoying her figure while Dex tried to politely look away but couldn't.

From a darkened corner came a deep chuckle that got Shelby's attention. Her face flushed hot and red as her arms instinctively flew in front of her under the water in a weak attempt at modesty. "Now, now, there's no need to be embarrassed, my beauty," the rich voice in the shadows said with a hint of a lisp on the 'r's. Benny locked eyes with Dexios, whose own had gone wide. Shelby, however, was too flustered to notice the lisp as she frantically tried to grab for her dress while simultaneously staying submerged. With the height of the rim, her clothes were just out of reach if she wanted to stay in the water.

Dexios gave a quick nod to Benny and Shelby, then walked as casually as he could to the far side of the stone basin. "General," he said with nervous cordiality, "good to see you again!"

"And you, Dexios," the man answered. "First Selagus and now you. What brings you to Persia?"

Dex disappeared into the darkness where the Athenian general reclined in the water and began telling him of Athens' plight in hushed voices. Since the general had managed to remain hidden unintentionally in the bath house, Dexios seemed worried that spying ears may be hiding in the shadows as well. Ever the soldier, he was loyal to his commander but cautious of a lurking enemy.

Shelby tried to take advantage of Dex's distraction to get out of the water and covered again, but Benny grinned down at her and pulled the fabric slightly farther away as she scowled up at him. Crouching next to her, he whispered, "Don't know how you did it, bella, but you found our man and got his attention. Try to keep it long enough to get his help." He winked at her.

"You can't be serious!" Shelby snarled.

Benny put a finger to her lips and kissed the corner of her mouth. "Just play along."

Movement in the water drew Shelby's attention away from her plans to throttle Benny into the next era if he left her alone in the bath with Alcibiades. The general and Dexios were moving toward the pair of Travelers. As much as Shelby knew that nudity and the human body were common and accepted in ancient Greece, it wasn't something she was comfortable with, even with the buzz she was currently sporting. As the men neared, she began to feel like she was in a nightmare where she walked into the wrong locker room at the YMCA. Her eyes pleaded with Benny to give her back her clothes as the rest of her sank below the surface of the dark water to her neck. Arms crossed over her chest and legs curled in front of her, she balanced on the stone bench carved into the side of the bathing pool. It was hard on her tailbone as she struggled to keep covered and from falling over at the same time. More effort than she would normally have put forth was being spent on seeming outwardly strong and confident in herself, at least the part that was above water.

"Benny, Shelby," Dex said as casually as he could. "I'd like you to meet my former commander, Alcibiades. General, my friends Benito Moretti and Shelby Starling."

Shimmering golden ripples flickered over the water's surface as the man stepped slowly out of the shadows into the torchlight. Shelby expected some grizzled old military man, wrinkled and gray, but was struck by the specimen of Greek physique that stood waist-deep in the water leaning on the edge of the basin shamelessly drinking in the sight of her. Even for middle-aged, he was in perfect physical shape, age only showing in the tiny wrinkles at the corners of his dark eyes. Muscles glistened in the glow of the flames and diamonds of water droplets sparkled in the dark curls on his head. Clean-shaven, his jaw was firm and strong, but his mouth curved playfully at the edges. Power and confidence met in every cell in his body, tempered by the mirth in his eyes. Without even trying, he had Shelby spellbound.

"My pleasure," Alcibiades said with perfect composure. "Dexios explained your... misunderstanding of the bath house, my beauty," he said with a grin at Shelby who finally remembered to close her mouth. "I, for one, am glad you wandered through the wrong door." The Greek was mesmerizing. Magnetic. Even the lisp wasn't off-putting. If anything, the soft 'r's gave his speech a silky sophistication, like a British accent.

Shelby forced a weak smile. "Thanks. Sorry I interrupted your bath." Blue sparks shimmered under the water as Shelby fought to hide them in the darkness. Seshat was urging her on. Shoving her hands behind her thighs, she curled her legs in front of her chest to cover as much as she could.

"No need to apologize. I'm glad you did," Alcibiades said still grinning at her. "I'll leave it to you, now. It's time I was going, anyway. However, I recommend the full Persian bath experience." His dark eyes twinkled as he leaned nearer to her. "There's nothing quite like being oiled and rubbed down."

Shelby could feel her cheeks flush and knew Benny was going to have a field day with this episode. "I'm sure you're right," was all she managed to say. Her voice caught in her throat and was barely a whisper in the cavernous room.

"I'm always right." His words were satin in his mouth. Seductive and playful. Straightening up to face the men standing behind her, Alcibiades said, "Dinner, tomorrow evening at my house. I insist you all join me. It will give me a chance to catch up on news from home," to the men, "and get to know you a bit better," to Shelby.

"We're honored," Benny said with a slight bow to the general.

"Of course, sir," Dexios added standing taller than he had in days.

Alcibiades chuckled again. "Good. It's settled then. Come, men, let's leave Shelby to her bath for a moment and we'll discuss details."

Shelby smiled faintly as the Greek ascended the marble steps next to her, water pouring from his body, shameless in his nakedness. Alcibiades was clearly enjoying the hell out of this. As much as Shelby willed her eyes not to look, the damned things were traitors.

The general strode across the floor, pausing to shake loose a folded sheet on a wooden table by the door as Dexios followed him down the columned hall toward the other rooms. Glancing over his shoulder, Dex motioned for Benny to come on.

"You ok, bella?" Benny asked, his grin close to getting him a slap across his handsome face.

"Fine," Shelby answered. "Just go. I'll be out in a minute."

Benny kissed the top of her head. "At least you're clean. Most of you, anyway."

"Shut up."

The Roman laughed as he turned to catch up with Dexios and Alcibiades. "We'll meet you in the main room. Assuming you remember which door you stormed through."

"I mean it, you sadistic twit. Shut up." Benny only laughed harder. His voice rang in the high ceiling as Shelby sank under the black glittering surface of the water, as much to wash the road dirt from her hair as to vanish from the embarrassment she was feeling more of as her buzz wore off. A significant part of her wished there was a time jump portal in the drain of the pool that would get her the hell out of here. Apollo had done nothing to prepare her for this shit, and she had a serious bone to pick with the god.

CHAPTER 6

Shelby had to hand it to Alcibiades. There really was nothing quite like the full Persian bath experience. Parts of it were like being at the Y, only with marble everywhere instead of mildewed carpet and funky tile. Other elements were completely and uniquely ancient Persia. Deep inside the ornate bath house structure was a massive sauna room where she was told to lay for almost an hour on the warm slab of striated stone. At first, she was antsy and wanted to look around at the carved basins on the walls and other intricate details, but the watchful eyes of the attendants kept her from wandering around. Eventually, she settled into the experience like she was sunbathing on the beach, only without sand in her bathing suit and tinny reggae steel drums on a portable radio. This time, however, instead of a stray naked Athenian general, there were a handful of other women of various origin with her. Once more she was reminded of a YMCA locker room, only this time it was the women's one. There were a few bashful women who tried to keep a cloth pulled over parts they were self-conscious about while others walked brazenly around in the buff. Shelby was somewhere in the middle of that. She knew she was in good shape and didn't have much she was self-conscious about except for the birthmark on her back in the shape of Massachusetts, but she wasn't really one to go parading around naked. A bikini, maybe. But nothing at all? Great big nope on that one. Of course, Alcibiades would probably find that one hard to believe after her escapade the night before.

Once she spent enough time sweating to satisfy the attendants, she was taken to another room where more servants waited to slather her in scented oils and rub her with a rough cloth before scraping off the grime and oils with what looked like a bone honed to a just-under-sharp edge. She could almost imagine herself getting a massage at a spa right up until the attendant started pulling her arms and legs all over the place getting all the dirt and dead skin off her with the buffing. After being scraped down like an icy windshield, she was buffed once more with a softer cloth.

After that step, she was sent to the women's pool which was not nearly as ornate as the men's. However, there was something comforting about knowing there shouldn't be a ridiculously attractive man sitting across from her. Instead, there was a very bashful young woman who nearly lost her footing trying to get into the tub while keeping herself covered and avoiding the eyes of the other women. Shelby felt a twinge of pity for her since she had very recent experience knowing exactly how she felt. Sucking up her own self-doubt, Shelby slid into the water and leaned her head back on the edge of the basin like the other women did. Much of her experience was simply watching what the others did and following their lead. This time, once all of them were settled, attendants came and kneeled beside each of them on the outside of the pool with an embossed metal basin full of perfumed water. Carefully, the attendant girls unbraided and unwound the hair of the one they were seated next to and lowered it all into the water basin to soak. This was a part Shelby could definitely get used to. Her favorite part of going to the hair salon was the shampoo and scalp massage. While there were no suds this time, it was just as good. And maybe even better because it also lacked the gum-smacking narrations of the New York hair stylist's personal life. By the time she was finished, she was cleaner than she ever thought possible with no soap, and more relaxed than she'd been in ages. No burning hands, no sparks, no Alcibiades. At least for the moment. She knew all of that would change at dinner.

* * *

The sun was sinking in the Persian sky setting fire to the buildings in brilliant swaths of orange and gold. Carvings and artwork on the facades shimmered in the fading warmth giving a sense of life and movement to the massive images and intricate stonework. The city that was full of life and sound during the day seemed to grow quieter with each shift in color. By the time the light faded from blazing golds to muted blues, the town had lulled itself into a gentle hush.

The peace of the evening grated in sharp contrast to the apprehension in the guts of the trio making their way through the winding streets toward the general's house on the edge of town. While they needed to get close to Alcibiades, none were exactly sure how to explain their mission to him, much less garner his support. No matter how they rehearsed what they wanted to say, it sounded ludicrous.

"How do we even start this conversation where it doesn't sound like a trap?" Dexios asked as they neared the house.

Shelby shrugged. "I don't know. Political intrigue isn't really my thing. I'm more of a 'drink a lot and let the world take care of itself' sort of girl." She rubbed at her hands that began to burn harder with every step closer to Alcibiades' house. Mercifully, Seshat had enough sense not to send the blue sparks for her to contend with during a dinner party.

Benny rolled his eyes and grinned at her. "I hate to say it, Shelby, but you've got the best chance of convincing him. I doubt he gives either one of us a second thought once he sees you. Play along. It's a means to an end."

Shelby sighed. "Great." For a moment, the image of the sculpted Greek getting out of the bath flashed before Shelby's eyes. There was a time when only her self-consciousness would have kept her from falling blissfully in bed with a man like that - at least until she had enough wine in her. Then, all bets were off. Now, though, things were very different. Part of her worried about her own self-control. She lost her heart to Benny, but she was still human. It was hard enough to resist the flirtations of Gael in Paris, and Alcibiades had already proven himself to be even more magnetic. Another part of her wasn't happy about Dex and Benny throwing her under the bus when it came to getting Alcibiades to Athens. "Play along, huh? Sure about that? I'll see what I can do," she added with more snark than necessary.

Music and voices spilled with the light through the windows of the general's house as they approached. Far from being the awkward dinner of the three outsiders and the great general, it was a gathering of modest number. "I thought this was going to be a more intimate dinner," Benny said quietly.

"Sounds more like a party," Shelby said warily. As awkward as it would have been to have only them and Alcibiades to make small talk, this was bordering on disaster. A house full of people made it even harder to broach a sensitive subject, much less know which side listening ears could be on. The last thing they needed was to be betrayed to the Persian authorities and sent to Lysander before they could convince Alcibiades to return to Athens on his own.

"Just act normal," Benny whispered.

"What exactly does normal look like in 404 BC?" Shelby hissed as a servant held the door open for them with a low bow.

* * *

Small talk with the men and flagrant flirtation with Shelby was the theme of the small gathering over a multi-course meal of richly spiced vegetables, roasted meats, and decadent fruit desserts. Conversation steered clear of anything political or controversial, letting the three newcomers know that either they or the other guests weren't completely trusted by their host. Charming and attentive, Alcibiades made Benny and Shelby feel as welcome as the general's former soldier. Vague innuendo about her bath house flub brought a blush to her cheeks that seemed to make their host bolder and more determined to keep the blush going. Benny and Dexios exchanged grins as Shelby's eyes widened with Alcibiades' brazenness in front of the more demure Persian guests, who seemed to be oblivious to the sexual tension or were too polite to react.

Between Benny and Shelby was a wordless sparring match of one-upmanship as Alcibiades turned up the heat. Benny egged him on, and Shelby squirmed before slowly flirting back making Benny squirm. Dexios found himself on the fringes drinking good wine and enjoying the show the Persians were oblivious to. By the time the locals decided to call it a night, the young hoplite had drunk himself halfway under the table and had pulled Benny into a detailed account of his exploits at sea under the general's command that had somehow failed to impress his father.

"Come, Shelby," Alcibiades said silkily. "Let young Dex entertain Benny for a while. I'm sure you'd prefer a stroll around the garden over a soldier's ramblings."

A nod from Benny over Dex's shoulder let Shelby know she better take her chance to talk to Alcibiades alone. Shelby, however, wondered how much talking Alcibiades had in mind. "Sounds perfect," she answered slipping her arm into the crook of the general's.

Behind the house was a small garden courtyard with a tall stone wall shielding it from the street and houses around it. In one corner, under a flowering vine that climbed the wall then reached across to the other corner, was a carved wooden bench. Nearby were torches in metal holders sending shadows scuttling through the leaves of the vine.

"It's beautiful," Shelby said taking in the delicateness of the space that seemed strangely soft in the city of carved stone.

"As much time as I spent on ships, I came to love intimate spaces almost as much as the open sea. There's something peaceful about this courtyard that draws me here," the general said as he led Shelby to the bench. "But tonight, it's beauty pales in comparison to yours."

Shelby chuckled in spite of not wanting to offend Alcibiades. "How many women has that line worked on?" she asked as she gathered her dress around her legs and curled up in the curve of the warm wooden bench.

"More than it should have," Alcibiades answered with a grin. "Of course, none were quite like you." Stroking her cheek with the back of his hand, he sat down next to her. "There's something about you that doesn't seem to fit this place," he said leaning back. One arm draped across the back of the bench, and he let his hand trace the curve of her shoulder as it found a resting place behind her. Alcibiades' face was cast in shadow from the vine above, so Shelby couldn't read his expression to know how much of that statement was flattery and how much was suspicion.

"Persia? I should say not," she answered coolly.

The general laughed and turned her chin to get a look at her face in the torch light. Sweat ran down Shelby's spine between her shoulder blades as nerves began to betray her. "Or Athens. True, you have the dress and the hair all right, but the attitude is refreshingly un-Athenian."

Shelby's uneasiness amplified with the stinging in her hands as the general spoke. He was doing his best to sound conversational and relaxed, but she could tell there was a layer of distrust under the schmoozing. "How so?" she asked, pressing the palms of her hands flat against the seat on either side of her trying to stem the pain.

Alcibiades leaned forward and faced her, looking straight into her dark eyes. "You don't talk like an Athenian, for one thing. It's enough to fool the Persians, but your accent is all wrong and your words and actions too brazen. Too confident. Too Spartan. Maybe that's what draws me to you."

With his last words, the flirtatious tone returned along with a smile, but Shelby had already seen behind the mask. Alcibiades didn't trust them. If she hoped to get him to come back to Athens at her request, she was going to have to make him want to, which was going to mean laying it on thick.

Shelby crossed one long leg over the other, letting the drape of her dress fall open mid-thigh. Just enough to remind him of what he'd already seen. "And just what is it about Spartan women that appeals to you?" she asked with a wink.

Running a finger up the nape of her neck, the general relaxed into the back of the bench again. "There is something captivating about a beautiful woman who says what she thinks. Something sensual in a confidence like that."

"Then why keep Athenian women subservient? Why not encourage them all to be more Spartan?"

"Because then the men would be too distracted to run the place." He sighed and closed his eyes. "Sometimes I wonder if we would be better off if women ran the government."

"Pretty radical thought for an Athenian general," Shelby teased.

He chuckled. "Perhaps you don't know as much about me as I thought. There's nothing conventional about much that I've said or done."

Shelby ran a stinging hand down her thigh letting the fabric catch on her finger and pull the opening a little wider. "I've heard enough to know that you are as fascinating as you are attractive."

"But where has that gotten me?" Alcibiades stood and paced. Muscles in his arms tensed slightly then relaxed as he opened and closed his fists in what seemed like an effort to control his frustration. As much as he appeared carefree and flirtatious on the surface, Shelby could see the mighty general bubbling up from deep down. "Once I could command anything my heart or body desired in Athens. Women, men, power, prestige. Now, I bide my time in Persia in a precarious arrangement with an absent satrap who could turn on me any time the money is right. I suppose there's some excitement in that."

"Not the kind you really want, though, is it?" Shelby asked.

"No," he said softly to the far corner of the courtyard. "Now the only adventure is in my dreams."

This turn from sexual tension to actual tension was not helping Shelby get Alcibiades wrapped around her finger like Benny was counting on. She smiled up at him. "Tell me about them," she said gently tugging him back to the bench.

Creases around his eyes that had hardened moments before softened as a grin played at the edge of his lips. "I can think of better things to do than discussing dreams."

"So can I," Shelby answered returning the grin. "First, though, I want to hear about them. I'm a sucker for a good adventure story." Her heart thudded heavily in her chest as she fought to stay on the edge of making him want her and pushing him away. A dance that was harder than she imagined. Her only plan was to keep him talking until Benny decided it was time to get Dex home. Alcibiades brought her hands to his lips and kissed them gently sending electricity surging up her arms. Her breath caught sharply in her chest as the general's eyes widened. Had he felt it, too? Surely not. "Come sit with me again," she said patting the seat next to her as she curled her legs up again, letting the drape of her dress fall open once more. Alcibiades settled himself on the bench and traced the curve of her knee with his fingertip. A warmth washed over her that had nothing to do with the sting of destiny and everything to do with the beautiful Greek's touch on her bare skin. "That's better," she cooed, making herself feel a little nauseous at her own brazenness. "Now, tell me what a great general dreams about."

CHAPTER 7

Stars were slowly wearing out as the night sky dawned over the Persian city where two Travelers sat up talking while an Athenian hoplite slept off copious amounts of wine. It had taken another hour after Shelby got Alcibiades talking again before Benny came to see if she was ready to go home. By that time, Dexios was weaving enough to require both of them to steer him back to their rooms at the inn. After getting him upstairs and sprawled across the bed snoring, Shelby and Benny sat in the open window letting the night air cool their room.

"I'm still mad at you for making me throw myself at him like that," Shelby said as she leaned her head on Benny's shoulder.

"Come on, bella," Benny teased. "Could've been worse. At least he's not an ogre."

Shelby rolled her eyes but thought that an ogre might have been less awkward. At least less of a battle against her own libido. Alcibiades was incredibly handsome and charismatic, lisp and all, and there was no way she could deny finding him attractive. It made putting on the show of flirtation even harder. She knew she could never love the Athenian general like she loved Benny. Real, honest, handsome Roman tour guide that he was. Far more her speed. Alcibiades was almost electric, which both excited and frightened her. "At least there was something he wanted to talk about. He seemed to have his mind on other things when he first took me outside."

Benny took her hand in his, turning it over and kissing her wrist. "I knew you could take care of yourself. Maybe not giving him what he wanted kept his attention a little longer. Men always want what's just out of reach."

"Is that so?" Shelby asked with a grin.

"Worked on me," Benny answered playing with the edge of her dress. "So, what was so interesting it took his mind away from taking your clothes off?"

"Dreams. Weird ones." Shelby sat up and looked at Benny. "There's something not right about them, though. Most people dream of things that are unrealistic. Fantasies that can't happen, good or bad. But his were more like a page out of history. They seemed strange and mysterious to him because it's history he doesn't know, but, to me, they were almost familiar."

Benny's forehead wrinkled in thought as his rich Roman eyes darkened. "Like what?"

Shelby's gaze wandered over the Persian rooftops as she thought. The sun was just below the horizon turning the sky from inky black to steel gray. "One of them made sense. He dreamt he was serving under some Greek general back in Athens. Alcibiades said his name was Themistocles, I think. Anyway, the guy was apparently widely popular in Athens, and it made sense that Alcibiades might dream about serving on one of his ships. I guess if you grow up in a sea-faring military, you have dreams like that. That one wasn't weird, except that he was serving under the guy, not commanding himself. You'd think someone as sure of themselves as the general is would always be in command, even asleep."

"Maybe he isn't as confident as he seems," Benny suggested.

"Not likely. He didn't seem to like it that he wasn't in command in the dream. Like he was more capable than Themistocles and was irritated at having to take orders from the guy that he was serving as an advisor. The general was too cautious for Alcibiades. Not a risk taker. Too politically correct in his decisions."

Benny snorted a laugh. "Now, that sounds more like the Alcibiades we know and love."

"Definitely."

"What about the others?"

Shelby leaned back against the window frame and tried to remember what Alcibiades told her. Like her memories, she could remember them in exact detail. It was strange. Why should she remember something that seemed like insignificant time-killing? "The other two dreams were the ones that seemed so mysterious to him. In one, he was in what he called 'a great stone palace full of carvings and statues of rigid bodies with animal heads.'"

"Egypt," Benny breathed.

Shelby nodded and went on. "One of the things he found so strange was that he was in the court of a great leader, but it was a woman. Hatshepsut."

"That's no coincidence. No one pulls a name like that out of thin air," Benny said, his dark eyes widening.

"I know. Her name was familiar, but I don't remember much about her. Alcibiades was fascinated by the queen, which goes with his respect for Spartan women and their own strength. But, again, he wasn't in charge, and it annoyed him that he should be advising a woman who had the supreme power, even if she did seem to have the strength for it. He said in the dream, he was attracted to her and jealous of her position at the same time. At least she seemed to listen to him as her advisor, where the general guy didn't."

Benny leaned forward and rested his arms on his knees. "What else did he say about the queen?"

"Not much. Mostly, he was fascinated by the palace and the statues of the gods and talked about those things more than what he was actually doing in the dream. The beauty of the palace is what brought up the last of the dreams he told me about.

"This one was about a lush and beautiful palace with gardens that seemed to hang in mid-air around him while the entire place was surrounded as far as he could see by desert sands. There were great fountains and intricate ways to harness and move water around the gleaming palace city. Trees growing on the roofs of buildings, flowers draping the patios, and lush gardens. Could he be talking about the Hanging Gardens of Babylon?"

Benny shook his head. "Yes and no. That's probably what he was talking about, but now they think the gardens weren't in Babylon at all, but in Nineveh."

"Alcibiades mostly described the gardens and how he wished they could have palaces like that here and how Athens surely should be able to create something as magnificent. But, of course, he also complained about being a sidekick to the ruler, Sennacherib."

"Nineveh," Benny said matter-of-factly.

"What?"

"Nineveh. Sennacherib was a king in Nineveh, not Babylon."

Shelby ran a hand up the back of her neck that was starting to ache from her long night and stifled a yawn. "Alcibiades didn't spend much time talking about what he did in his dreams, probably because he didn't want me to think he was less than the great leader he thinks he is. Most of what he was obsessing over was the kingdoms themselves and what Athens could do to improve on the art and gardens."

Benny turned Shelby around so her back was to him and moved the hair not caught up in braids away from her neck. "Sounds like he still has a soft spot for the city that won't have him," he said as he took over rubbing her neck.

His hands were warm and gentle as he massaged the tight muscles. As much as she wanted to stay irritated with him about throwing her to the Greek wolf, she couldn't help but love him. In his arms, she was safe from the strangeness of the time-warp her life had become.

"It's weird, though," she said half-asleep. "All of his dreams fit the same theme - Alcibiades serving a leader instead of leading himself. Just different times and places." Shelby paused as her hands began to burn and sparks swirled around her wrist and the bracelet. The sleep that had begun to cloud her senses was yanked away.

In the gray of the dawn, the blue shimmer caught Benny's eye. His hands stopped working her neck and turned her back around to face him, taking her hand in his. "There's something about what you just said. Say it again."

"In all of the dreams, Alcibiades was serving a leader instead of leading himself." Sparks jumped wildly as a strange feeling settled over them. "There's something familiar about that. Something -"

"- that you've been told before by a goddess with an attitude," Benny finished.

Seshat's bracelet glowed under the sea of swirling blue as the meaning dawned on her. "These weren't just dreams, were they?" Shelby turned wide eyes up at Benny who slowly shook his head. "But then, that must mean he's a *Traveler*!"

"And the dreams are his way of being able to see the memories of his past. He wouldn't be likely to travel to Nineveh and Egypt to touch monuments and be pulled back into them. The universe must use different things for different Travelers."

Blue sparks flooded from Shelby's hands to Benny's, who instinctively pulled back even though he knew they carried no heat. Seshat was letting them know they had finally stumbled on the truth of it all. "I - I don't understand," Shelby stammered, suddenly feeling nauseous. This was far bigger than just bringing back a wayward general. This was cosmic.

"But," Benny began in his own confusion, "why didn't he have flashes in Athens? Why did the universe use dreams for that?"

"Continuity?" Shelby guessed. It was a shot in the dark. Who the hell knew what the gods and universe were ever thinking? Not much that they did made sense, anyway.

Benny swung his legs back inside the window. "Come on, bella. The city is waking up and listening ears will be in the streets." He helped her inside and closed the window.

"So, is helping Athens win the war Alcibiades' destiny?" Shelby asked.

"Maybe. Maybe all those lives advising great leaders helped him to become one."

Shelby shrugged and flopped down on the edge of the bed. She was mentally and physically exhausted and sleep was catching up with her. "But is he really a great leader? Did he really learn what he was supposed to? Seems to me that all he's managed to do is make a mess of things. He's a traitor who isn't really welcome anywhere. How can he be a great leader when the only thing that waits for him in Athens is death?"

Benny sat down beside her and rubbed her hands, knowing it didn't really ease the burning pain. "Something isn't right about this. We need to get some answers."

"From one asshole of a god who sent us out here on a wild goose chase."

"Or the journal?" Benny suggested.

Shelby reluctantly pulled her hands away from Benny's and dug the book out of the pouch. Her hands buzzed harder, but she didn't have a choice. Tossing it on the bed, she waved a hand over it as the cover opened and pages fluttered. At least that trick still worked. With a flick of her finger, she turned past the pages they already knew well. "The last thing we read was about him meeting Apollo on the ship to Athens and how he should go visit Delphi. Here." Her hand hovered just above the page not wanting to touch it. "It picks up again once he's off the boat."

Apollo had certainly not sold Athens short. It was a fascinating city of ancient wonder, but certainly not luxurious. More rustic in its charm. Once a city of gods, its marvels lay scattered across the landscape among the homes and businesses as if they were quite accustomed to centuries of co-existence. Rising above the city, buildings that seemed to be slowly climbing the hills, was the great Acropolis and the mighty Parthenon. Oh, to have seen it in its splendor rather than in ruins!

I deposited my belongings at the inn and had a drink at the bar while my body became used to the stillness of the land. It always surprises me how quickly one can become accustomed to the constant rocking of the sea and how still and lifeless the land can feel after that. After a rest and change of clothes, I am hoping to have time for a tour of the city before dinner.

"Pretty dull stuff so far, Eli," Shelby scoffed as she swished a finger to turn the page.

Once, I considered myself an experienced traveler. One with their wits about them. Yesterday, I learned how wrong I was about that. There is danger in even the most welcoming of cities. Athens not excepted. Last night, on my way back to the inn after a delicious meal, I must have been more exhausted than I realized. My thoughts wandered to plans for the next day and I didn't see the men approaching. It likely wouldn't have mattered anyway as they outnumbered me. Once they caught my notice, it was too late. Each with a blade in their hands, the men blocked my path. Hoping it was only my money they were after, I willingly gave up what I had on me. Most of my money and valuables were in the hotel safe, leaving carrying only what remained after my dinner bill was settled. This amount didn't satisfy the bandits. Mercifully, they left me bleeding and bruised, but alive. Perhaps they thought me dead as I lay on the ground as still as I could manage, stifling the cries threatening to escape my swollen lips. Even now, I shudder at what could have become of me.

Athens has much to offer in history and beauty, but little in the way of medical care. I have been brought back to my room in the small inn and am being seen to by doctors and the inn owner's wife. A kind old woman, but not qualified to nurse anyone. Pain is being dulled with medicines that make me sleepy, and wounds are being held together with bandages and poultices, but surgery in this place frightens me. The modern practices of London have yet to make it this far. I only hope it will not come to that, although the pain in my side grows worse, even with the drugs. There is no cut there, but the pain is staggering. From what I can understand of the doctors, they are considering the possibility of operating on me to find the cause of the pain. I pray it doesn't come to that.

"That doesn't sound good," Benny said.

Shelby shook her head. "Surgery in Victorian England doesn't sound good, either. Surgery in Athens then had to be really scary."

"I meant the injury, but yeah. Sounds like he's hurt inside and that isn't a good thing in modern times, much less the 1870s. What else does it say?"

A yawn stopped Shelby from continuing for a second, then she turned the page again and went on.

No one is telling me anything. I ask questions, and get vague answers. Doctors come and go, looking at wounds and pressing on my side. The pain is getting unbearable. Medications make me sleep through some of it, but the fog my brain is in is almost more than I can stand. There are times I'd rather be able to think and understand more clearly and deal with the agony. The only moments clear enough to let me write this are as the drugs are wearing off. Writing helps to keep my mind from the pain.

I thought if they wouldn't answer my questions about my injuries, maybe someone would at least tell me how I got here. I remember the men and the beginning of the fight after they took the money, but then the details are hazy. There are some memories that I am not sure are real and I am hoping someone will help me understand. I remember seeing two people standing over me. They spoke English, one of them with a heavy accent. Maybe the couple I met in town earlier that day. But I don't know for sure. Maybe I imagined they were there and am mixing memories with all the drugged visions. If it was the young couple who brought me here, I'd like to thank them.

"It jumps and his writing is badly scrawled. This isn't going well for Eli," Shelby said surprised by how much emotion the Victorian diarist's struggle was stirring. Elijah Faircloth, even though he didn't know it, had been a constant companion through her own journey to her destiny as a Traveler. Even though all she had were words written a hundred years before she was born, she was connected to him somehow. Reading his words of pain and struggle hurt her, too.

Fever has become too high. Doctors are concerned about infection, or worse. Cuts are healing slowly, but surely. My side is their concern. It grows worse, and I grow weaker. Tired. So tired. Too tired to object to surgery. Too weak to make the journey to London. Doctors will operate in the morning.

Tears pushed their way to Shelby's eyes as she fought them back. One snuck down her cheek as she looked up and met Benny's dark eyes. "That's it. There's no more. What happened?"

"Maybe the journal was just lost," Benny offered gently.

"Or maybe Elijah Faircloth didn't make it out of surgery, much less to Delphi." A sob caught in the back of her throat as she buried her face in Benny's chest. After all Eli went through, the mental stress of being yanked back into memories; he had no one to explain. He didn't make it. "It's not fair," she sobbed. "It's not fair that he didn't finish his journey after all that!" Sadness quickly gave way to anger. "Apollo. He knew. Why didn't he do something? Why didn't he help him? How is *this* supposed to help *us*?" Part of her wanted to cherish every word of Eli's journal. Another part of her wanted to shove it down Apollo's throat. "There's more to this than a war between Athens and Sparta. It's about time that asshole god told the truth," she spat. "Not a word to Dex. He'd never believe any of this."

Benny nodded as he laid down next to her and tried not to yawn. "Think he'll take us to Delphi?"

"Whether he does or not, we're going."

CHAPTER 8

"Delphi?" Dexios asked as he pushed his breakfast around the plate with a crust of bread. He had slept most of the day and was nursing a wicked hangover. Food was what he needed most but was the last thing he wanted. "Why?"

"There's someone we need to see there," Shelby answered simply.

The young hoplite shook his head. "I don't know. What if it's not safe in Greece right now?"

Shelby snorted. "The same way it's not safe in Persia? You know, that place we're sitting in right now with Lysander and the Spartan army in their back pockets?"

He shrugged and winced as he tried to take another bite of bread. "They may not be on our side here, but they aren't going around waving swords and spears at us, either."

"True," Benny said, "but it doesn't change the fact that we need to get to Delphi."

"Now," Shelby added.

For a long moment, Dexios stared at them, his glassy eyes drifting from one to the other as he thought. Shelby wasn't sure if it was the idea of getting back on the road with his raging headache and nausea that was the problem, or something else. She knew damn well it wasn't because it was dangerous. He was a soldier. His life was danger. They were no safer here than in Greece. It didn't matter anyway. Shelby was damned if the kid was going to keep her from facing off with Apollo about the shitstorm he dropped them in.

"Let me try this again, Dex," she began slowly so he could understand her through his hangover haze. "We're going to Delphi. Are you coming with us?"

"Without Alcibiades?" Dexios deflected. "I thought he was the whole reason we came here. Don't we need to take him with us?"

Benny leaned back in his chair and crossed his arms over his chest. He was losing patience. "Dex, Alcibiades isn't going to run back to Greece with us because he enjoyed a night talking in a garden with Shelby. There's someone in Delphi who can help us get Alcibiades where he needs to be."

Clarity was slow in its dawning on Dexios. "Are we going to see the Oracle?"

Shelby draped one long leg over the other and rested her arm on the table bringing her dark eyes level with Dexios'. "Probably. But that's not who we want to talk to."

Dexios squinted at Shelby. "Apollo?" It was barely a whisper, as if he couldn't believe the words coming out of his own mouth.

Shelby didn't react. She just stared back at him and asked, "Are you coming with us or not?"

Slowly, imperceptibly at first, the young hoplite nodded.

* * *

Nothing about their approach to Delphi was familiar to the two Travelers, but Dexios seemed to see nothing unusual about it, so they kept their mouths shut. Dexios thought they had come from the city before he met them in Athens, and they couldn't risk giving away the fact that the last time they saw the place it was a pile of rubble and ruin.

Rising above them now was anything but.

Gleaming polished walls surrounded the buildings nestled in the crook of Mount Parnassos. Statues soared overhead on giant columns next to intricately carved and vibrantly colored friezes on temples and treasury buildings that peeked over the walls. Gone were the grass fringed paths, lonely columns, and crumbled remnants of a fallen civilization. Only the surrounding hillsides and staggering view were familiar in any way. The twin Phaedriades, or 'Shining Rocks', flanked the mountain rising to a precipice almost a thousand feet high. Voices carried on the wind drew their attention to one of the peaks as a steady drumbeat began. The people were too far away for the Travelers to see what they were doing, but a blood-curdling scream let the three of them know that whatever it was, it wasn't good.

"What's happening?" Shelby asked squinting in the direction of the scream that was now echoing off the hillside.

"Sacrilege," the hoplite answered.

Benny shielded his eyes from the midday sun and tried to focus on the tiny figures above them. "What are they doing that's sacrilegious?"

"Not them," Dexios answered. "Whoever is screaming. Sacrilege is punishable by death, and you can be thrown from the heights of the Phaedriades. Usually Phleboukos instead of Rhodini."

"That's horrible!" Shelby said shocked at the brutality of people claiming to be so religious. Clearly, forgiveness was not part of the theology here.

Benny, slightly more pragmatic, asked, "How did they choose which mountain to throw them off of?"

Dexios shrugged. "That, I don't know. Maybe the direction the wind usually blows? It would ruin it if the person was blown back into the cliff before they hit the bottom." It may have seemed like a reasonable explanation to the soldier, but Benny and Shelby just stared at him, mouths agape. "Not- not that either way is a good way to die," he added trying to salvage the conversation.

As they watched, tiny figures gathered at the peak, like ants swarming a piece of fruit at a picnic. Drumbeats intensified as the screaming quietened. The condemned had apparently accepted his fate. Seconds later, the drums stopped, and the mass of bodies grew still. Then, one shadow of a form became airborne as the screaming began again, but only for a few seconds. From such a height, the man died, or at the very least lost consciousness, before his body finished falling. His form grew momentarily larger as he fell to the level the three of them stood, then shrank again as he tumbled in the air to the valley below. Shelby turned her face into Benny's chest as her breath caught in her throat unable to watch the final moments of the man's punishment.

"It's ok, bella," Benny said wrapping his arms around her. "It's over."

Shelby didn't really want to look, but her eyes involuntarily went to the valley. There was nothing to see. The scrubby trees concealed wherever the man had landed. "What a horrific thing to do to someone."

Dexios rested a hand on the hilt of his sword and looked uneasy. "The gods don't like being offended. What they could do is even worse." With that, he led them to the gates of Delphi.

As they approached, they could see the marble or red-tiled roofs of the various temples and buildings that surrounded the massive structure in the middle. The Temple of Apollo. As much as she wanted to get to the reason for coming here, she couldn't. Not yet. "Wait," Shelby said tugging on Benny's arm to stop him. "There's something we need to do first." Her hands had burned and tingled worse and worse the closer they got to the city but the agony was almost more than she could take as they stood at the gates. Rubbing them, she remembered the only way she had been able to deal with the pain the last time they stood here. "We need to get to the spring first."

* * *

The Kastilian Spring in the valley below the walls of Delphi was transformed in much the same way as the city. Vegetation no longer reclaimed the carved stone. Instead, reliefs along the stone backdrop of the sparkling water gleamed in the dappled sunlight that tumbled through the trees on the hillside. Penitents knelt at the water's edge as priests mumbled rites of purification while pouring water over the heads of the seekers of the gods. Their last time here, in the hour before dusk after the tour buses departed, the Travelers had the spring to themselves. Now, there was a small crowd waiting their turn.

"Could be worse," Dexios said. "You should see it on the day the Pythia speaks to the people."

"What do you mean?" Shelby asked while scanning the crowd at the edge of the stream or gathered around small fountains dribbling water into carved basins.

Dexios led them to a shaded area with benches carved from the trunks of fallen trees and sat down shaking dirt from his sandals. He looked up at Benny and Shelby seeming to measure his words. Finally, he said, "Apollo sent you to Athens, but you don't know how all of this works?"

It was the most pointed thing the young hoplite had ever said to them. Most of the time, he went along with whatever the pair asked of him, seeming to put his faith in the scrap of fabric with the god's symbol on it. When they arrived in

Delphi, suspicion snuck into his expression. Now, it found its way into his words, too.

"Things are a little different since the last time we've been here," Shelby said trying her best to sound more confident than she was.

It didn't seem to work on the soldier. "Things have been the same here for over a century," he said flatly. He said no more, but it was enough to let the Travelers know that he wasn't sold on the story they had spun for him all along. The question, then, was why had Dexios gone along with it all this time if he didn't believe them?

"Come on, bella," Benny said giving her a warning look to say no more. He took her stinging hand in his as she stood to follow him. It was strong and sure where hers were trembling and hurting. Faint blue sparks began to sparkle on her fingertips as she laced them through his but were too faint to be seen by passers-by in the sunlight. Benny noticed, though. "I think we need to find a place without a priest."

"Blue sparks would be a little tough to explain. Wouldn't want to find ourselves being hurled off a cliff."

With a nod, Benny scanned the valley for a place that was less popular than the picturesque spot the priests occupied. Shelby needed the water to calm the burn in her hands and insulate her from the power of the temple, but it didn't matter where it came from. She didn't have the rites last time either, so they figured the priests were really just for show. Reluctantly, Dexios followed them away from the ritual space to a fountain set away from where the faithful gathered at the water's edge.

Shelby turned to look at the young hoplite. "Is this the same water that comes from the spring?"

"Yes, but you need the priests to purify you before you enter the temples."

Shelby shook her head. "Look, Dex, I know this isn't the way things usually work, but it's not the first time we've done this." She took a deep breath and decided to let the soldier in on more than she originally planned to. "There's something we haven't told you. Well, there's a lot we haven't told you, but one thing you should probably see for yourself to understand why I'm doing things the way I am." Shelby let Benny's hand go and held hers out in front of her, slowly turning it over. Sparks danced merrily, swirling around the bracelet.

Dexios' wide dark eyes reflected the tiny sparkling lights. "I- I've never seen anything like it," he breathed. "What is it?"

Benny touched her hand, and the sparks flooded his and wrapped their wrists. "Messages," he answered. "In a way. Apollo isn't the only god leading us. There's another, but now isn't the time for all that. The sparks don't hurt us, but there's pain in Shelby's hands when she's near certain people or places that the gods want her to pay attention to. It's a message like the sparks."

"But we can't let the priests see them. They wouldn't understand, and we damn sure aren't about to get thrown off a cliff," Shelby added. "Last time, the water stopped it long enough for me to go into the temple."

Eyes still glued to the blue swirling mass, Dexios nodded and motioned to the fountain. "The water here is the same. It should work."

Pretending to be standing by the fountain in deep conversation, Benny and Dexios shielded Shelby as she knelt in front of the trickle of water. Diamonds of light shimmered on the small stream as it twisted on itself down to the small basin on the ground. Droplets splashed out creating dark spots on the sand-colored stone and made flecks of mud from the dust on the ground. A familiar pull in her hands let her know they sought the water as much as she did. Slowly, she eased her fingertips under the cool water and let it wash over her hands and wrists then let it flow down her arms to her elbows. As she did, the sparks flickered in the flow of water then vanished, and the pain numbed. Splashing her face with the cool liquid, her mind that raced with questions began to calm and focus. Shaking the dust from her dress as she stood, Shelby traded places with Benny for him to do the same. Even though he didn't have the sparks and the pain, he was still a Traveler seeking the god and would need to at least purify himself, even without the rites of the locals.

Dexios went next. His glance flickered from Benny and Shelby to the priests, likely wondering if it was enough for him to wash in the water without the rites, but he said nothing. He knelt and held his hands under the flowing water. As it touched his hands, he jerked them back and rubbed his right wrist through the leather guard. Benny and Shelby exchanged confused looks but said nothing of the strange reaction to the cold spring water. A shrug and glance over his shoulder, then Dexios put his hands back in the stream letting it run down his arms. Cupping his hands, he caught enough to pour over his head like the priests did to the others, then splashed his face. Standing his left hand absently rubbed his wrist again.

"You ok?" Shelby asked.

"I'm fine," Dexios said. "Old injury. Comes and goes." It was a lie and Shelby knew it, but since she hadn't exactly been truthful with him, she didn't press the issue.

"Ready, bella?" Benny asked with a glance up the path toward the city.

She nodded and held her hands out in front of her. No pain. No blue sparks. "As I'll ever be."

CHAPTER 9

Delphi rested in the slumber of the long-deceased when Shelby first laid eyes on her a lifetime ago. Quiet, somber, and half-buried under time and destruction. Only footprints remained where giants once stood. Legends and archaeologists constructed her history from puzzle pieces scattered across her hills and hidden under her blanket of eons past with mere shadows to tell them where each piece belonged. Rising from the dead before Shelby's eyes, Delphi stood in brilliant splendor radiating spiritual power across the face of Mount Parnassos. Where she had once seemed cold and dead, Delphi now opened her arms to the Travelers in warm welcome.

The same path wound up the hillside to the commanding structure at the heart of it all: the Temple of Apollo. Along the way were smaller temples and treasuries given to the city to honor the gods for their benevolence or aid in battle. Shelby wondered as she passed one of these monuments how much was for the god's glory and how much was for the victor's. Intricately painted and gilded carvings depicted scenes of ancient mythology, the modern religion of Delphi, that wrapped the exteriors of the buildings with special attention paid to the peaked roofs supported by huge stone columns. Treasuries and shrines were built in a hodgepodge with no real plan as new ones were dedicated, shoved in wherever they could fit as more were added over the centuries. Each vying for prominence and dominance. Statues and towering columns seemed to compete with one another to see who could reach the heavens first. Gold glinted in the sunlight from frieze work overlays and gilded statues nestled into every available nook and cranny. All faced the processional path so that their gods and the patrons who paid for them could be properly honored.

Crowning the hill was the ornate and massive Temple of Apollo. All around were small statues on pillars and columns, but one seemed to stand guard high above the rest. Rising nearly a thousand feet in the air on a column, a stone creature sat perched surveying the surrounding city. "What the hell is that thing?" Shelby asked squinting up at the massive sculpture that had the body of a lioness, the upturned wings of a bird, and a human head seated atop an Ionic capital.

"The Sphinx of Naxos," Dexios said, eyeing Shelby as she stood in awe of something that had stood in that spot for over a century and a half.

"Oh," she said, realizing she should keep her mouth shut about things that had probably been there forever if she didn't want to give herself and Benny away as outsiders. "Of course." Shelby shrugged sheepishly at Benny who rolled his eyes as they walked toward the temple entrance.

Standing on Apollo's portico, the temperature dropped several degrees. A chill ran through Shelby, but she wasn't convinced it was from the cooler air. Something about standing here again made the hair on her arms and neck stand on end. It was almost electric.

Dexios stopped at the top of the stairs and turned to face Shelby. "So, do you have a plan for getting inside?"

"What do you mean?"

"Only men are allowed in the inner chamber and only on days when the Oracle sees visitors. You're no man, and today is not that day," Dexios said crossing his arms over his chest. It was almost a challenge to see what she could pull out of her bag of tricks to get what she wanted, especially since he seemed doubtful she was who she said she was. So far, Shelby had been able to track down the elusive Alcibiades and get into his good graces without much effort. Dexios seemed to think this was where her luck ran out and, if she was reading his face right, he was amused by it.

"To be honest," Shelby said, "I hadn't thought that far."

"I didn't think so," Dexios answered, his lips curling into a smirk. "Good thing I decided to come with you."

"What do you mean?" Benny asked.

Dexios winked. "It's my turn to be vague. There are some things I can tell you, and some things I can't," he said throwing Shelby's words in her face. "Stay here."

Shelby watched him go, torn between being confused and amused at the young hoplite's brazenness. "What the hell was that all about?" she asked.

Benny shook his head. "No idea, but I think we need to keep an eye on Dex. I don't think he believes half of what we've told him."

"He doesn't, I'm sure," Shelby answered with one hand on her hip. "But why doesn't he challenge us about it? Why go along with us?"

"I'm sure he has his reasons," Benny answered. Vagueness was running rampant around Delphi.

While they waited for the soldier's return from inside the temple, the Travelers did their best to seem inconspicuous. Like their arrival in Athens, being dressed the part did little to prepare them for the customs of the place. After seeing what sacrilege could earn you, neither one was willing to risk it. Standing out of the sun on the expansive portico, they watched the penitents making their way up the path, pausing to pay homage to some monuments, ignoring the treasuries, placing offerings at the bases of statues. While the setting was serene and reverent, there was a certain energy about the place humming just beneath the surface. It was a flurry of anticipation and gratitude, fear and repentance. Emotions ran the gamut, from weary soldiers and weeping mothers to expectant couples and youths on the verge of the independence of adulthood. Each bringing with them a petition for the gods that they prayed would meet them there.

Shelby sat at the base of one of the huge columns and curled her legs up under her dress. Her hands weren't burning, but she still felt strange, like the place was pulling the energy from her somehow. Unlike the stillness the grounding of the Parthenon gave Shelby her first time in Athens, Delphi seemed to be reaching for her, pulling her in. Tugging at her soul in a way she struggled to understand, so she didn't mention it. Instead, she rested her head on the column and pretended to be rapt in the beauty of the place.

Pressing her hand against the column, Shelby pushed herself up to adjust the cloth of her dress. The familiar and unwelcome surge of electricity shot up her arm. *Goddamn it! Not here. Not now!* A flash of white light blinded her as images of Delphi past and present collided in a kaleidoscope of colors. Brilliant temple facades crumbled to ruin while others rose from the rubble. Dina's gentle smile and

Apollo's defiant smirk swirled into faces she didn't know. Faces that seemed familiar, somehow, even as she struggled to understand who they were. The faces seemed to pulse as they changed, morphing quickly from one to another, always on the edge of familiarity.

Finally, the flood of images slowed, and blurred into a wash of color. Stepping through the haze was Alcibiades, his dark curls falling into his face as he grinned at her. Strength coursed through every muscle as he approached, but amusement danced in his dark eyes. Shelby squinted trying to focus on him as a wave of nausea washed over her. He chuckled and cupped her chin in his hand. "Surprised?" he asked, the creases around his eyes deepening with his grin.

"You could say that," Shelby answered.

He laughed again and brought his lips to the corner of hers. Electricity shot through her, but there was no blinding flash of light; nothing to break the vision. She wanted to pull away, to resist, but gave in just enough to let him kiss her without returning the gesture. For a moment, she felt like she was back in Hadrian's litter being carried through Athens as the emperor's mouth and hands roamed her body. She was connected somehow to Alcibiades like she was to Hadrian, but how?

He pulled away from her slightly and whispered in her ear, his lips grazing the curve of her neck. "You're wondering why you can see me here, aren't you?" he asked silkily, as if he knew a secret and was teasing her with it.

She nodded as her back stiffened with suspicion. "You're not really in Delphi. You can't be," she whispered.

"You're right, my beauty. And you're not who you said you are. So, we both have secrets." His hand that had slid around her waist clutched the fabric of her dress, holding her tightly against his chest. The general in him seemed to have taken control over his Casanova side as he struggled with wanting her and not trusting her.

"Where are you? Where are you *really*?" Shelby asked, trying not to squirm and give her fear away.

Lips brushed her shoulder as Alcibiades answered, "Nowhere. Anywhere. It doesn't matter anymore."

"I - I don't understand."

A deep chuckle. "No one really does, do they?" he asked. "No, I suppose some do, but they don't tell the truth. I've never had much use for the truth. Most people don't believe it when they hear it."

Shelby was getting nowhere with the enigmatic Athenian, so she changed tactics. "Alcibiades, I'll tell you the truth. I need your help. I was sent to find you. To bring you home. Athens needs you." Her words were urgent, not knowing how much time she had left with the vision. "*I* need you."

Alcibiades' mouth came down hard on her lips, kissing her as he held her close. She needed his help, so she gave in more this time and relaxed into his embrace. After a moment, he pulled back from her, looked into her eyes, and his expression seemed to wilt from confidence to sadness. "Then, come find me," he whispered.

The blur of muted color around them began to shimmer as nausea washed over her again. Shelby swayed as Alcibiades let her go then stepped back into the growing mist of color and light. "No!" she cried. "Don't go!" Her hand shot out to try to grab his, but there was nothing to hold onto. Nothing solid about his form as he faded into the nothingness around her. Once more, white light flooded her vision, blinding her and taking Alcibiades with it.

CHAPTER 10

"Get her inside," a familiar voice said as she began to come to. Dexios. Shelby was on the ground leaning against the column where she was before the vision, but her hands were being held tightly in Benny's so she couldn't touch anything. "She's too close to the temple. The spring water can't insulate her against the power of it. Let's go. Now!" the soldier ordered in a whisper.

"But you said she can't go inside," Benny argued.

"I told you I'd take care of that part. Let's go before people start asking questions."

Dexios took one of Shelby's hands and helped her up to unsteady feet. For a second, she was afraid she was going to vomit on her protectors, but the wave passed as she regained awareness of where she was. As quickly as they could manage without looking suspicious, the three of them made their way to the temple entrance and up the steps. Before, there had been a small crowd outside waiting to enter, but they were gone. The temple itself was deserted. Not even the priests were loitering in the doorway anymore.

"Where is everybody?" Shelby asked, her voice a raspy whisper.

"The Pythia said there was a heretic in the Temple of Athena. They've gone to flush them out and toss them off the mountain."

"Jesus!" Shelby cursed. "That's horrible!"

"Not really," Dexios said. "They won't find anyone. The priests made it up."

"But - how -" Benny started.

Dexios held up a hand to stop him. "I told you, there are some things I can't explain to you. Not yet. Come on. We don't have much time. I managed to buy us maybe an hour."

As they crossed the threshold into the temple, Shelby looked up at words that were all too familiar. 'Know thyself.' The words of the sages. *Easier said than done, assholes.* All those words did was lead her here, to a place of more confusion about who she was and what she was supposed to do than anywhere else in her life. Or lives.

Stepping into the interior of the temple, the temperature dropped several degrees. It wasn't cold, but Shelby still shivered. Her skin pulsed with electricity and the hairs on her arms stood up. Huge carved columns surrounded her like they had in Egypt, but they lacked the vibrant color of the desert temple of Karnak.

"There's so many of them," Benny said looking up in wonder.

"The Forest of Columns. I never understood the reason for them. I guess to make you feel small as you approach the inner sanctum of the god."

Shelby's eyes peered through the maze of towering stone and shadows. "It works."

"This way," Dexios urged as he moved through the columns toward the center of the temple.

Far from the empty chasm Benny and Shelby expected, the interior room of the temple was ornate and full of statues and altars of various sizes. Standing in the midst of it all was a towering gold statue of perfect Grecian physique. Shelby squinted up at the face glinting in the reflected light from the flame in the eternal hearth. "Is that supposed to be Apollo?" she whispered to Benny. She'd learned her lesson about asking Dexios things she should know.

"Probably. I wonder what he thinks of it. Doesn't look much like him."

"Not in the face, anyway." The statue had the typical facial features of what Greeks considered handsome, like the true Apollo did, but it lacked the attitude of the real thing. The indignant scowl when he was challenged, the curl of his grin when he was amused, and the firm jaw when he took aim with his bow. If she wasn't usually annoyed at the god most of the time, Shelby would have found him perfectly gorgeous, even more than the striking gold image on the pedestal above her.

Dexios waited impatiently for them at the far end of the temple next to another set of columns and steps leading down to the inner sanctum. "This feels familiar," Shelby said, rubbing her hands that were beginning to throb again despite the dip in the Kastilian Spring.

"It should," Benny said. "The steps are in better shape than the last time we went down them." Crumbled shadows of steps in the temple ruin were now polished and gleaming, surrounded by Ionic columns heralding a place of sacred reverence and power. No more skittering pebbles followed them down into an unknown abyss. Now, Dexios led them silently and slowly down into the darkness beneath the temple.

Torches burned low in sconces in the corners as the familiarity of the place washed over the Travelers. In the center of the room, a tripod stool stood in front of a large lattice-carved stone shaped like a pineapple with no leafy top. "The Omphalos," Benny breathed. "The Navel of the World."

"That's right," a woman's voice said with a chuckle. Three heads whipped around to find the owner of the voice. From the shadows stepped a woman with laughing eyes and a quiet, elegant strength.

"Dina!" Shelby cried as tears welled up in her eyes.

The Oracle opened her arms as Shelby rushed toward her. "It's good to see you, too, Shelby," she said laughing. Releasing Shelby, Dina looked her over. "You make a stunning Athenian."

Shelby glanced at Dexios, who stood with his mouth agape watching the women greet each other. "But not a convincing one. Right, Dex?"

Slowly, he shook his head. "Yes. Um, no. I mean -" Then to Shelby, "You know the Pythia?"

Dina walked over to the young soldier and took his hand in hers. "Thank you for taking care of them, Dexios. Shelby and Benny are very special to us. You've done well."

"Thank you," Dexios said with a deep blush. "Us?"

A deep voice behind him answered, "The Oracle and I both thank you." Dexios spun around and came face-to-face with Apollo in the flesh. Realizing instantly who he was, Dexios fell on his face kneeling before the god. "While I appreciate the fealty, Dexios," Apollo's sonorous voice dropped gently, "I assure you, there's no need for kneeling." Dexios stood, but struggled to let his eyes meet Apollo's.

Benny stood at Shelby's side and whispered in her ear, "Careful, bella, he's still the god here, no matter how mad you might be at him."

"He *needs* me, remember?" Shelby snapped. Her back stiffened, and, despite her outward show of brazenness, a bead of sweat ran down between her shoulder blades. "Apollo," Shelby said stepping forward, "we need to talk."

Benny shrugged at Dina. "That doesn't sound any better in 404 BC than it did when girls told me that in school."

Dina grinned at him. "Surely, Shelby hasn't come all this way to dump a god," she whispered.

Apollo strode across the stone floor with his shoulders squared against whatever Shelby had to say. Confidence radiated, but there was something else lurking in his eyes. Something reminiscent of their last encounter and Shelby's ability to disarm the God of Light. Measured words veiled his unease. "I didn't expect to see you so soon, Shelby."

"Why doesn't that surprise me? You gods never seem to have a good handle on what's going on with us mere mortals," Shelby spat.

Apollo tisked at her. "Now, now. I thought we got past all this."

"Hardly. Especially since you managed to leave some key information out of our destiny deal."

Dexios had regained his senses enough to know that arguing with a god might not be a good thing. Inching over to Benny, he whispered, "Should she be talking to him like that? He's a *god*!"

"It's okay, Dex," Benny said pushing his hair out of his face, a quirk that gave his own nerves away.

"If you say so." The young hoplite stepped back into the shadows as though he didn't want to be close enough to be hit by a lightning strike if Shelby pushed the god too far.

Shelby paced the floor, furtive glances darting to the place where the tripod stool stood. She knew full well what was lurking underneath the temple in that spot and was keeping her distance. "Let's try this again," she said stopping in front of the god, one hand on her hip. "You let us believe our mission was stopping Athens from losing the war to Sparta."

"I didn't say that," the god volleyed.

"But you didn't correct us."

"No."

Shelby resumed her pacing, but her eyes never left Apollo's. Nervous energy moved her feet, but anger kept her gaze locked on target. "Maybe you just didn't know what *we* know now. After all, you didn't know about Benny."

Apollo crossed his arms over his chest and planted his feet, meeting her challenge to his omnipotence. "And what is it that you think you know that I don't?"

A mirthless grin stole across Shelby's face, flickering there then dissolving back into steel. Shelby's voice was flinty. "Alcibiades is a Traveler."

The god's shoulders fell slightly. Humbled, he said softly, "I know."

Benny's dark eyes widened, and he made a move toward the god. Dina's hand caught his arm and wordlessly cautioned him. Sulking, he stayed where he was letting Shelby face-off with Apollo.

"Why didn't you tell me?" Shelby snarled.

"Would you have made the leap over another Traveler? You're the only one who can do this, Shelby. I needed you to want to go."

Benny couldn't take it anymore. "You *tricked us?*" he roared, his voice ringing on the stone and echoing around them.

Apollo's eyes met Benny's. "I'm sorry, Benny. I had to. Chasing down another Traveler doesn't seem like much of a destiny, but there's more to this than you know."

Shelby planted her feet and put both hands on her hips. Dark eyes narrowed as she glared viciously at the god in front of her. "Spill it, Apollo, or we're done. We'll ride back to Athens, or Sparta, or anywhere the hell else, and live out our days leaving you to clean up your own damn mess."

The god stared hard at her before slowly answering. "You're right," he admitted. His words were low and firm. Gone was the swagger of the mighty god replaced by a serious calm. "You're right that I lied, and you're right that I knew what Alcibiades was. You're right about everything." Apollo walked over to the stone wall and leaned against it. He seemed to age some, weary and hurt at having to admit to everything Shelby accused him of. "Don't think I liked lying to you, Shelby. I'll tell you the truth, but I need you to do something first."

"Why should I help you?" she said, quickly losing her patience. Standing there in the center of the crypt, her mind darted across the Greek countryside imagining places she and Benny could live happily and humbly without the neediness of the immortals. She was over it. All of it. Over the gods' ineptness. Over the weight of the universe being forced onto her shoulders. Shelby Starling was done. Making up her mind to walk the hell out on the damn god, she turned to go only to be stopped by a word.

"Please." It hadn't come from Apollo. It was Dexios. Shelby wheeled around on him. Before she could let loose her anger on him for siding with the gods, the young hoplite spoke again. "Please, Shelby. If you go, I've failed. I've disappointed my father my whole life. I can't fail at this, too." Tears ran down his cheeks unchecked. Shoulders that had proudly squared off against his father in the Athens streets returned to the slumped defeat Shelby had seen in him kneeling at the fountain washing away the tears.

"Dex," Shelby said gently. "This isn't your fight. You haven't failed at anything. They already told you; you've taken good care of us."

"That was only part of my job," he said. "Please, let me finish it."

Shelby smiled at him, and Benny put a hand on the hoplite's shoulder. Shelby's eyes found Dina's. Having had enough of Apollo's riddles, she aimed her next question at the Pythia. "What's he talking about? What's his job?"

Dina's expression softened as she walked over to Dexios. Taking his hand, she began to unlace the leather guard on his arm. Dropping it to the ground, the oracle raised his wrist up for Shelby and Benny to see.

Shelby's breath caught in her chest, tight and suffocating. The room swam for a minute as she tried to process what she saw. There, on pale skin untouched by the Mediterranean sun, was a clock and compass tattoo. "You're a *Watcher*?" Her voice was strained as her breath came rushing back to her.

Benny cocked his head to one side, taking in the soldier in front of him. "That would explain why it didn't take much convincing to get you to come with us."

"I don't understand," Shelby said.

Dexios' eyes searched the floor as he tried to explain. "I told you my father brought me to the Oracle when I was young, but I didn't tell you what she said. I went in alone. Even my father didn't know." His eyes darted up and met Dina's before lowering again.

"But you said she had a silver tattoo of the bow and arrow," Shelby said turning to Dina.

"I do," the Pythia answered, "but only when I'm speaking for Apollo."

The god, still leaning against the wall, said, "Think of it like my signature. It lets the petitioner know her words are mine."

"You never needed to see it," Dina said to Shelby. "You had the real thing to tell you what he wanted." The oracle paused, then said, "Go ahead, Dexios. Tell them."

"I was the only one in my family to be born with the gift. My father would never have let me fulfill my destiny as a Watcher. I was supposed to follow in his footsteps in military service and politics." Tears once again filled his eyes. Shelby's heart ached for the young soldier who feared failure so deeply.

Dina rested her hand on his arm to try to reassure him. "But that's not what you were created for. It's never felt right, has it?" Dexios shook his head as tears fell. "So, we gave him his brand as a Watcher where it could be hidden and used his military service that would please his father to help with part of his destiny."

"Alcibiades," Benny said.

Apollo spoke up again. "Right. You see time as a linear thing. To the immortals, it twists around itself -"

"Like threads that need untangling," Shelby said remembering the words of Seshat in the temple at Karnak.

"Exactly," Apollo said.

Slow steps carried Shelby across the stone floor to the young soldier with pleading eyes. Lifting his hand, she turned it over in hers and ran a fingertip across the tattoo. "You trusted us more than we trusted you. I'm so sorry, Dex." Her own eyes blurred as tears gathered on her lashes. Barely above a whisper, she said, "You haven't failed us. We've failed *you*. We didn't do what we came here to do, despite your best efforts to help. Let's finish this." She smiled up at him, then turned to look at Benny, who nodded. "Alright, Apollo. What do we do?"

"Bring me Alcibiades. If you brought Alcibiades back to Athens and they won the war like you thought your destiny was, it would've been easier to get him back here to me. But the city has fallen to Sparta."

A sob at the loss of his precious Athens caught in Dexios' throat. *He can't take much more of this. Poor kid's going to crack*, Shelby thought.

"Now," the god went on, callously ignoring the young soldier's heartbreak, "you'll be harboring a fugitive and traitor. Your job just got a lot harder. I'll explain everything, but first, bring me the Traveler."

CHAPTER 11

Smoke curled over the distant city walls in long lazy tendrils against the gray sky of dawn as the Travelers and the Watcher made their way back from Delphi to complete their mission. Conversation was scarce on the return from the temple as each processed the task that now lay before them and the loss of the city they had all hoped, in one way or another, to save. Gazes were fixed on the city walls looming larger ahead, but none really saw them. The smoke was a detail completely lost in their haze as the trio approached.

Ahead, a lone rider thundered toward them down the dirt road that led to the paved ones within the walls. Vaguely, Shelby mused that the vision in the rising dust reminded her of something, but her thoughts were too far into the depths of the universe to put it together. Benny's spine stiffened in his saddle as the figure drew nearer. He saw the faint glint of light and heard the familiar clank of a shield on the horse's flanks. It wasn't until the blue sparks began to swirl around her wrist that Shelby focused enough to see what Benny saw. Selagus.

"What the hell is he doing here?" she asked Benny, pulling her horse alongside his.

"I don't know. He was headed away from the city last time we met him on the road. Why would he be coming *from* the city now?"

Dexios glanced at the Travelers and jabbed his horse in the side, surging ahead toward Selagus. He tried to seem like it was no big deal to see his old friend on the road again, but the Travelers saw the Watcher's hand go to the hilt of his sword as he rode.

"Come on, bella," Benny said with a snap of the reins, "but stay behind us." Shelby nodded and followed suit.

"I don't care what business you had with him," Selagus was saying, "you can't go back into that city!"

"What's going on, Dex?" Benny asked.

"I've always trusted you, Selagus, but this can't be true," Dexios said, ignoring Benny's question.

Selagus fidgeted uncomfortably in his saddle and glanced over his shoulder. Dexios may not want to believe whatever the soldier was telling him, but it was clear Selagus was genuinely anxious about whatever was happening in the city. "You see the smoke?" Selagus asked. A nod from the three of them who were truly seeing it for the first time. "That's what's left of his house. Smoldering ruins. Assassins torched it to flush him out. As Alcibiades ran out to safety, they were waiting for him."

Dexios was rigid in his saddle. "How?"

"Arrows to his chest. He was unarmed and unprotected. He didn't stand a chance."

Shelby's eyes narrowed. "How do you know all this? And why are you even *here* to know any of it?"

Selagus' eyes swept over her as she spoke to him for the first time. "You're not Athenian," he said flatly.

Shelby was getting tired of games. "No, I'm not. But if you don't start talking, it won't matter who or what I am. You'll be dead." Benny and Dexios both gripped the hilt of the swords at their sides as Shelby's fingers wrapped the handle of the dagger at her waist. Soldier or not, Selagus was outnumbered.

Dropping his eyes, the soldier admitted, "What I told you before about being in too deep was true. I've been serving as messenger for Alcibiades since he came here to the Hellespont. He needed to know what was happening in Athens and a soldier was the best way to get that knowledge. I could slip in and out of the battles and feed him information that might help him make a return. As long as the Persians here were indifferent, I could come and go fairly easily." Selagus paused and looked at Dexios. "But I didn't even make it back to Athens this last time. I only got as far as the coast before I got word that the city had fallen to Sparta and that Lysander had a bounty on the head of the wayward general."

"So, you came back to warn Alcibiades?" Benny asked.

Selagus nodded. "I begged him to leave the city in the cover of darkness. To go somewhere - anywhere - else, but he refused. He said his destiny wasn't finished with him yet, or some such nonsense."

"He was right," Shelby said, "but not in the way he thought. Finding us on the road to town was just a happy coincidence?" Her question was barbed. Trust wasn't something Shelby Starling gave away easily.

Selagus shifted uneasily under the icy glare of the non-Athenian. "Yes, actually. I looked for Dexios at the inn, but was told he and his companions had already left. Knowing there was nothing else I could do here, I made a run for it." He paused as a question of his own dawned. "How did you manage to get all this way without getting wind of the city falling?" Selagus asked.

"We heard," Benny said cautiously, "but we didn't know about Lysander coming for Alcibiades. For all we knew, Persia was as safe as it was when we left."

Selagus glanced over his shoulder again toward the city in the distance. "You can't go back inside those walls. You were seen with Alcibiades. *They'll find you.*"

Shelby nodded as images flooded her mind. Alcibiades in a haze on the steps of the temple. Nowhere and anywhere. It made sense now. Alcibiades was dead. "He's right," she said slowly. "About everything."

Dexios and Benny looked at her for a long moment. "How do you know?" Benny asked glancing at the wrist she was keeping tucked in the folds of her dress.

Shelby shook her head. "I can't explain it. Not now." Her eyes flicked to Selagus, then held steady on the Traveler and Watcher. Dexios and Benny nodded leaving Selagus confused.

"I- I *am* telling you the truth, Dex," the soldier said earnestly.

Dexios held his hand out to his friend, who clasped his arm, the ancient equivalent of the modern handshake. "I know. And if Shelby believes you, it's enough for me. I trust her instincts more than my own." Releasing Selagus' arm, he said, "Good luck, my friend, wherever fate takes you. May you find safe refuge."

Selagus nodded, "You too, Dex. We'll meet again," he said. Shelby seriously doubted that.

* * *

Apollo paced the floor of the inner sanctum angrily as Shelby and Benny waited for an answer. Finally, he stopped and faced them. "This wasn't supposed to happen!"

"Seriously?" Shelby shot back. "You send us on a wild goose chase for a traitorous womanizer who manages to get himself killed because he can't pick a damn side and *that's* what you have to say for yourself?" Shelby's face was unadulterated fury. "How could you not know he was dead? You're a goddamned *GOD!*" she shouted. The word thundered around them off the stone walls. "What the hell do we need *you* for if you can't do anything right? You get the glory, the power, the fucking statues, and for *what?* Complete and total incompetence? What *now*, Apollo? What is our destiny *now?* Tell me! What did we give up everything we've ever known for?" Shelby's hands tore at her dark hair in frustration giving them something to do so she wouldn't punch Apollo in his perfectly straight nose.

Apollo sank down on the tripod stool and put his head in his hands. Dina stood with Dexios in the shadows out of the crossfire of the showdown between Shelby and the god. Benny glared from his corner, but let Shelby stand her own ground knowing she was most important in Apollo's plan, and her rage was enough to terrify the god into submission.

After a long moment, Apollo raised his eyes but not his head. "Shelby," he began quietly, "there's nothing I can say to change your opinion of the gods because you're right about so much. We're flawed. Terribly flawed, but we aren't all bad. My people mean so much to me, but I don't always know what's happening to them. I'm not all-knowing, no matter what the mortals may think. And, like it or not, free will plays a huge part in what we can and cannot do. I needed Alcibiades to live so he could be brought back here and be punished for his crimes. Lysander wanted to punish Alcibiades and snuff out the only real Athenian threat to his power. Lysander's assassins got to him first. It's as simple as that." Standing, he ran his hands through his dark curls and rubbed the back of his neck. His human form was feeling his immortal stress. "But, as you no doubt understand by now, time and destiny aren't linear things. He may have slipped through our fingers this time, but that doesn't mean this is over."

Benny spoke. "Why shouldn't it be? He's dead. What possible trouble can he be to you anymore?"

Apollo sighed. "Dead? Come on, Benny. Death isn't the end of anything. How many lives has Shelby lived? You know better than that."

Benny sulked back into his corner aggravated with the god's patronizing but was too angry to say anything else. Shelby knew Apollo had a point, damn him. "Something tells me living out our days in the countryside isn't an option you're about to give us," Shelby said.

Apollo shook his head. "I can't. I wish I could, but this is your destiny. It always has been. It's woven into the very fabric of who you are. I could let you live out this life, but we'd be back to square one in the next. It doesn't end until it ends, Shelby. You have to find him."

Shelby sighed and looked over her shoulder at Benny who nodded. "Tell him, bella," he said.

Apollo cocked his head to one side. "Tell me what?"

"I knew Alcibiades was dead before we ever walked into the temple last time. I just didn't understand what he meant."

"What?"

"I touched the temple and thought I was being pulled into a memory again, but it wasn't the same. It was more like Karnak, where I saw things between the planes. Alcibiades tried to tell me what happened, sort of. Mostly, he was trying to get his hands on me and figure out who I really was, but he did tell me something was wrong. He said he was nowhere and anywhere. He was already dead when we were standing here. But his last words were strange. He told me to come find him."

"But," Dexios said, then blushed at his interruption of the conversation. "Sorry."

"Go ahead, Dex," Benny said gently.

Dexios took a deep breath and said, "But why would he appear to Shelby? He just met her. I know he wanted her, that was obvious, but why would he come to her after he died?"

Dina took his hand and Apollo nodded for her to explain. Dexios seemed more comfortable with the gentleness of the Oracle than the abrasive god. "Like you're connected to Benny and Shelby as their Watcher," Dina explained, "Shelby is connected to Alcibiades since he's part of her destiny. Having gotten that close to her in life, it makes sense his soul would seek her in death. Finding him in Persia was easy enough for Shelby because of that connection. She didn't know it, but she was drawn to him, too. Hopefully, it will serve her well going forward."

Shelby turned to face Apollo. "Well? What does 'going forward' look like, oh mighty one?" Sarcasm dripped thickly from her words as arms crossed defiantly over her chest.

"You do exactly what I told you to do. What Alcibiades told you to do. You find him and bring him to me," Apollo said without a hint of negotiation in his voice. It was a decree, not a suggestion. "And fast. He's caused enough trouble already. I'm not going to put up with more eons of his nonsense."

Shelby wrinkled her nose. It sounded more like the god was irritated with a naughty child, not bringing a fugitive to justice. For a moment, Shelby stood in silence in front of the god. Her eyes traveled over his perfect face looking for cracks in his armor. He seemed so sure about his plan yet, nothing he had sent her to do had gone well so far. She wasn't entirely sure this quest was worth giving up her life over. "How?" The god and Oracle said nothing. "Another jump?"

"You're kidding," Benny said leaving his corner to intervene. "No. You can't be serious."

Apollo sighed. "I wish there was another way, Benny, but there isn't."

Shelby rolled her eyes and paced the floor. Torchlight flickered around them as shadows swayed on the polished stone of the walls. Once more, she was overcome with how insane her life had become. Standing in one corner of the room was the Pythia of the temple of Delphi. Standing next to her, an Athenian Watcher masquerading as a soldier. In the middle of it all, the God of Light, Apollo. Just standing there. A freaking god. A freaking pain in her ass. "And what happens if we can't find him? Or he dies? What then? We're stuck in some god-forsaken place in some god-forsaken time, and we have to find our way all the way back here? Over and over? No. I'm not spending eternity on the road to Delphi."

"Then, you better get moving."

CHAPTER 12

"Goddamn you, Apollo," Shelby snarled. She was angry and didn't even know why. She knew they had to go, and that the universe was never going to be through with her until she did what her destiny demanded of her, but she didn't like not having a choice. Taken for granted that she would just bow down to whatever the idiot gods wanted. It went against every grain in her defiant body.

From the shadows where she had been comforting the alarmed Watcher, Dina spoke softly to diffuse the rage building between the god and his Traveler. "Apollo, is there no other way once they jump this time? Shelby may have a point." It was risky to take sides against a god even with her voice gentle and not challenging. A small pale hand went to Apollo's cheek as she smiled up at him. "Please, surely there's another way. Think of the time wasted on trips back here. If they only had to make one trip back with Alcibiades, that would be one thing, but he's slipped through your fingers so often it seems unlikely even Shelby can return him on her first try."

Shelby's anger with the god flickered to a grateful smile at Dina for an instant before her jaw tightened again.

Apollo was silent for a moment and thought, lost in the oracle's pleading eyes. Then, his expression softened into a smile at Dina. "You're right," he said after a while. "You always are." Taking the Pythia's hand in his, Apollo turned it over and kissed her wrist where his silver bow and golden arrow would be when she spoke for him. His connection to her. "I've never given control of the leap to any Traveler before," he said to Shelby, "but it may be time to break the rules."

"Well, they're *your* rules. You can break them any time you want," Shelby answered, strength mingling with gentleness in her words as the god's armor cracked. Finally, they were getting somewhere, and it was a good thing, too. Time was running out. Her hands burned as the spring water wore off. Sparks swirled around her fingers as they flexed against the pain. Whatever Apollo was planning, Seshat was on board, but they needed to move.

The god nodded at Shelby. "Your first time here, you had to come on your own. Lessons learned; destiny sought. A choice you as a Traveler made. The ceremony and the arrows took you both from a mundane life to one of ethereal destiny," he explained. "None of that is essential to the actual moving through time and space. It's only essential for you and the connection to your fate. You've done that. Your destiny is sealed. Now, we get you where you need to go."

"How?" Benny asked, coming to Shelby's side. He may have been content to let her wage war against the god, but his protective instincts kicked in when it came to the time jump.

"A connection to the temple and the chasm. A key to turn, so to speak," Apollo answered. "But first, we open the gate." Wordlessly, Apollo held a hand over the tripod, which slid forward a few feet. "Dina, are you ready?"

The Oracle nodded, gave Dexios' hand a squeeze, then took her place on the tripod stool. Seeing the Watcher's face whiten, she said gently, "It's alright, Dexios. Whatever happens, it's alright - no matter what it looks like." The young hoplite said nothing and stared at the Pythia as she seemed to transform from the approachable beauty to the ethereal voice of the gods.

Once more, the Travelers watched the sybil breathe in the sweet-smelling vapors that rose from the depths of the earth through the hairline crack in the stone floor. Dina's arms hung limply at her side as her eyes closed and head tilted back. Slowly, she began rocking from side to side as the peace of the vapors engulfed her mind. The gentle sway was short-lived, though. Arms rising as if she was a marionette, Dina slipped deeper into her trance. Dexios' eyes widened as he watched tremors begin to wrack the small frame of the Oracle. Clearly, as a child, he was spared the trauma of watching her go into her deepest trance. Even as a young soldier, he wasn't handling it well. His skin turned ashen as Dina's head whipped back and forth, her long hair spider-webbing across her face. Hands rotated at the wrist as she lifted slightly above the stool. A deep rumbling began to shake the earth beneath their feet and dust drifted from the ceiling of the inner sanctum as it had before. With a thrust of her hand straight out in front of her, the tripod stool skidded across the stone floor leaving the Oracle suspended over the crack that was rapidly widening beneath her. Blood ran from her mouth in a tiny rivulet as the tremors in her body subsided with the ones in the ground.

Apollo gently gathered his Pythia in his arms and wiped the blood away as he kissed her. Once more, breath rushed into Dina's lungs as her eyes fluttered open. Cradling her like a baby against his chest, he stroked her sweat soaked hair. Shelby watched with fascination as it dawned on her how much the arrogant god changed when he held Dina in his arms. She was his voice, his confidante, and his love.

Dexios swayed for a moment, then caught himself on the temple wall. "Is- is she going to be alright?" he asked Apollo. His voice was strained even though he tried to hide his fright at what he had just witnessed.

Dina smiled at him as Apollo gently set her on her feet. "I'm fine, Dexios. It just takes a lot out of me. It has for centuries."

Assured the Oracle was unhurt, the young soldier turned his attention to the gash in the stone floor. "Where does it go?" he asked, peering into the blackness from a safe distance.

"Anywhere destiny would take you," Apollo answered. "It's different for each Traveler."

Shelby's mind flashed back to the shimmering void she dropped into with Benny. It had been only a matter of days, but felt like a lifetime ago. Standing here again on the edge of time and space, she once more felt the insanity of it all pressing in on her. Most of her wanted desperately to be back in a hotel room in Rome knocking back the last of a bottle of chianti as she fell into bed with Benny. Now, she stood at the edge of the unknown. "Where will it take us?" she asked Dina. "You saw it last time."

"Rome."

A sharp breath caught in Benny's chest at the word. "Home," he whispered. Dexios' eyes narrowed as the question of Benny's origin was answered, but he said nothing.

"Almost," Dina said. "Same place, different time. Ancient Rome."

Shelby sighed. "Great. I was hoping for indoor plumbing and deodorant."

"Not this time," Dina laughed.

Holding his strong hands out in front of him, Apollo's silver bow and a golden arrow shimmered into existence across them. "Hang on," Shelby said. "I thought we weren't going through all that this time. You're going to shoot us again?"

Apollo chuckled. "I could, but I won't. No, these have a different purpose this time. Something to connect you to me and the temple so you can make the jumps when you need to." Torches in iron sconces on the stone walls burned and flickered in rich oranges and reds, except one. It shifted from yellow warmth to blues, then to white-hot. Apollo brought the glowing torch to the chasm and held the tip of the bow above the flame. Almost instantly, the end of the bow began to glow deep crimson before a single drop of molten metal fell into the abyss. Then, the god did the same with the end of the golden arrow. As the second drop fell, a flash of white light burst from the crack in the earth followed by an eerie hiss. As the group watched in breathless silence, two tiny threads of gleaming metal slithered over the edge of the chasm and into Apollo's hand. "Give me your hand, Shelby," the god said.

Shelby hesitated for a moment then cautiously extended her left hand as she looked at the shining threads in Apollo's palm. "Holy shit. They're snakes!"

The god nodded. "My bow and arrow and the soul of Python. Your keys to the chasm." As he explained, the tiny silver snake slithered from his palm, down Shelby's fingertips, then wrapped itself around her ring finger in a delicate shining coil, tucking its tiny diamond head against muted scales.

"How does it work?" Shelby asked, holding her hand up to the light as the snake settled into a solid silver ring, delicate and subtle.

"Turn it a full turn with the words you already know: 'The Traveler follows the serpent.'"

"That's it?"

Apollo shook his head. "No, it's not that simple. There are two Travelers. Like the two of you, the keys must work together. Benny, your hand." Benny tentatively stepped forward and extended his hand. It was shaking despite his best efforts to keep it still. The golden thread uncoiled itself and slid around Benny's finger, then settled into a gleaming band with only shadows of scales giving it away as a snake. "After Shelby, a full turn of yours with the words: 'The Watcher follows the Traveler.'"

"Watcher?" Dexios asked.

Dina smiled. "Not you this time, Dexios. Your work is finished."

Shelby tore her gaze from the ring around her finger and looked at Apollo. "Then, who?"

"You. Both of you," the god answered.

The Oracle stood behind Shelby and put her hands on her shoulders. "You will always be a Traveler on a journey until you've fulfilled your destiny. But that's not all you are. There's so much more than you realize. Today, you're a Watcher, too."

Apollo smiled down at her, more tenderly than he ever had. "She's right, Shelby." A strong hand eased the edge of her dress away from her chest by her shoulder. Pressing his palm against her skin, he said, "Trust your heart to show you the way."

Sparks shot from Shelby's fingertips and cascaded onto the temple floor as her chest tingled under his touch. While Dina held her still, he pressed harder then gently pulled his hand away revealing a clock and compass tattoo. "It's just like Naomi's," Shelby whispered.

Apollo nodded then turned his attention to Benny. The god wrapped his fingers around Benny's wrist. "Trust your strength to carry you through, but know strength comes in many forms." Benny's face winced slightly with the tingling but held his arm still letting the god brand his wrist. Dexios smiled at him and turned his own wrist over. Apollo pulled his hand away leaving behind an exact replica of Dexios' mark.

"What happens to Dex?" Benny asked as the god released his arm. "He's lost his home and his mission. He's served you his whole life. It isn't fair."

"Dexios will be well rewarded for his service. He'll have my protection for the rest of his life."

Shelby glanced over her shoulder at the young hoplite standing sheepishly in the shadows. "But where can he go? Athens fell to Sparta. Persia isn't safe."

The Oracle spoke up. "The loss of Athens to Sparta is tragic, and there will be suffering, but it's a fragile occupation. Unrest will follow and Sparta will lose allies in Greece and Persia. Athens will rise again."

Tears poured unchecked down the young soldier's face as he struggled for words that wouldn't push past the raw emotion. Rescuing him from the struggle, Apollo placed a hand on his head in blessing. "You and yours are under my watch. You've earned that. The restoration of Athens won't be quick or without struggle, but it will come. Know that and rest easy." Releasing Dexios, the god smiled.

"Thank you, Dex. I won't forget this. Neither will they," Apollo said with a glance over his shoulder at the newly branded Watchers. "You're connected forever. If Shelby succeeds, you'll meet again."

Dina grinned. "So, it's not goodbye, really."

"Are you ready, Shelby?" Apollo asked.

"Almost." Shelby took Dexios' hands in hers and kissed him on the cheek. The young soldier blushed crimson and smiled at her as tears continued to stream down his handsome face. "We'll see you again, Dex. I promise. Thank you. For everything." Another kiss and she stepped back to let Benny say his goodbye.

Standing side-by-side at the edge of the chasm, the new Watchers received their final instructions from the God of Light. "Find him and bring him back to me. It isn't as easy as it seems. He won't know you and may not even look the same. Use what you know about him to make him trust you. Look for my messenger and know that you will have what you need to succeed."

"Messenger?" Benny asked.

"My raven."

Shelby wasn't sure how a bird would be much help, but Apollo wasn't one to give everything away all at once. Somehow, they would figure out what he meant. Dina kissed her on the cheek and said, "I'm so proud of you, Shelby. Know that. I'll be waiting for you." A kiss from the sybil for Benny and the Watchers prepared for the leap to Rome.

Sweet smelling vapors rose from the opening in the floor and the pair took deep slow breaths. Their bodies began to relax as the room around them shimmered. Apollo raised his hands in front of him and their feet left the stone floor. Gently, the god pushed Shelby and Benny forward, suspending them over the gaping hole in the earth. "Your destiny awaits. Trust your heart and your strength to guide you." With those words, Apollo's jaw set like it did when he took aim with his bow, then he released them into the shimmering blackness.

CHAPTER 13

Intimidating and polished, the behemoth rose from the ground in magnificent splendor against the cloud-dappled sky. Flags and banners in gilded crimson whipped in the wind around the rim of the massive structure. Gone was the mangled corpse, battered by time and destruction, whose skin had been chipped away to coat the surrounding city. Lazarus stood once more. The Colosseum shimmered in the sunlight, massive, strong, and pulsing with the energy of the crowd inside.

Muffled shouts and the dull rattling of cart wheels broke slowly through the white light and rising dust. Once more, the Watchers were insulated from the world around them as it came into focus. Voices of the passersby were unintelligible but excited as they walked like moths to a flame toward the shadowed arches. Hawkers sold food and trinkets from carts or small tables on the perimeter. The smells of bread and roasted meats filled the air and attracted flying pests that the cart keepers worked furiously to shoo away. Other carts reminded Shelby of the stalls in the Egyptian market overflowing with cheap souvenirs, small flags, and ribbons on sticks drifting on the warm breeze. Togaed people waved, shouted, and embraced one another as they hurried into the main event. The atmosphere was electric.

"It's like a football game. There's even tailgaters," Shelby said looking around wide-eyed.

"I don't know much about American football, but I'm sure most of the players don't have their lives on the line," Benny answered.

"No, just endorsements." Shelby squinted through the sun that broke through the clouds at the swarm of faces around her. "How are we going to find him in this crowd?"

"How do we know he's even *in* this crowd? When we were looking for him in Athens, he was in Persia. He could be anywhere." Benny sighed as he took in the sheer numbers of people milling about and making their way inside. From the sounds of the shouts and cheers, the Colosseum was already filling up. Alcibiades was the needle in a haystack.

"The Watchers follow the Traveler. We have to be close," Shelby said trying desperately to rationalize the situation. She ignored the fact that there was nothing at all rational about leaping into a Delphi abyss in 404 BC and landing in Rome in whatever time this was. "Any idea when we are?" she asked Benny hoping his well of knowledge of Roman history was deep enough to figure it out.

"There are a few centuries this could be based on clothes and what's happening in the arena. It would be easier to tell if I knew who the emperor was."

Shelby bit her bottom lip as she thought. "We could ask somebody, but that might raise some eyebrows." Her voice lost the hollowness as the sounds around her rose when the world came into full vibrance, which meant they could be seen and heard, too.

Benny shook his head. "No, we don't want to do that."

Spectators picked up the pace inside the building as the crowd surged and drums beat loud and strong. "What's happening?" Shelby asked.

"The games are starting. Come on, bella. Maybe we can get some answers inside." Benny took her hand and led her into the same entrance they had gone through together weeks ago, only then it had been full of tourists and crumbling travertine.

The Watchers joined the throngs of Romans flooding the stadium seats but stayed in the corridor shadows instead of the stone bleachers. Inside, the arena thrummed with sound as the opening ceremony concluded. Shelby looked around as a strange feeling came over her. Blue sparks on her fingertips told her to pay attention but were vague about what. Her palms stung and tingled as she looked toward the royal box. Hanging from the carved stone railing of the box was a banner edged in gold with a large black raven on the blood red field. The raven. Was Apollo trying to tell them something, or was it coincidence? People crowded into boxes around the royal box, leaning over the sides, filling goblets, and exchanging money in bets. Inside the emperor's box, veiled women stood serenely. Vestal virgins. But something was missing. Or, rather, some*one*.

"Something isn't right about this. It's familiar somehow, but not quite a perfect memory. The emperor isn't here."

Benny glanced up at the open box where the royalty gathered away from the plebian crowd to see what Shelby was talking about. Lots of fat rich men, but none of them with a golden laurel of royalty. "Strange. He should be here. Unless-"

Before he could get the words out, drums began to beat loud and strong as the crowd surged with excitement and anticipation, then erupted into a roar as the gates on the far side of the dirt arena opened. Standing in the opening in gleaming splendor was a man who could only be the emperor himself. No common gladiator could have afforded the gilded armor and elaborate engraving. In his hand was a polished blade. He stood, arms wide, soaking in the adoration of the people. "Holy shit," Benny said. "He's going to *fight*!"

"Who in their right mind would take on royalty in the ring? Much less the *emperor*?" Shelby asked.

"Someone who didn't have a choice," Benny answered with a deep frown. "All his opponent can hope to do is make the emperor look good while trying not to hurt him."

Shelby wrinkled her nose at the thought. "What an ass."

"A royal one. I'm not sure who it is, though," Benny said trying to make out the face in the helmet.

Another door opened, and a horse trotted out to meet the strutting would-be gladiator who sheathed his sword and swung up onto its back. The crowd cheered again, and he rode around the perimeter of the dirt ring waving at the people who bowed as he passed. As he neared the opening where the Watchers stood, the crowd knelt, and Shelby could finally see the face of the emperor. And he could see hers. Dark eyes winked at Shelby and her knees buckled. Benny's hand shot out to steady her and confusion settled on his brow. Shelby steadied herself and whispered, "Hadrian. It's fucking *Hadrian*!"

* * *

Pomp and circumstance gave way to civil savagery as the exhibition match between Hadrian and the chosen gladiator began to escalate. Showboating with swords and footwork began to become more riddled with testosterone as the gladiator struggled with restraining the skills he'd worked hard to hone. The emperor's pride wouldn't let him be outdone by someone beneath him, although the fighter spent his entire life training while the emperor had spent his politicking. Whoever was on the other side of Hadrian's sword wasn't following the rules of royal engagement and didn't seem to care. Both men crashed together and parried away from one another, then stalked each other around the ring, before colliding again and spinning away. Thrust and parry. Collide and spin. Over and over as the emperor wore out. The gladiator barely broke a sweat putting Hadrian through his paces.

Rather than plead royal privilege, Hadrian seemed to seethe and get more competitive the more the gladiator held his own against the emperor. Soon, however, Hadrian's anger shifted from his own lack of ability to fury at the gladiator for letting that ineptness be seen by thousands. "You'll die for this," Hadrian snarled at the gladiator as they crashed together.

Then, the gladiator did something that would surely seal his fate. He grinned at the emperor. "But isn't this all for show, your holiness?" the gladiator asked in mock innocence. "Or should we give the crowd some real excitement?" The gladiator raised his sword against the ruler's throat, holding it hovering at a distance just far enough to be safe so long as Hadrian didn't flinch.

Shelby stared in wide-eyed amazement, not at the potential horror of an assassination veiled as competition, but at the gladiator himself. "Did you hear it? It's him!" She had to yell in Benny's ear over the roar of the spectators pressed close around them. A soft lisp on the 'r' sounds in the arrogant gladiator's words. Benny nodded that he'd heard it, too. "Shit! Hadrian's going to kill him before we can bring him back!"

There was nothing they could do but hope Alcibiades would come to his senses and let Hadrian recover whatever was left of his pride and win the match in some spectacular way. Shelby held her breath hoping Alcibiades wouldn't die in the process. After a few more turns around the ring for good measure, the rogue Greek finally appeared to be wearing down, or at the very least making a good show of it. After one last dramatic struggle, Alcibiades staggered back from Hadrian and held his sword out horizontally in front of him before letting it drop to the dirt at his feet. The crowd roared and laughed at the defeated gladiator, knowing it was the only possible outcome.

Hadrian strutted like a dirty sweaty peacock around the arena before turning back to his opponent. "I won't forget this," said the emperor through his teeth, "*slave.*" Hadrian spat the final word at the gladiator removing any hint of smugness from the face of the superior warrior. Alcibiades went white even under the layer of sweat-streaked dirt on his face.

"What just happened?" Shelby asked.

"Some of the gladiators were slaves, but not all of them. Apparently, Alcibiades wasn't - until now."

"Maybe he'll be more likely to go with us if it means escaping slavery," Shelby said more hopeful than she felt.

"Or maybe he won't want to risk any more."

"It's a chance we have to take. We've got to get to him."

Benny sighed knowing it didn't matter how much he objected to anything. The mission was to get Alcibiades back to Delphi and that would mean risking their necks to get to a damned gladiator. "Alright, but not now. Tonight. The gladiator barracks at the Ludus Magnus are where we'll find him."

* * *

A sliver of moon leaned heavily on torches to light the darkened Roman streets around the massive structures at the city's heart. Even in silence, the shadow of the Colosseum was foreboding. The temple of death and savagery slept soundly with the rest of the city. Just behind the east walls of the colossus was the Ludus Magnus, training grounds and quarters for the gladiators. Where the Colosseum rose in arches and curves, the Ludus Magnus was angles and straight lines. As rigid in form as the discipline it harbored.

Far from the imposing gladiator or the commanding Athenian general, the man in the Ludus Magnus cell seemed to have lost his swagger. Shoulders that once squared against an emperor now sat hunched as he held his face in his hands. "Just put it over there," he said not bothering to look at the two people who let themselves into his room.

"Put what over there?" Shelby asked.

Alcibiades' looked up and blinked heavily trying to bring the vision of her into focus. "I thought -" he began, then reconsidered the explanation. "Who are you? Did he send you?" the gladiator asked thickly. From the sound of it, he had been medicating wounds to his body and pride heavily with alcohol.

"Hadrian?" Shelby asked. Alcibiades nodded. "No."

"Although, he probably would be interested to meet the one who did," Benny said flatly remembering Hadrian's fascination with all things Greek and his run in with Shelby in Athens. Alcibiades' eyes settled on Benny and narrowed as the meaning of the newcomer's words escaped him. Rather than try to explain, Benny changed tactics. "We saw what happened out there today. Seems you let your pride run away with your head."

"Pride," Alcibiades scoffed. "No one but his royal pompousness is allowed to have any pride." He rose painfully and slowly paced the small cell. "Does he try to outdo the merchants? Does he try to bake better bread than the bakers? Does he try to build better bridges than the masons? No. Just the gladiators. In one show of arrogance, he stripped away everything I've worked for and trained for my entire life." He stopped and faced Benny, swaying slightly on his feet. "I could have killed him. For an instant, it crossed my mind. Would've served him right."

"But you didn't," Shelby said. She stood with her stinging hand on her hip, hiding the blue sparks from the bracelet in the folds of her dress.

Alcibiades let his eyes wander over her figure, then let them rest on her face. "No," he answered, his voice barely above a whisper. "I didn't. But maybe I should have. Maybe I should have chosen death over slavery."

"So, he's made you a slave, but you still live here? With the gladiators?" Shelby asked genuinely confused.

Alcibiades sat on the edge of his bed and sighed. "I'm here because of the emperor's divine mercy, if you can call it that."

"Explain," Benny said.

Shifting his focus, the gladiator's eyes narrowed again. Somewhere in his drunken stupor, he realized he was spilling his guts to complete strangers. "Who *are* you?"

"Old friends," Shelby said sitting next to him. "I'm not sure you'd believe us if we told you. Certainly not in this condition. We want to help, but you need to tell us what's going to happen to you. What did you mean about Hadrian's divine mercy?"

For a moment, the gladiator stared at her as if he was weighing her words but could very well have been on the verge of passing out. Apparently deciding she could be trusted, he said, "He made me a deal."

"What deal?" Benny asked.

"One you'd expect of an emperor. One that only benefits him. He said he liked the way I fought and didn't want to lose a gladiator that could captivate the crowds the way I did, so he gave me a choice. I do something for him or spend the rest of my life in the mines."

Shelby's brow furrowed. "Something tells me what he asked you to do isn't much better than the mines."

"And you'd be right," Alcibiades replied. "There's a match tomorrow after the animal fights and dramas. Valerius, one of the gladiators in the match, fights for a manager named Calvus. Hadrian wants Calvus taken down a notch but is afraid to kill him. Calvus might manage gladiators but makes most of his money spying for politicians. You'd be surprised how loose their tongues can get after a long day drinking and watching fights. They come to congratulate him on his wins, and thank him for fattening their purses, and he gets them talking."

"Which makes him a dangerous man to offend. He passes information to Hadrian, but he's got something on the emperor, too?" Benny asked.

Alcibiades nodded, then paused as suspicion settled in his inebriated thoughts and expression. "Who are you?" he asked again.

Shelby decided to feed him just enough information to keep him talking. "My name is Shelby, and this is Benny. You have friends who want to keep you safe, but you have to trust us, or we can't help you. There are things we can tell you, but it would be dangerous for you to know too much."

Benny nodded. "Like Calvus does."

That hit home with the gladiator who started his pacing again. "Then, don't tell me. I know too much as it is. Not that it will matter for long." He ran his hand through his hair and sighed.

"What did Hadrian ask you to do?" Shelby asked gently.

"Kill Valerius."

"But that makes no sense!" Shelby said. "Why? Why not kill Calvus and get rid of the spy?"

"Because, murder, even murder disguised as an accident, could raise suspicions. Calvus has as many enemies as friends. Some who are both. If he dies, it could spark dissention among the elite to find the killer and what they were hiding worth murdering a man over. No, Hadrian wants to teach him a lesson about crossing him that will hurt, without raising suspicion."

Benny pulled out a chair and sat trying to figure out the ancient intrigue. "And having Valerius die in the ring will do that?"

Alcibiades nodded. "For people like Calvus, there's one place to really hurt him. He has no family, no heart, nothing that can be taken from him, except for the only legitimate way he makes money - Valerius."

Benny nodded as the logic came together. "Valerius is the reason the senators come to him with information. Take that away and he loses the income from the fights *and* his connection to the politicians. He would lose everything."

Alcibiades nodded. "And he wants me to do it."

"I don't understand," Shelby said. "Can't he just get another fighter to make money and draw the senators to him?"

"He could," Alcibiades admitted, "but that takes time. By then, he would have fallen out of favor. The political tide turns quickly around here."

"If you kill Valerius," Benny said, "you go free?"

Alcibiades nodded. "A life for a life."

Alcibiades leaned against the stone wall. For a moment, he reminded Shelby of Apollo and the way he did the same thing when he was thinking. "We've trained together for years. He has a family. Kids. His wife just had a baby. Valerius has done nothing but work his ass off for Calvus and his family. He's a good fighter, but a better man."

The three sat in silence as the weight of the gladiator's words settled on their hearts. An innocent man would pay for the treachery of his manager, or Alcibiades would be sent to the mines. Better than death, but only slightly. And even harder to escape with the supervision he would be under there. They needed to get him to Greece before he had to make that choice.

"You can't do this," Shelby said. "How do you know Hadrian won't still send you to the mines after you do what he wants? You can't trade Valerius' life for freedom that may never come."

"I don't know," Alcibiades conceded, "but if I don't do this, I'm a slave anyway. There's at least hope that Hadrian will keep his word."

"You're a free man, now. What's keeping you here?" Benny asked. "Run. Tonight."

Alcibiades stared at Benny with glassy bloodshot eyes. "What?"

Shelby put a hand out to touch the gladiator's but pulled it back as she remembered the shock the last time she touched Alcibiades in the vision. "You can stay here and live as a traitor to a man, a friend, who never wronged you, or you could run. Come with us."

Turning his dumbstruck stare to her, Alcibiades slowly shook his head. "I don't know who you are or where you're from, but any fool knows you don't run from the emperor. The arms of Rome reach around the world. He'd find me, and when he does, it would be far worse. No, I stay here." Resigned to his fate, Alcibiades laid on the bed and faced the wall to sleep off the alcohol before his gruesome task tomorrow. "Go," he said, "whoever you really are. There's nothing left for you here."

"We'll go," Shelby said softly, "but we aren't giving up on you as easily as you give up on yourself." With one last look at the crumbling gladiator, she and Benny slipped back out into the night.

CHAPTER 14

Blood coated the sand floor of the Colosseum shed by hundreds of animals for the gratification of the commoners packed into the seats clamoring for more. Their thirst for death would be disappointed for the time being, quelled by the dramas staged during the midday hours. Evening would bring the chance for them to scream for the life and death of humans who were valued merely for the sake of spectacle. Only this time, there was one life they would have little choice over. One fate was already sealed.

Shelby and Benny watched from the arched openings in the corridors trying to stay out of the chaos in the stands as Alcibiades was introduced. Doors opened and he stood in the shadow of the gladiators' tunnel. For a moment, he hesitated as if he had changed his mind. Then, his shoulders squared, and Alcibiades strode out toward the center of the arena to thunderous applause.

From his royal box, Hadrian scanned the crowd, and reassuring himself that he had made the right choice in sparing the popular gladiator. Gone was the crumpled heap of a man torn between two fates from the night before. The man in the center of the ring was once more the embodiment of the Athenian general the Watchers knew him to be. Tenuous muscles flexed as Alcibiades knelt before the emperor, then raised his head to lock eyes with the ruler. Shelby watched as a silent pact was made between them, sentencing Valerius to death. Alcibiades stood, glanced once more up at Hadrian, then stood ready for his opponent to be introduced.

Even more fanfare was built around the second gladiator's entrance as though Hadrian wanted to make certain that Calvus understood the value of the fighter he was about to take from him. A lesson amplified by the roar of the bloodthirsty crowd. When the doors opened revealing Valerius, the Colosseum shook with the fervor of the people inside. Minutes passed before Hadrian could get them calmed enough to start the event.

At the emperor's signal, the two gladiators began their match. Both sized up their foe with controlled swings of their swords. Each was dodged or deflected giving the fighters a chance to study their opponent's reactions and moves. Skill and brutality combined in a morbid dance across the sand. Soon, the fight began in earnest, and they clashed and spun away from one another as Hadrian and Alcibiades did the day before. However, this time, there was more force behind the blows, more strength in every swing, more concentration in every block and parry. The gladiators were evenly matched and could easily have gone to a stand-off had Alcibiades not been fueled by desperation that gave him an edge over Valerius.

The sun beat down on the gleaming metal blades that rang as they collided in front of the fighters. Armor on the arms holding the swords glinted with each swing. Wood cracked as shields crashed together. Sweat poured down clenched faces and tightening muscles. Leather darkened as sweat pooled from the blazing heat and physical strain. Soon, Valerius began to flag and go on the defensive more than the attack. He lacked the adrenaline of Alcibiades to keep up the fight much longer.

Shelby's hands burned savagely as the match progressed and Alcibiades gained the upper hand. Something about it all was familiar and sickening as she stood in the shadows watching two men struggling for their lives for very different reasons. The crowd roared and money changed hands as a stab missed its mark, only nicking Alcibiades on the shoulder of his shield arm. Crimson blood ran down his arm, but he didn't flinch. He couldn't show weakness to the crowd. Valerius raised his sword above his head to strike again but staggered back under its weight and his own exhaustion. This was it. Sadness flashed across Alcibiades' face as his eyes flitted to the emperor in his box. Shelby followed his gaze in time to see the slightest nod and narrowing of Hadrian's eyes.

Fingers tightening around the hilt of his blood-soaked sword, Alcibiades raised it high for the emperor before giving Valerius the only mercy he could - a swift strike and a quick death. Overpowering the weakened Valerius, Alcibiades drove his blade straight at his heart. The heart of a friend, husband, father, and innocent man. Valerius' eyes widened in shock as he realized what was happening in a match that did not have to end in death. Blood bubbled from his lips as Valerius sank to the sand clutching the sword protruding from his chest. It wasn't the death-blow Alcibiades had counted on. Maybe it was guilt that shifted his aim slightly to the left. Whatever the reason, Alcibiades had missed the heart of Valerius.

A thousand eyes turned to the man in the gold-wreath crown standing in the first tier Podium. Hadrian neither moved nor signaled. He stared hard at Alcibiades whose face contorted in grief and fear. Slowly, the fighter turned to face his suffering friend and Shelby saw his mouth move but couldn't hear what Alcibiades said. It didn't matter. The words were for Valerius alone. Numb, Alcibiades bent slightly and pulled the dagger from the sheath on his leg and slit the throat of his friend.

Blood spurted onto the sand as Valerius fell forward and the crowd roared its rage or approval, depending on the wager. Alcibiades turned away from the carnage at his feet, still clutching the dagger, to face the emperor. A smile curled the corner of Hadrian's mouth before he turned his back on Alcibiades and went down the royal tunnel that would lead him safely out of the Colosseum. The crowd continued their shouting and jeering as Shelby braced herself on the wall next to her. Her hands felt like they were in flames and sparks flew unchecked from the bracelet, but her heart was too broken to care anymore. Benny stepped closer to her to hide them when he realized she wouldn't and laced his fingers through hers. The sparks spun around his hand and hers.

As they watched, a raven began a slow circle over the lone fighter in the center of the ring staring down at his fallen friend. Fingers tightened on the dagger that had almost slipped from his hand. "No!" Shelby shouted as she realized Apollo's message. Pushing off the wall, she tore through the opening in the stone bleachers toward the edge of the railing. "*No!*" she shrieked again, but her voice was lost in the din around her. It didn't matter. She was too late. Alcibiades raised his hand and drove the dagger soaked in Valerius' blood into his own chest. A white-hot shock surged through Shelby's body as Alcibiades sank to the ground alongside the man he'd killed for Hadrian. The traitor couldn't live with his treachery, even if it meant saving his own life.

Shelby ran with tears in her eyes back to the shelter of the corridor and Benny's arms. "Bella, there was nothing you could do. He made his choice." The words were hollow. No, there was nothing Shelby could have done, but it didn't take away the feelings of horror and failure for either of them. "It's not over until we get him back to Apollo."

Dark eyes under glistening lashes looked up into the gentle face of the Roman she loved, then down at the silver serpent around her finger. Nodding and taking a deep wavering breath, she put two fingers on either side of the ring as Benny did the same with his. Turning it one full turn, she said, "The Traveler follows the serpent."

Benny turned the gold snake with the words, "The Watcher follows the Traveler."

CHAPTER 15

Muffled voices and footsteps surrounded the Watchers. Churning dust in the dry air stung their faces. Sun in a cloudless sky beat down and glared off the polished stone arches soaring above as if it was watching the activity and disapproved. Apathetic palm trees swayed lazily in the distance, oblivious to the panic in the city. It was anything but business as usual in the crowded marketplace. People rushed around shouting across the heads of others going in different directions. Parcels were shoved into the arms of slaves who hurried away with them. Something was putting the people of the desert city into a fervor.

As the time and space around them solidified and the sounds and sights became clear, Shelby took in the scene. "Where are we? *When* are we?" Remembering Dina's advice to use the clothes to determine time, Shelby searched the crowd. "The people are dressed like Romans, but this doesn't look like Rome to me."

Benny shook his head slowly as his eyes scanned the landscape. Stone pillars and buildings rose in ancient Roman architecture that seemed strangely out of place amidst the expanse of sand, rock, and scrubby palms. Massive carved arches rose overhead forming a grand promenade while triangular peaks and honed columns adorned other buildings. A Roman oasis in the middle of the desert. "Palmyra."

"What?" Something about that name seemed familiar to Shelby, but she was too overwhelmed to think about why.

"We're in Palmyra, in what we know as Syria."

"But it looks so Roman," Shelby said confused.

"It is."

Shelby turned in a slow circle as the locals rushed around her. "Alcibiades was right. The arms of the Roman empire stretch around the world."

"Most of the known world at that time, anyway." Benny stepped quickly out of the way of a slave laden with packages he couldn't see around, and tugged Shelby out of his path seconds before she was trampled. "This may not be the best place to figure out what's going on. There," he said, pointing to a stone porch a few yards away. "Come, bella."

Wagons rumbled down the paved road through the center of town as the Watchers darted through traffic to the one place they could find out of the commotion. Under the safety of the shadowed portico, Shelby shook the sand out of her sandals and caught her breath. "This place is madness. What's got everyone so worked up?"

Benny shrugged. "Not sure. Carmelita once told me if you want to know what's going on, shut up and listen."

"Well, since asking questions would make us stick out like the strangers we are, let's go with that." After everything that had happened to her lately, Shelby wasn't about to question the advice of the elderly glam psychic who helped her figure out who and what she was.

Standing in the shadows of the columns appearing to be deep in conversation, Benny and Shelby watched the crowd over each other's shoulders catching snippets of information.

"... it's madness riding out against him like that..."

"... empress will do what she wants...."

"... emperor will kill her first chance he gets..."

"... leading them all to slaughter..."

"... can't let him get away with treating us like his slaves..."

"... she and her soldiers will be here soon... won't like what she sees if we aren't ready to go..."

Shelby squinted at Benny. "Who are they talking about? If this is Roman territory, who's the empress?"

Benny thought for a minute searching his mental files of ancient Roman history, pushing a hand through his dark hair. "It has to be Queen Zenobia. That's the only thing that makes sense. She named herself empress and challenged the emperor Aurelian because she didn't like what he was doing in the Roman East. She was a powerful ruler here and loved by her people. Zenobia encouraged the arts and intellect, but she was also a formidable force on the battlefield. If anyone stood a chance taking on Aurelian, it was her."

"She's a badass."

"You could say that, just not to her."

Rubbing her stinging hands, Shelby looked back out over the city from her vantage point on the covered porch. Opulence surrounded her in the middle of nowhere. The flat horizon stretched out until it shimmered into nothing in the heat miles away from the glittering city. Merchants bartered their exquisite fabrics and gilded treasures in the middle of the huge promenade. Spectacular buildings surrounded them, carved, painted, and shimmering with metallic accents. Palmyra was staggering in its beauty and strength and ruled by a woman who reflected the city itself. "How in the world did a place like this spring up out of nothingness?"

"The nothingness actually helped it become the treasure that it is. Palmyra is on the Silk Road, which means travelers and merchants passed through on their way to Europe and other parts west of here with things they were bringing back from the Orient. Some decided here was a good place to stay and set up trade. The city grew in wealth and power as a result. Of course, Rome wanted anything that could turn a profit and control the exchange of goods, so, naturally, they took the city."

"Naturally," Shelby said rolling her eyes.

"For a while, they left Palmyra alone and fairly autonomous, but different emperors over the centuries of Roman rule had different ideas about how to control the wealth coming through. Some Palmyrians were content to let Rome do what it wanted in exchange for the protection of the empire, but others wanted their independence."

"Enter Zenobia."

"Right," Benny said. "She cut off supplies to Rome and pissed off the emperor Aurelian who decided he'd had enough and tore through Persia to get to her."

Shelby's eyes narrowed, searching the horizon. They weren't just dropped into a busy market day. Something was very wrong. Where only shimmering heat and shadows of palms and rocks had been on the horizon before, a cloud of dust was rising. "What's that?" she asked. She wasn't the only one that noticed it. Horns blew and panic followed. People that bustled through the Grand Colonnade moments before were screaming and running for cover. Mothers scooped up their children who had been happily chasing each other around the carts, oblivious to the building tension around them. Men grabbed anything they could use as a weapon. "What's happening?" Shelby screamed over the explosion of chaos. "Zenobia?"

"Worse," Benny shouted back. "Rome!"

"*Shit*!"

* * *

Dust swirled and panic intensified as the citizens fled or became impromptu soldiers pushing the well-organized ranks of Rome out of the heart of the city. Fires raged on wooden carts and buildings struck by flaming arrows sent ahead of the lockstep ranks of Roman soldiers. Arrows missing flammable marks smoldered on the ground or wedged in stone cracks. One man was struck in the chest and fell screaming to the ground as his clothes ignited, burning him alive before the wound bled out. People fled the rain of fire emerging only to loot carts and shops not ablaze for anything that could be used as a weapon against the invading troops.

Benny grabbed Shelby's arm and pulled her back down into the fray in the streets hoping to find something they could use to arm themselves. Gone was the hoplite sword and daggers from Athens. The only thing that remained was Shelby's pouch. They were completely helpless. Racing through the chaos, the Watchers wove through the city streets in search of something, anything, they could use for a weapon. Rounding a corner, Benny tripped over the fallen body of a Roman soldier, whose sword and dagger had been mercifully left with his corpse. Only his shield was missing. Kneeling over his fallen countryman, Benny stripped the body of the sword and hilt, then gave the dagger to Shelby who tucked it into the cording at her waist. Benny grabbed Shelby with his free hand and pushed her behind him, protecting her as they took off running again toward the Colonnade where they could get their bearings.

Standing in the middle of the street, panicked and crying, was a little boy about five years old. Sand and dirt on his little face under black curls was streaked in muddy tear tracks as he screamed in blind terror. Shelby looked around for his mother but couldn't find anyone looking for him. Instead, all she could see were horses thundering toward the child. Turning on her heels, she tore back down the street to him and scooped the boy up and out of the way just as one of the huge war horses reared in front of him then raced onward. From behind one of the columns, a terrified woman appeared whose tears were a mix of fear and relief as she took her crying child from Shelby's arms then vanished between the buildings to safety. Relieved and exhausted, Shelby sank to her knees, the hoofbeats of the horse echoing in her ears.

As Benny caught up to her trying to catch his breath, he looked down at her hands. "Bella, sparks!"

Sure enough, blue sparks were swirling around her wrist and sizzling hand. She hadn't noticed the searing pain in the adrenaline of saving the child. Benny helped Shelby to her feet as they searched the cacophony of sounds and bodies around them for what Seshat wanted them to see. The only thing out of place was a dumbstruck slave watching the terrifying approach of the queen's army slaughtering the Roman soldiers trying to stop them. Other than the two Watchers in the shadow of the columns, he was the only one left standing in the street. Everyone else had the good sense to run for their lives. The man seemed disoriented by the panic and blinked blankly up at the woman on the horse in front of him.

A soldier shouted at the slave, but the stunned man simply stared back. Finally frustrated at being ignored, the soldier slapped him across the face.

"Slave!" the woman on the horse shouted as he blinked out of the trance that held him. Under a layer of gilded armor, she was stunning. Fierce dark eyes glittered in the Arabian sun as she looked down at the man standing in her path. Swinging herself off her horse with one fluid motion of her long legs, she stood to face the man in her way. Her shoulders squared and one hand on the hilt of her sword as if deciding whether to talk to him or kill him where he stood.

"What?" the man stammered in shock.

A soldier standing beside the woman raised his arm to strike, but the woman stayed his hand. Her head cocked to one side as her expression softened. "No, let him be. Poor fool is frightened. He won't survive here if he hasn't any wits about him. Bring him," she said to the soldier next to her. Then to the stunned man, "Come, slave. We're riding out of the city. I won't be a Roman trophy."

"You're leaving the battle? The people?" the slave stammered. "But, you're the-"

Shelby's breath caught in her throat as she heard the slightest lisp on the 'r's in the man's words. "Alcibiades," she whispered as her breath returned.

The armored beauty stood tall, proud, and spoke firmly. "I'm Empress Zenobia and I will not be questioned by a slave!" She paused, then with more compassion, said, "I won't let them sack my city. It's me the emperor wants. Aurelian can come to me in the desert and find his own death there." Zenobia paused, letting her words sink in. "Bring him," she ordered again to the soldier who grabbed the slave by the clothes and began herding him to a cart behind the horses.

"Damn it!" Shelby said, as Alcibiades was led away. "Now what?"

"We go after him," Benny said. He pulled Shelby out of the shadows and knelt before the queen, Shelby following suit. "Highness," he said with his eyes on the ground, "we want to fight for Palmyra."

"*We*?" the queen asked.

Shelby looked up at Zenobia and rose to her feet. "We," she said simply.

The two women stood for a moment with matching steady stares. Benny got to his feet beside Shelby but said nothing. Zenobia broke the stare down and said, "But you're a woman."

Shelby, never wavering, answered, "So are you."

A moment passed, then a smile curved the corner of the queen's mouth. "So I am." A nod of her head at Shelby, then Zenobia turned to a soldier who had taken the other's place at her right hand. "Arm her. She won't be much use to me with that dagger. And find them horses." The empress grinned down at Shelby as she mounted her own heavily armored horse. "Come, my girl. Let's show those men how it's done."

In a flash, confused but obedient soldiers brought horses and a sword to follow their queen's commands. Once they were properly armed and mounted, Benny and Shelby followed Zenobia's soldiers out of the city and into the desert making sure to stay inside the ranks and away from the Roman soldiers breaking formation to attack the caravan. As they rode out, the stray soldiers were fewer, and the Roman army began to pull out of the city to regroup and re-form their ordered lock-shield ranks on the desert battlefield. Zenobia wanted the fight with Aurelian on her own terms, and she was going to get it.

CHAPTER 16

Torches burned low in the tent camp on the only rise in the vastness of the desert outside the city. A low rocky slope defined the word 'rise' in the loosest of ways. In the distance, pinpricks of light gave away the Roman encampment at the edge of the expanse of palms. Clearly, the Romans were trying to use what little coolness the shade of the palms would provide to protect soldiers unused to the scorching desert climate. Zenobia knew her soldiers could take the heat and used the openness of the rise to keep an eye on the enemy.

The setting of the angry sun gave way to a star-filled sky as cloudless as the day had been. Even darkness did little to quell the heat. The moon, cut neatly in half, cast a blue glow on the sands. Shadows, silent as the stars, moved between tents. Only the sounds of sharpening stones sliding along dull blades made any sound at all, and that was muffled through tent fabric pulled shut. The only voices were whispered reports of the soldiers changing watch. Sound traveled like light across the stillness of the open desert, so Zenobia ordered silence.

Shelby sat curled in Benny's lap inside their makeshift tent watching the soldiers and slaves slipping mutely by. Benny rubbed Shelby's burning hands, more out of affection than helping them to feel better. Nothing stopped the searing pain as long as Alcibiades was within reach. With the soldiers surrounding them and the queen's order for silence, there was nothing they could do but watch and wait. At first, Zenobia's new recruits had been a curiosity among the troops, especially Shelby, but once the camp was set up and the battle plans were drawn, they were mostly forgotten, except for a few sideways glances from horny soldiers toward

Shelby, and a couple toward Benny. Being too wrapped up in protecting Shelby, Benny hadn't noticed the glances that made her giggle and only rolled his eyes at her when she told him. "Some of them have better taste than others," he said.

Now, they sat in the eerie quiet of the night waiting for the dawn. It wasn't what Shelby imagined. In the movies, there was always frantic activity the night before a battle. Lots of coming and going, working on weapons, hammering dents out of armor, replacing worn straps, checking ammunition, messages being hurried through the camp. Some of that was happening, but in a vacuum. Before they retreated to the solitude of their tent, Shelby and Benny watched Zenobia stand at the edge of her camp in the shadows of the tents. Out of armor, her hair flowed down her back like a black river rippling in the wind. Her back was straight and strong, but her curves gave away the queen's softer side as she stood listening to her enemy in the distance. The Watchers didn't know what she could possibly hope to learn from the ghosts of sound that floated across the desert, but she was focused intently on them. Soon, the Roman camp fell as silent as hers and she turned to go back to her tent. Seeing the pair of newcomers, Zenobia nodded, her dark eyes glittering in the torchlight, as she passed by. Her movements were effortless and graceful, strong and purposeful. Power and beauty in perfect harmony.

Sitting tucked into the crook of Benny's strong arm later, Shelby's thoughts drifted back to the woman standing at the edge of battle and wondered what made her so sure she could take on Aurelian and his army. So sure that she could risk the lives of the people she was fighting to protect. The Watchers had seen enough of ancient Rome to know this was suicide, but there was no way they could convince the queen of that. Zenobia would never back down, and it wasn't their job to change history anyway. She had to fight, and she had to lose. Their mission was Alcibiades, who had somehow managed to gain the pity of the empress. One more anomaly in this strange place.

After he was shuffled off into the cart back in the city, the Watchers didn't see him again until they made camp. Zenobia had Alcibiades brought to her as the tents were being raised. He stood stripped to the waist as she walked a slow circle around him. His muscles tensed slightly as her gaze traveled across his chest and arms. "You're strong for a slave," she said more surprised than impressed. His blank stare in the marketplace and the lisp that suggested weakness had concealed the fact that he was actually physically strong under the billowing toga. A small straight scar marred the muscle of his chest and faint raised marks on his arms drew Zenobia's attention. "You've been wounded. How?"

"Some masters are better than others," he said vaguely.

Zenobia narrowed her eyes critically. "No, those aren't the marks of a whip. Those came from a blade. The truth, slave."

"My master was trained with the sword and needed practice. It took some time before I was as good with the blade as he was." Soft lilting 'r's masked a hardness in his words.

The queen's eyebrow raised on the last word but said nothing. *Was*? Had he murdered his master, Alcibiades would have been killed. An accident was different. If he was skilled enough, he could easily have made it look like one. "You've given me a difficult decision, slave," Zenobia said, resuming her circle around him. Alcibiades stood straight but kept his gaze respectfully on the ground in front of him. "When I plucked you from the market, I intended to give you a duty safely out of the fighting to protect you. Now," she stopped in front of him and put her finger under his chin, raising his eyes to hers, "I see you are not quite the weakling I thought you were."

Alcibiades flinched slightly at being called a weakling by the woman in front of him but respected her authority. "No, Highness, I am no weakling."

Zenobia released his chin, but not her gaze. "So, what shall I do with you?"

Alcibiades hesitated for a moment as if unsure whether the question was rhetorical. As he formed his answer, sparks leapt from the bracelet on Shelby's wrist to her fingertips. She crossed her arms quickly at her waist hiding her hand under her other arm, but a fleeting glance from Alcibiades told Shelby she hadn't been fast enough. Turning his attention immediately back to the queen, he answered, "Let me fight."

Benny leaned close to Shelby and whispered, "And get himself killed again."

Shelby nodded but was in no position to interfere. "Maybe not. He hasn't died in battle yet. Maybe if he's armed, he'll actually survive." Benny shrugged but didn't seem convinced.

It didn't matter what the Watchers thought. Zenobia wasn't going to pass up muscle trained with a sword before a battle. She had her men fit him with armor and weapons then placed him under the command of one of the men who pulled him from the market street. Before she let him go, she reminded her new recruit that arming him wasn't the same as granting him freedom. He was still her slave, but she wasn't one to overlook loyalty and bravery on the battlefield. Alcibiades bowed with grateful respect as Zenobia turned to walk away, but there was something that struck Shelby as odd in the way a grin stole across his face as he watched the queen go back to her tent.

"Why do you think he looked at her like that?" Shelby asked Benny softly from her spot in the curve of his arm.

His fingers played in her hair as he answered, "Who knows? She's beautiful and powerful. Death can't have changed him that much. He was probably imagining her naked."

Shelby turned just enough to toss a playful sideways glance at him. "Were *you*?"

Benny grinned and his dark Roman eyes danced. "I'm a man. It's what we do, bella."

She punched him playfully on the arm before settling back into his embrace. She sighed and watched the stars through the opening in their tent flap as she thought. The camp had long since gone to sleep except for the night watch posted around the perimeter. Inside the tight circle of tents, there were only the sounds of slumber. "It wasn't like that, though," she said after a moment. "I've seen his undressing-you-with-his-eyes look, and that wasn't it. There was something else behind that grin."

"We may never know," Benny said kissing the curve of her neck.

She was inches from giving into Benny's caress when her hands began viciously burning. Sparks flew around her wrist and jumped toward the tent opening. Shelby's gaze followed the sparks to see a familiar figure pass the tent with a furtive glance over his shoulder. "Or we could find out right now," she whispered. "Look!"

Benny scrambled to his feet and peered into the darkness. "Where's he going?"

"I don't know, but this might be the only time we see him alone and alive. Come on." Shelby pushed the tent flap back and eased into the night keeping well out of the pools of torchlight as she followed Alcibiades through the tent maze.

Once more he glanced over his shoulder and caught sight of the Watchers following him. Alcibiades wheeled around and a flash of a glare crossed his face before he remembered his place and lowered his eyes. "I-I couldn't sleep," he whispered. "Thought maybe a walk would help."

"Sure," Shelby whispered back. "Us, too." Alcibiades shifted his weight uneasily as it sank in that neither side was being entirely truthful. Shelby took a step closer, then stopped with one hand on her hip. "We need to talk to you," she said flatly.

Alcibiades' eyes looked her up and down pausing longer on her curves than a slave should. "It's late and I should get to bed. Maybe this can wait until morning?"

"You just said you couldn't sleep," Benny countered. "I think now is a good time."

Alcibiades crossed strong arms over his chest. "What about?"

Shelby knew time was running out and dawn would bring a battle that Alcibiades could very well not survive. Cutting to the chase, she said, "You don't belong here."

Fear flashed in the dark eyes of the slave in front of her replaced quickly with defiance. "The queen herself brought me here. How dare you say I don't belong!?"

"That's not what I mean. I mean you don't belong *here*," Shelby said with her arms wide, gesturing to the vastness around them. "In Palmyra. In this time."

"You're insane," Alcibiades said after a moment. "Beautiful, but insane." He turned to walk away, but Shelby's hand caught his arm. A shock went through her as he jerked his arm away. Wide eyes searched hers for an explanation. "What was that?" he asked breathlessly.

Shelby turned her hand over slowly. It burned fiercely. "I'm- I'm not sure."

Benny's cooler head jumped in to salvage things. "Maybe the gods are trying to get your attention," he said to Alcibiades depending heavily on the superstition of the ancients. "Maybe you should hear what she has to say."

The slave held Benny's gaze for a moment, then searched Shelby's face for answers she wasn't going to give just yet. "What do you want?" he asked slowly.

Shelby cocked her head to one side and replied, "Haven't you always felt like you didn't belong here? Like you were disconnected from this life?" She paused to see if he would react. There was no sign of anything but cautious confusion on the face of the slave. "My friend here," she said with a wave of her hand toward Benny, "is right. I'm-" She paused again trying to find a way to convince him without seeming more insane or overdramatic. Realizing everything she was trying to say was overdramatic as hell, she finished, "I'm a seer. A prophetess. The gods do have a message for you," she said. It sounded ridiculous, but it was all she had at the moment.

He wasn't buying it. "A *seer*? *You*?" Alcibiades looked her over once more and shook his head. "I don't have time for nonsense. Goodnight." Turning on his heel, he started once more to go.

"You're destined for more than this," Shelby called as quietly as she could after him. "You're supposed to be doing great things. You weren't meant to be a slave!"

The same sly grin danced on the corners of his mouth as Alcibiades turned to look over his shoulder at her. "You might just be a seer, after all." He winked and disappeared around the corner of the next tent.

Shelby's shoulders dropped with a defeated sigh. "Well, that could have gone better."

Wrapping her in his arms, Benny whispered, "You tried. At least you gave him something to think about. We'll try again tomorrow."

"What if we don't survive tomorrow?" Shelby asked looking up into the dark eyes she loved so much, tears gathering on her lashes.

"We will," he said holding her closer. "Apollo won't let us off that easy." The words were a hollow promise, but Shelby clung to them as tightly as she clung to him.

CHAPTER 17

Exhaustion weighed heavily on Shelby's body, but her mind tore down a twisting racetrack of thoughts and possibilities. Sleep was an elusive bitch. Benny tossed and turned on the hard ground for a while before finally drifting in and out of a fitful slumber. As much as she wanted to rest before the impending battle, Shelby lay awake scanning the stars through the tent door that let in only the slightest breeze in the stifling night.

At first, she wasn't sure she'd actually heard the footsteps, but soon they were unmistakable in the silence of the dead of night. Thinking it was the soldiers changing watch, she ignored them, but something wasn't quite right as they drew nearer. They lacked the purpose of a soldier taking the watch or the weariness of one relieved from watch. No, these steps moved with cautious stealth. Sitting up as silently as she could, Shelby watched whoever it was approach, concealed in the blackness of her darkened tent. Soon, the footfalls became a shadow that emerged from between the tents across from hers. As it skirted the edge of the torchlight, she could make out a familiar profile.

"Benny!" she whispered shaking the sleeping Roman awake. He grunted and blinked up at her confused and mostly still asleep. "Come on! He's up to something!"

"Who?"

"Al!"

"Al?"

Shelby tugged at his arm. "Alcibiades! Now!"

"Al?" Benny asked again, trying to push the fog of sleep from his brain as he heaved his reluctant body from the ground and followed her out of the tent. They crept along being careful to stay completely hidden in the shadows and far enough away that they wouldn't be heard. All around them, only the sounds of snoring, some more vehement than others, and the occasional grunt or grumble from inside a tent broke the silence of the night. Ahead of them, a furtive Traveler was intently focused on his mission.

Alcibiades slowed his progress as he neared the queen's tent. Her only protection, a soldier stationed outside propped up by his spear as he drifted in and out of sleep. Inching through the darkness, Alcibiades skirted around to the rear of the large tent. The Watchers followed at a safe distance.

"What's he doing?" Shelby mouthed to Benny who shrugged.

They stopped and watched as Alcibiades ran a hand along the back of the tent looking for an opening. Soon, his fingers found an overlap in the tent fabric and parted them slightly. Waiting on all hell to break loose as a slave broke into the tent of the queen, Shelby and Benny held their breath. Instead of indignant fury, a soft feminine chuckle greeted the royal intruder. One more glance over his shoulder, then Alcibiades slipped inside.

Benny stifled a laugh as Shelby turned a disgusted face toward him. "Oh my god!" she whispered. "He's seduced Zenobia!"

"I told you death couldn't change him that much. Come, bella," he said looping her arm through his, "time you got some sleep."

The pair slowly made their way back through the shadows toward their own tent trying not to giggle at the soft groans coming from the queen's bed. Glancing back, Shelby could see that the dozing guard had perked up a little but was clearly not going to interrupt the queen's tryst to check on her well-being.

Rolling her eyes at the thought that anyone could be that horny before facing a Roman army, she fell back into step with Benny then stopped dead in her tracks as something fluttered through the torchlight just overhead. The huge black bird dipped and circled before heading skyward to dive again. Shelby dropped to her knees covering her head with stinging hands as it barely missed her. "What the hell?" she gasped, scrambling to her feet.

Benny's eyes tracked the movements of the winged maniac. "Raven!"

The bird dove once more then flew off in the direction of Zenobia's tent. "Shit!" Shelby hissed and took off after it. The bird wove through the tents and circled back on itself pulling the Watchers along the path it wanted them to take until it settled itself on the peak of the queen's tent. Alcibiades was evidently as adept at lovemaking in this life as he'd been in others if the sounds coming from inside were any indication. Both seemed to be well into the throes of intimacy when the cries of the queen suddenly changed.

Rather than rising passion, her shrieks were fear and anger. Clanging and thrashing inside seemed to confuse the guard who couldn't tell if he should interfere or not. A shrill call from the raven pierced the night and sent Shelby and Benny into action. "Don't just stand there, stupid!" she yelled at the guard. Other soldiers awakened by the raven began staggering sleepily out of their tents thinking the battle had begun. In the chaos, Alcibiades made a run for it through the back of the tent before the soldiers could put together what was happening. Benny and Shelby didn't wait for them to figure it out and took off after him with the raven soaring above them.

Weaving through the camp, Alcibiades threw anything and everything he could in their way to slow them down, but still the Watchers stayed on his heels. Knowing he would need something faster than his own legs to escape, Alcibiades slowed down just enough to try to untie one of the horses. It was the break the Watchers needed. In a flash, Benny tackled Alcibiades, slamming his head on the ground. Stunned, the slave blinked up at him before beginning a valiant struggle to free himself.

Shelby stood over him with a sword she'd pulled from one of the wagons next to the horses. "What the hell are you doing?" she said holding the blade inches from his neck.

Ceasing his struggle for fear of having his throat slit, he glared up at her. "My job," he snarled.

"Explain yourself or there won't be anything left for those soldiers to find."

"You were right about one thing, seer. I don't belong here. I'm Roman. And if you would have let me do my job and kill that whore on the throne, I could have saved your lives. Aurelian will kill you all in battle!"

"You're an assassin?" Benny asked.

"The best there is. At least, I was until that bitch decided to fight back." A purplish bruise was beginning to emerge on the edge of his jaw where the empress managed to land a punch.

"You should've gotten to know your target a little better. Zenobia's a badass," Shelby spat.

Soldiers rounding the bend with swords drawn distracted Benny and Shelby enough for Alcibiades to make his escape, but he didn't get far. Without the horse, he was only fifty yards outside camp before the soldiers overtook him. Vigilante justice took him down in a flurry of swords. Shelby fell to the ground clutching her chest in pain as Alcibiades collapsed under his wounds. Benny dropped to her side holding her head in his lap as she gasped for air, the bond between Shelby and her Traveler severed once more. Her stomach rolled as the men trudged by with the mangled body of the would-be assassin to present to their queen. With heavy steps, the Watchers followed behind.

Zenobia, wrapped in bedsheets with a frayed strip from the bottom tied over a seeping wound on her left arm, stood watching the bloody procession with flashing angry eyes. Her men dumped the corpse at her feet in the sand as the queen stared down at the man who seduced her then tried to kill her. "Who is he?" she asked her commanding officer.

"Roman. One of Aurelian's men. He cursed us all to the tip of the emperor's sword as we took him down."

Slowly, Zenobia knelt beside the body and lifted Alcibiades' dagger that was laid across the bloody shredded fabric on his chest. Running it along the palm of her hand, she made a tiny cut, just enough to bleed. A thin dark streak glistened on the edge of the blade in the torchlight. "You wanted my blood for Aurelian," she said to the corpse at her feet. Turning the knife in her hand, she let the light play on the line of shining crimson. "Then, bring him this!" With that, she plunged the blood-stained dagger into the dead heart of Alcibiades. Coldly, the queen stood then turned her back on him with the order to send the trash back to Aurelian.

"I failed again," Shelby said as the men returned to their tents to prepare for battle. The eastern horizon was beginning to lighten signaling the coming dawn and the bloodbath that would come soon after.

"*We*," Benny corrected. "We failed again. You don't do this alone, remember?"

Shelby nodded, grateful for Benny's support, but the sting of failure burned. She wrapped her arms around his waist and stood on tiptoe to kiss him. He smiled down at her, his eyes showing the strain of his sleepless night. With her arms still around him and her head against his strong chest, she turned the silver snake ring on her finger behind his back. "The Traveler follows the serpent."

"The Watcher follows the Traveler."

CHAPTER 18

Mountain ridges rose and fell like the green scaled back of a mighty dragon resting on the expanse of wilderness. The breath of the serpent drifted through the hillside and hovered among the trees and stones. Dirty fog rose from the stamping feet of hundreds of restless horses in the valley that had come as far as they could carry their riders. Now, the masses of armored muscle were stymied by the snaking structure on the crest towering coldly in front of them. Their riders had heard of the massive thing, this feat of engineering by weak people that could not fight so they built walls around them to protect their fragile shells. It was lifeless stone, yet the sheer size of it terrified the riders who hid their fear from a leader who frightened them even more.

Bravado could not conceal the fear that rippled through the ranks. Voices with brave words were muffled as the battleground came into focus for the Watchers, and the riders lacked the poker faces needed to hide their terror. Shelby blinked through the gathering dust trying to focus on the horde in front of her to determine where and when they were. Benny, his hand holding hers, did the same. Horses and riders maintained a show of strength on the mountainside as leaders fell back to the valley camp to make a plan against an immovable enemy. On the wall, archers stood drawn and ready, as still and immovable as the stone beneath their feet. A warning to the army before them that they were not as weak as their wall made the horde believe.

"China," Benny whispered. The word shimmered in the space between time.

"Strange," Shelby answered, her voice just as hollow.

"What is?"

Shelby pulled her hand away from Benny's and flexed her fingers. "My hands. They aren't burning. He's not here."

Benny scanned the mass of bodies on both sides of The Great Wall. "Or he's just too far away right now. Patience, bella."

"Not something I have a huge supply of at the moment." If she was honest with herself, and she rarely was, Shelby would have to admit that this whole 'save the world' gig was wearing on her. At the moment, she would have given anything to be sitting on a beach diving lips first into a drink with one of those useless paper umbrellas. "I guess we should figure out how we fit into this mess."

Benny nodded as the sound came rushing at them with the solidifying of time and space. He looked up at the expanse of stone in front of them from their vantage point amid the trees on the hillside. "You think you can imagine what it's like, then you see it for yourself and it's even bigger," he said in awe of the Wall.

"Seems to be a common feeling," Shelby said as she looked at the faces of the soldiers in the distance. "They seem so rough, so savage, yet they are clearly afraid of this thing."

"Not the Wall, but what it means," Benny explained. "The Mongols were used to descending on a place like locusts and attacking en masse with arrows and huge crossbows. Part of what made them feared was the fact that they came like a tidal wave of weapons. A surge of force. Here, they can't attack like they normally do, and they don't know any other way. It's not the Wall that frightens them, but having to abandon tactics they know will work for ones they haven't proven."

"Fear of the unknown."

"Right. As huge as this is, it's actually not one of the higher parts of the wall."

Shelby scanned the massive structure. It was definitely big, but Benny had a point. It seemed like it should be higher if it was supposed to keep out invaders. This section seemed more like a medieval city wall on steroids than the wall you can see from space. And there were gates in it. She didn't expect that. She'd expected a solid swath of stone. "The gates are unexpected. This doesn't seem right from the pictures you see in textbooks."

"You're right, bella. The weaker parts of the Wall wouldn't be as impressive to photograph. This spot isn't formidable as far as its height, so there must be a significant fortress behind the stone wall. This spot wasn't chosen by accident, though. The attackers knew exactly what they were doing when they decided to come here where the Wall is lower. Likely, there was some help from the other side. Spies or allies. From the looks of it," Benny said, his dark eyes scanning their clothes, "we're working for Khan, too."

"Khan? *Genghis* Khan?" Shelby asked, her mouth unflatteringly agape.

"That's the one."

"But he's- he's-"

"A murderous, womanizing, loose cannon hell-bent on world domination?"

"*Yes*! There's no way I'm kneeling to that maniac!" Shelby stubbornly dug her heels in and pouted.

Benny chuckled and settled on a rock jutting out of the hillside. "There was a lot more to the man than that. If you can overlook his faults, he was actually one of history's great civilizers."

Shelby snorted. "Tell that to the people he conquered."

"You going to pout your way back to Apollo and tell him he crossed a line, then?"

"Maybe," Shelby answered folding her arms defiantly over her chest.

"Look around, bella," Benny said gently. "Think you'll live long enough to do it?"

Shelby scanned the horde in front of her and let her eyes drift to the arrow-wielding troops atop the wall. Damn if the Roman wasn't right. "No," she said sheepishly.

"That's better. Now, get used to taking orders from Genghis Khan if you want to live long enough to find Alcibiades."

Shelby's shoulders drooped as much with fatigue as frustration. She didn't need to be a seer to know this wasn't going to go well. "A woman in a Mongol military camp. This can't be good."

"Not as bad as you might think. You actually have more rights and freedoms now than you did in Greece or Rome."

"Really?" Shelby asked. That was not at all what she expected.

Benny shrugged and nodded. "Don't let it go to your head. You're still not equal to the men here."

Shelby fidgeted in her clothes and twisted the turned-up pointed toe of her shoe in the dust. The long red silk skirt, fitted bodice, and beautifully embroidered vest were uncomfortable after the loosely wrapped fabric of Greece and Rome. Instead of intricately styled hair, her dark locks were more simply woven with a sparkling comb tucked into a twist at the top of her head. Although far from the over-the-top costume of royalty, she was clearly not a common nomad and certainly not a slave. Other than that, she had no idea what or who she was to Genghis and his army. "Fine. So, who are we supposed to be?"

"Lucky enough to not be slaves. Other than that, who knows?" Benny glanced down at his own clothes. A long tunic with splits up the sides that almost completely covered a pair of loose pants. Cinching the tunic at his waist was a belt with a long dagger in a hilt. Armed, but not armored like the men mounted on horses in front of the wall. "There's one way to find out. Walk through camp and wait for someone to tell us what to do."

Going into the lion's den wasn't exactly what Shelby had in mind. "You're nuts, you know that?"

"Got a better idea?" Benny asked standing up and shaking the dust from his tunic. "If we stay on the outskirts, we'll draw even more attention as deserters, or worse." Shelby shrugged reluctantly but didn't argue. "Listen for anything useful and try not to pick a fight with anybody."

Shelby rolled her eyes and followed closely behind him into the Mongol camp. "At least you aren't wearing a skirt anymore."

Benny grinned. "I was getting used to it. Very freeing. You can thank Khan for the pants. Part of that great civilizer bit."

"I didn't like the long toga," Shelby teased. "I liked the short one in Athens better. You've got great legs." Benny's face reddened as he walked but let the comment pass.

* * *

Only the occasional glance from a passing soldier greeted the Watchers as they walked through the Mongol camp site that looked more like the movie scenes Shelby was used to than Zenobia's camp did. Small fires that had burned down to glowing coals were scattered throughout the valley with men sitting around them casting furtive glances toward the mountain crest and the fearsome structure riding the top of the ridge as they roasted unidentifiable meat on the ends of their swords.

Messengers scurried back and forth, horses and their armor were being checked over by their riders, and soldiers inspected the sharpness of their weapons. "Either everyone is too preoccupied to notice us, or us being here is expected so no one cares," Shelby whispered to Benny.

"Our arrival hasn't seemed strange to anyone yet. It's as if wherever we go, we were there all along. At least to everyone else."

"Not sure I like that explanation. Makes me feel like a body snatcher."

They walked slowly between the clumps of soldiers and gear sprawled in the shadow of the Great Wall. Occasionally, there would be a tent top stretched across poles made from trees felled to clear the valley that shaded space for the men to work, but most of them were largely exposed under the passing clouds of the China sky. Dotting the landscape in the distance were larger round tents with smoke rising from a hole in the center of the roofs. The outside seemed to be wrapped in white fabric or animal hides. It was hard to tell at a distance, but whatever they were made of, the tents almost gleamed in the sunlight on the dirty trampled landscape.

"Those look like yurts the hipsters go glamping in."

"They're called *gers* in Mongolia, but, yeah, same thing," Benny, ever the tour guide, explained. "Fewer hipsters here, though."

"Thank god." Shelby scanned the expanse on the hillside. One of the gers was considerably bigger than the others and had a huge tent tarp pitched next to it. "That one looks important," Shelby said. "Command central?"

Benny nodded. "Khan."

"So, stay far away from that one."

"Not necessarily," Benny said. "If we want to know what's really happening here, that would be the place to start."

Shelby groaned. He was right, and it wasn't fear that made her want to keep her distance. She knew she'd have a hard time keeping the eye-rolling snark out of any encounter with Genghis Khan. Once you've gone toe-to-toe with an obnoxious Greek god, earthly pissing contest winners aren't exactly intimidating. There was something freeing about knowing the universe was protecting her from the vileness of humanity, but it also had a tendency to make Shelby reckless. "Fine. Let's go see his Royal Assness."

"Shelby," Benny cautioned.

"I'll behave," she groaned. Benny's lips pressed into a thin line, obviously unconvinced. "I promise. Really."

The Watchers trudged toward the massive ger in the distance listening for anything that could be helpful. Most conversation, if there was any, surrounded the imposing structure in their way. Some didn't see the big deal since they conquered walled cities before, while others called them out on their stupidity about this wall being in any way comparable to the others. A few even cautiously questioned Khan's intentions and suggested they turn back to find someone else to conquer. Those comments were few and far between as they smacked of cowardice. It wasn't until the pair was in earshot of Khan's tent that anyone seemed to care about them.

Under the expanse of red fabric stretched between four large poles with one in the center for support was a large wooden table with maps strewn across it. Men in armored tunics stood around it haggling about their own theories and strategies for breaching the Great Wall. Genghis Khan stood at the head of the table scowling down at the maps, largely ignoring the bickering officers except for an occasional grunt at something one of them said. He was shorter than Shelby imagined him to be but barrel chested and strong. His armor and furs draping his shoulders intensified the effect. Eyes like obsidian narrowed in thought in a bronzed face hardened by sun and conflict. A thin mustache and beard traced the defined jaw set in sheer determination. As Shelby and Benny approached, he cast an irritated glance up at them, then his gaze softened as it settled on Shelby.

"Ah, my girl," he said, leaving the men to their argument. "Did you enjoy your walk after being confined all that time in the wagon on the journey?" Genghis Khan slipped his arm around her waist and Shelby quickly figured out what she was. Then to Benny, he said, "Thank you for bringing her safely back. She will let you know when she has need of you again."

Benny nodded, seeming to understand that he was a guard to the ruler's concubine. His Roman face darkened as Khan turned away from him, but a shrug from Shelby was all she could do to reassure him. He mouthed at her, "I won't be far," then turned reluctantly to go as ordered.

"Yes, it felt good to stretch my legs," Shelby answered trying not to vomit as Genghis Khan ran his hand along the small of her back. "I hate to distract you from your battle plans."

"Nonsense. I welcome the break. Besides, it will give those fools some time to get the bickering out of their system. It's tiresome."

"But you're the khan. Can't you just tell them what you want them to do?"

The Mongol laughed. "I could, but that doesn't make for good leadership. They have to *want* to do what I need them to do. If I give them enough time, they will see for themselves that my plan is the only sound one."

"Do you have that kind of time? What if China decides they've had enough waiting for you to make a move and decide to attack?"

He chuckled again. "Let them. It would be easier to take them down on this side of their wall." Genghis turned to look at her and placed a strong calloused hand on her cheek. His almond eyes scanned her face. "Why the sudden interest in the battle? You've never cared before."

Shelby tried desperately to still the trembling she could feel growing at her core. She couldn't let him see through her. Her only way out of this life was with Alcibiades and she had no idea where he was. She couldn't risk making the leader of the Mongol nation suspicious. "I've never seen anything like their wall before. It fascinates me. And the men seem so afraid of it. It sparked my interest. Besides, there's nothing much to do out here in the middle of nowhere."

A smile drifted across his lips. "I could think of a few things better to do than worry about China's wall."

God, Shelby thought, *Genghis Khan is flirting with me.* Her stomach rolled as she thought of the many times a line like that must have worked on his concubines and wives in the past. Not that they were in any real position to deny him. The more she thought about it, the stranger the flirtation was. He could just take whatever he wanted, making flirting completely unnecessary. Why go through the motions unless he simply enjoyed the sport of lovemaking? *Just another form of conquest,* she thought bitterly. "As could I," Shelby said playing the game, "but the wall does capture my interest. What do you think should be done?"

Khan sighed and gave her cheek a playful pat. He seemed to see her deflection as playing hard to get rather than impertinence, which was good. "Even safely behind their stones, they have likely heard of the might of the Mongols. I will begin the way I always do: give them the option to join us and save their own skins."

"As slaves? Who would take that bargain?"

"No, any that come willingly would come as soldiers. You know that, child. Only the ones we capture in battle become slaves. That's why so many take the deal I give them before the fighting begins. And why my army continues to get stronger while those we conquer grow more vulnerable."

Shelby had to admit it was a good strategy. Take on more numbers before the battle ever begins. And soldiers who know the moves and weaknesses of those being attacked. The defectors wouldn't dare turncoat again and risk the wrath of the Mongol nation. They would be slaughtered on the spot. Brilliant. "And if they decide to fight instead?"

"Then we mount the wall. I already have men constructing ladders to get enough warriors on the top to push the archers back. Some will make the right decision and defect once they realize all is lost for them. Others will stupidly decide to keep fighting. Then," he said as simply as if he was ordering a pizza, "we slaughter them, and China is mine."

"Many of your men will die at the hands of the archers on the wall before they can make it over. Is there no way to spare their lives?"

"Sacrifices must be made in battle. No warrior wants to lose any of their men, but a successful one counts the cost of winning. And, that cost is one I must pay." Khan pulled her closer and wrapped a strong arm around her waist. As he kissed the curve of her neck, his mustache and beard tickled her, making her squirm. He misinterpreted it as being turned on, which spurred his affections.

Over her shoulder, Shelby was grateful to see one of the officers waving his arms at them. "I think your officer would like a word with you."

"Let him wait," Khan said as his hand found her breast.

Shelby gently pulled away before she lost her temper and her lunch, and forced calm words, "He seems insistent. Maybe they've decided you're right after all."

Stroking his ego seemed to have the effect Shelby hoped for as Khan released her and turned to see what she was talking about. "He always had the worst timing." Turning back, he kissed her on the cheek and said, "We'll continue this later. Take another walk if you wish but always have your guard with you."

Shelby bowed and smiled. "Of course," she said sweetly as he strode away to take command of the battle.

CHAPTER 19

The day and night passed in relative monotony as the standoff at the Great Wall carried on. Thankfully for Shelby, Genghis' aggravation at the tenacity of the Chinese soldiers quelled any amorous designs toward Shelby he may have had earlier. Morning light only brought more of the same. Chinese archers lining a formidable structure and the frustrated Mongols at its base. Benny escorted Shelby on her walk as they hoped like hell to get information about Alcibiades before the fighting broke loose. "Why the hell am I always getting pawed by some obnoxious asshole?" Shelby grumbled as she and Benny walked through the camp. "What's Apollo's deal? Why can't he make me like Xena, Warrior Princess, or something? Why do I have to be sexy and weak all the time to get men to talk to me? Doesn't it bother you, too?"

"I don't like it, but you have a job to do. I trust you. I don't think Apollo has anything against you, bella, he just knows how the men work that you need information from. I doubt he'd make you a concubine if you needed information from a monk."

Shelby smacked Benny on the arm and gave him a sideways grin. "Maybe Al can be a monk in his next life."

"We've got to get through this one first. Maybe we won't *need* a next life."

Shelby spread her fingers out in front of her. No stinging pain. No blue sparks. The universe had been eerily uncommunicative since their arrival. "I'm starting to think we've been let off at the wrong stop."

"Still nothing?" Benny asked.

"Zilch."

"He has to be here somewhere. Focus on keeping Genghis at arm's length for now. Your hands will let you know when to look for Alcibiades."

"Well, it better be soon. I don't want to end up in the middle of another battle." Shelby tried to shake the image of Benny running the Spartan soldier through from her mind. Blood spurting and the sickening look on the soldier's face. Benny wiping dripping blood from his sword. Her stomach turned with the thought. She was glad he was there to protect her, but Shelby never wanted Benny to need to use that hidden talent ever again.

"Neither do I, bella," Benny said moving to put his arms around her, then pulling away before Khan's men saw him getting too amorous with one of the ruler's women. More than anything, Shelby wanted those Roman arms around her, but understood why he resisted. "Khan sent a messenger this morning to the Wall with an offer, according to what some of the men said earlier."

"The 'defection in exchange for their lives' thing?"

"Right."

"Did they say how long Khan was giving them to decide?"

Benny shook his dark head. "No, but he won't wait long. The ladders are almost ready, and he's ordered the crossbows to be brought toward the front line. Won't be much longer." One of the most intimidating weapons the Mongols had were massive crossbows that, had it been the 1800s instead of the 1200s, would have been cannons. Seeing an arrow that size being loaded into a crossbow of gargantuan proportions would bring even the bravest soldiers to their quivering knees. Add that to the sheer number of Mongol warriors, Khan's reputation for savagery, and the defection began to look better and better.

"I guess The Great Asshat is ready to get the show on the road."

"Apparently."

"That gives us no time to find Alcibiades before the fighting begins."

Benny shrugged. "Maybe it's time to stop trying to control everything and let the universe bring Alcibiades to us."

Shelby hated that idea, but he had a point. Being a control freak had done nothing to find the wayward Greek in the Mongol camp, but she didn't want to just sit around and wait. The universe and the half-baked gods that controlled things weren't very good at getting things done. Leaving it up to them could mean sitting in Khan's army camps for decades. However, having zero leads on Alcibiades meant she would have to just sit and wait. "I hate waiting," Shelby said sitting on a rock under a small stand of trees at the far edge of the camp.

Benny chuckled. "I know, bella." They were far enough away from prying eyes that he ventured to take her hand in his. As he did, his arm brushed the edge of something hard at her waist. "What's that?" he asked.

"The pouch I've had all along. It would be too out of place in this get-up, so I put it underneath the skirt." As she talked, blue sparks began to spin around their hands and jump toward the sharp angles of the book in the pouch.

"Looks like Seshat has a clue for us," Benny said.

"At least someone is talking to us now." Shelby undid the clasps on the vest and shoved her hand into the waistband of her skirt. As she wiggled her fingers into the pouch, they immediately began to burn like fire. For a moment, she pulled them back out and shook them before sucking it up and reaching back in again. Her hand closed around the small leather book and pulled it free. Sparks swarmed the book as Shelby dropped it to the ground in front of her, in too much pain to hold it anymore.

"How can Eli's journal help?" Benny asked squinting down at the small diary.

Shelby thought for a moment and rubbed her hands. "I don't know, but there must be something. Wait!" she yelped as the answer dawned on her. "Eli was here! On the Wall!" Her hands hovered over the book and spread apart, opening the cover. With flicks of her finger inches above the pages, she turned them until she got to the entry Elijah Faircloth wrote about standing on the Great Wall of China. "In one of his past lives, he was in the battle that's about to happen. Look!" Shelby and Benny reread Eli's account of the Mongol siege.

The Wall was under siege, and I was standing in the middle of it! The Chinese soldiers in their armor sprang to the parapets firing arrows down on the advancing horde below. Archers stood ready in the openings, being fed arrows from men crouched below the wall, raining a shower of death down on the invaders. Men on the ground fell as arrows found their targets in the vital organs of the poorly protected advancers. Most of those below were on horseback wielding spears against the onslaught of arrows. This wasn't going to go well for them. As I watched, hundreds were taken off their horses spurting blood from chest wounds. Many were shot in the head, their fur hats being better protection against cold than weapons. Ladders were being carried toward the wall, but they were woefully short. Realizing this, the men fell back to lash them together to make them taller. Precious time would be lost in this effort and the Chinese soldiers were using the delay to pick off more of the attackers quickly reducing their numbers.

Watching from my corner of the fortification, I began to feel a panic for my life that felt very real. I could smell the sweat and blood around me. Dust rising from the horse hooves below stung my eyes. And yet, no one seemed to notice me. No one shoved a crossbow in my hands or pushed me out of the way. They seemed to look around me and through me, but the sensations I felt were very real indeed.

Sparks flew wildly around them as Seshat became more insistent in her message. Even though Shelby held her hands still over the book, the pages fluttered again. Once they settled, the Watchers read on.

The jolt of electricity raced up my arm with more force than before and the white light enveloped me again, blinding me to my surroundings. As my senses came back to me, I found myself in the midst of another battle. However, this time, it was tearing through a marketplace being overrun by soldiers. Wooden shop stalls lined the colonnade filled with all the treasures of the East spilling out of toppled shelves and shattered pots. Fabrics, spices, and trinkets once admired, now trodden over. A mixture of an Arabic language and Latin filled my ears as soldiers raced by shouting orders. On a horse, leading the charge, was a woman. Armor and the sword in her hand was a stark contrast to the feminine braids in her long dark hair. She was fearless as she rode in front of her troops against the Roman regiments. The Palmyrian troops were rougher and less organized than the disciplined Romans who marched with swords and shields locked and protecting them against the Arab onslaught. All around me, the battle raged and the fear in me mounted, though I wasn't sure why.

"Holy shit," Shelby breathed. "Eli has been with us in Palmyra and here at the Wall!"

Benny's eyes narrowed in thought. "Maybe other places, too, but he just didn't go there when he was writing the journal."

Shelby looked up at him with a realization that seemed too far-fetched to be true. "You don't think Elijah Faircloth could be --"

"Alcibiades."

Searing pain ripped through Shelby's arms as sparks burst like the Fourth of July from her fingertips. It took an Egyptian goddess and the journal of a Victorian to put the pieces of the life of a rogue Greek together for a Roman and an American in the middle of China. "Holy shit," Shelby said again.

"Turn back to the part about the Wall," Benny said. "There's something I need to see." Shelby did as he asked, hovering her hands, that were hurting less now that the riddle had been solved, over the journal. She turned the pages until Benny stopped her. "That's it. Right there. He's on the Wall."

"That's why we haven't found him in Khan's camp. But why would Apollo make us Mongols if Alcibiades is on the Chinese side of the Wall?"

Benny leaned back and looked at her. "What's the one thing that's been consistent with Alcibiades?"

Shelby thought for a minute and flicked a bug off her knee. Thoughts fluttered back in time across eons to the various lives of Alcibiades. Finally, one characteristic came to the forefront. "He's a traitor."

"That's my girl," Benny said with a grin. "So, he may be on the Wall now, but he's not likely to stay on that side."

"He's going to take the defection deal," Shelby said nodding.

"Likely. But he doesn't do it right away. Eli describes the battle. He defects when he realizes the Mongols are going to breach the Wall in order to save himself from slavery."

A silence fell between the Watchers as both of them put the puzzle together and tried to anticipate what the missing pieces were. Knowing who Alcibiades was, or rather who Elijah Faircloth was, made finding him easier, but getting to him was another story altogether. He was on the Chinese side of the Wall before the fighting, which meant if they wanted to get to him before the battle, they would have to get over the Wall themselves. Not likely to happen, and they had both seen enough episodes of *Star Trek* and *Dr. Who* to know that changing the past had a ripple effect on the future. Al would have to be in that battle like he was supposed to be. That's the past Eli saw. What they would have to change is what happened after that. Once he defected. It was the only thing that made any logical sense. As if anything in the whole mess made any logical sense.

"So," Shelby said as they came to the end of the mental acrobatics, "we're back to waiting again."

Benny nodded. "Yes, but at least we know what we're waiting *for*."

CHAPTER 20

Orders from Genghis Khan to stay out of the way and in her ger only meant that Shelby would have to make sure she wasn't seen by the Mongol when she directly disobeyed them. Benny managed to steal some clothes from a soldier's tent and smuggle them to her so she could walk more freely through the camp and battle zones. As badly as she wanted to get to Alcibiades, Shelby wasn't an idiot and stayed far enough back that she could watch safely out of range of the Chinese archers' arrows. Having spent the night pouring over every word of Eli's journal account of the Mongol siege of the Great Wall, she knew exactly what was going to happen. The beginnings of the battle itself was like being forced to watch reruns of a Cecil B. DeMille film in 3D and HD. Brutal and sad, but she couldn't look away from the sweeping epic playing out in front of her.

Dust rose from the feet of the horses stamping impatiently in front of the Wall as their riders took aim at the rows of Chinese archers peering down at them with steeled resolve. If there was fear of the Mongol horde, it didn't show in their measured movements. With the first Mongol arrow released, hell rained down from the Wall. Arrows pierced the armor of the attacking soldiers as they tried to get off shots of their own. As soldiers fell, others took their place, leaving the bodies where they landed. Horses took a beating, too, but most were saved by the heavy armor covering their vital organs. Gaps in the armor of the soldiers on their backs meant that riders changed frequently as one after the other was taken down by flaming arrows. Each new wave of Mongols began their attacks behind the ones that fell, inching backwards.

"Are they retreating? Why are they moving back instead of toward the Wall?" Shelby asked as she watched from the hillside. "It looks like Khan is using his own men to test the range of the Chinese archers."

"No, he knows the range. He's using his men as a distraction. Look." Benny pointed across the valley. Felled trees had been stripped of their branches and lashed together into enormous ladders for breaching the wall. Rows of men hoisted the huge ladders onto their shoulders and carried them like savage pall bearers to their own deaths.

"They aren't tall enough," Shelby whispered remembering Eli's journal. "They'll die trying to get them in place for nothing."

In the middle of the attacking horde, Genghis Khan sat astride his massive war horse surveying the progress and yelling orders to the battalion leaders. Shelby watched him lean forward in his saddle as the ladders approached. Men continued to draw the fire of the Chinese archers as the Mongols parted the battlefield like the Red Sea for the ladders to pass. Archers walked alongside them ready to step in front of the foot soldiers who would be hoisting the ladders. Human shields. At such close range to the archers on the walls, there was little the Mongol archers could do to protect the others except add to the confusion.

On cue, just like Eli's journal entry said, a flame tore across the top of the wall as the archers lit their arrowheads preparing to rain fire on the Mongols. As the ladders found footing at the base of the Wall, arrows were released. Men fell as the ladders settled far shorter than they needed to be. Rage burst from Khan as he shouted to the men to take the ladders and fall back. The Chinese had picked off many of the men leaving the remaining ones struggling under the weight of the ladders. Orders were shouted sending more men to the Wall to pull the massive things away from the fighting and lash them together. The retreat of the ladders seemed to give the Chinese soldiers confidence that their Wall had defeated the invaders. The volley of firepower slowed some for a moment.

"Why aren't they still trying to kill the Mongols? Why are they backing down?" Shelby asked.

"They don't want to waste ammunition if they don't have to. Khan's breach has been stymied for now. They're holding back to see what he'll do. If he advances again, they'll be ready."

As Benny said, shouts came from up and down the Wall as the ladders, now twice their height, were set on the shoulders of the rows on Mongols and marched toward the Wall. Footing was found once more as archers sent arrows into the faces of the men on the Wall. Once the ladders were up, the foot soldiers that had carried them shifted gears and began climbing to the top of the Wall, swords slashing at anything and anyone in their way. Archers struggling to reload their crossbows were slashed down where they stood by the horde turning the balance to the Mongol favor.

From where she stood, Shelby could see Genghis Khan smile as a hand went up in a signal to the men behind him. "What's he doing?" Shelby asked.

"I think he's signaling for the rest to advance, but how is he going to get his whole army up those ladders? No! Wait!" Benny shouted, grabbing Shelby's arm and turning her. "Look!"

The massive crossbow cannons lumbered forward on carts drawn by armored horses and pulled into position across the battlefield. Shelby watched, expecting them to be aimed toward the top of the Wall, but that wasn't what happened. Instead, they took aim low rather than high. "I don't understand. What are they aiming at?" Squinting through the dust and humanity, she saw them. "The gates!"

Benny paced as he watched the battle unfold. "The ladders and men on the Wall were another distraction. He pulled the defending soldiers up there so he could use the crossbows as battering rams." As he said it, three massive arrows were released simultaneously into the gates with a deafening crash. "None of this is in the history books," Benny said mesmerized. The gates held, for the moment, but the huge arrows were splintered. More were loaded as the confused Chinese took in what was going on around them.

Then, something unexpected happened. Chinese soldiers began flooding the ladders coming down to the Mongol side of the Wall. "He was right! Khan was right!" Shelby cried. "They know he's beaten them and they're defecting!"

Crossbows were released again damaging the gates further as more men raced down the ladders. Again, and again, the crossbows battered the gates until they finally gave way under the attack. Men swarmed, pulling them apart and flooding through to take the fortress on the other side. Khan sat back in his saddle as the newest defected recruits bowed in fealty in front of him. Shelby's hands began to burn savagely as she scanned the crowd of Chinese soldiers at the feet of Genghis Khan. "He's there! One of those men is Eli. Or Al. Whoever the hell he is now."

Benny nodded. "Now to figure out how to get to him."

* * *

Night fell as smoke curled up from the other side of the Great Wall where the Chinese had tried to burn provisions before the Mongols could seize them. The metallic smell of blood hovered in the stillness of the air wafting alongside the stench of corpses that littered the shallow valley beside the foot of the wall. In the morning, they would be stripped of their armor and weapons then burned. For now, they lay under the swath of stars in a clear black sky staring into the vastness with vacant eyes. Smaller fires burned in the camp as soldiers cooked what meat they could find and dressed wounds. There was lighter conversation than there had been in the days leading up to the battle. Bravado-soaked fear was replaced by the adrenaline of victory as soldiers told their tales of conquest, each attempting to outdo the others around their campfire.

Benny and Shelby walked the camp searching for the defectors that had been scattered within the ranks of Mongols, likely to keep them under scrutiny and preventing a unified uprising should they decide defection was a bad idea. "Think we'll know Alcibiades when we see him?" Shelby asked. Her heart pounded in her chest as she rubbed at her stinging hands. She wanted desperately out of this Mongol camp and was no closer to finding the key to the door. The bracelet that could give her clues had been pushed up into her sleeve so the shining blue sparks wouldn't draw attention in the darkness of night, which left her dependent on her hands to tell her if her target was close.

Benny shrugged. "I don't know. He's looked similar the last two times, but that's because he was Roman. Not that different from the Greek version. He couldn't look like that here since he's Chinese. The last two times, he's had the lisp, so let's hope that's true this time, too."

"And that he's not so scared of the Mongols he's afraid to talk." There was a palatable difference between the Mongol groups and the bands of deserters. While the Mongol troops boasted of their conquest, the Chinese soldiers mostly sat silent and sullen around their campfires. They were alive but seemed to be struggling with the shame and dishonor of defection. "I don't even know what to say to him when we *do* find him. So far, all I've managed to do is convince him I'm insane."

"Worry about finding him first. After, you can decide how crazy to sound. You thought everyone was crazy, too, remember? Even yourself sometimes."

Shelby shrugged and nodded. From the electric shock and visions to the Watchers and snarky goddess Seshat, Shelby had certainly doubted her own sanity and the entire situation. The visions felt so real that they were the main reason she even believed any of it, weren't they? So much had happened since then it was hard to remember. It all seemed very far away and long ago now. If some chick had walked up to Shelby and told her the gods needed to see her in Delphi, she would have laughed her ass off.

Minutes seemed to fade into hours as they walked slowly through the camp from one end to the other. Nothing. No sign of Alcibiades or his lisp. Shelby's hands stung letting her know he was nearby, but without hearing him, he could have been right next to her, and she wouldn't know it. That is, if he even had the lisp at all.

"Living as a defector has more honor than dying as a slave," one of the Chinese soldiers said as he settled around the smoldering fire remnants as the Watchers passed. Shelby knew it was a half-truth the man was trying to get himself to believe as much as the men he was talking to. The ones who died on the battlefield were the only ones seen with any real honor.

One of his compatriots agreed with Shelby's thoughts. "You're wrong, you know. There is no honor in either one. There are only differences in how we avoid death. We must fight to avoid it; the slaves must serve."

Shelby's spine stiffened as the man spoke and her feet rooted to the dust under them. Slowly, she turned to face the man whose soft 'r's caught her attention. "What did you say?" she asked.

The soldier looked quizzically at the woman brazen enough to question a man, then let his eyes wander over her. Standing rigid, she was as commanding as she was beautiful, this Mongol vision before him. Shelby gave him a moment to remember that Mongol women were more equal to the men around them than their Chinese counterparts before she pressed him for an answer. She didn't need to. Slowly, the man stood and faced her, not wanting to be looked down on by a woman anymore, even one as lovely as the one in front of him. Benny took a step back to let Shelby handle things but had a hand on his dagger lest the new recruit get carried away.

"I said," the soldier replied with a crooked grin that turned up the corner of his mouth, "there is no honor in defection, no matter what my friend here thinks. There is only life awaiting a different death."

"Having second thoughts about your decision?" Shelby asked with one hand on her hip trying to still the trembling. The other was held slightly behind her in case the sparks became more than her sleeve could hide.

"In China, our women don't question the decisions of the men."

"Sounds like the women need to be questioning a lot of things. Like, why the men would be afraid of their opinions." The soldier crossed his arms over his chest insulted by the comment, so Shelby changed tactic slightly to play on his machismo. "Or, maybe strong women are just too much for the men on that side of the Wall to handle. Maybe the women would prefer Mongolian men, who listen to them and can... handle them." Her stomach lurched as she once more played the tart to get information from a man. At this point, she was really hoping this worked or the monk thing played out in the next life. She couldn't see his face, but she knew Benny was behind her struggling to keep from laughing at her.

The soldier chuckled and grinned. Her change in strategy worked. "No, we handle our women just fine. At least, some of us do."

Shelby raised an eyebrow as her dark eyes glittered in the dying firelight. "Is that so? It's not what I've heard," she lied. "I'd need some proof of that one to believe such a story." Benny gurgled and coughed behind her trying to cover the laugh that wouldn't be controlled any longer. Shelby's face reddened, which only seemed to egg the soldier on.

He bowed slightly to her and said, "I'd be happy to prove it to you, my lady."

Shelby stared at him for a moment considering how dangerous her next words were going to be. She needed to get him away from the others to talk and convince him of his own destiny, but doing that could put both of them in danger. She knew Genghis Khan was open about the number of women he was with, but wasn't sure he'd tolerate the same from his women. Not that Shelby had any intention of letting the soldier prove anything to her about the prowess of Chinese men. She knew what it could look like if she was caught alone with him. There was no choice, and he was giving her an open invitation to see him alone. Sickening and dangerous or not, she had to take it. "Come to my tent later. We have things to discuss." She nodded to Benny who followed as she turned to go.

Behind her, whisperings around the campfire drifted to her ears. "Careful, she belongs to the khan," one soldier warned.

Chuckling from the one with the lisp as he answered, "Khan may think so, but that one belongs to herself."

A grin stole across her face as she walked back to her ger. Except for the part of her that was all Benny's, Alcibiades was right. Now, if she could just keep it that way.

CHAPTER 21

Night dragged on under a peaceful twinkling canopy of stars draped languidly above the camp. The peace didn't cross the threshold of the small ger a stone's throw from the large imperial tent of Genghis Khan where Shelby paced, quivering with apprehension and nerves. On one side was a blanket-covered cot across from a narrow chest for clothes. A delicately carved dressing table and stool stood beside the trunk. The floor was covered in tapestry rugs to keep the dust off her clothes and feet. Pillows piled on one side reminded Shelby of nicer versions of the bean bags she had on the floor of her first apartment in Queens. Had there been air conditioning and indoor plumbing, it wasn't half bad.

The long-sleeved shirt, floor length skirt, and tight vest had been replaced by a light robe with long bell sleeves whose trains nearly brushed the ground. Shimmering threads of vines and flowers chased each other over the cream silk that was cinched shut with a tie at her waist. Her hair, released from the comb and pins, flowed loosely down her back. If she hadn't been wound so tightly, and Benny had been in her bed, Shelby would have happily gone to sleep. As it was, she was a ball of nerves with a job to do.

As she was beating herself up mentally about her idiotic plan and the very real danger she was putting herself in, Benny nudged open the small carved door. "Bella? You ready? He's here."

"No, but I don't have much choice, do I?" Shelby took a deep breath and nodded.

Benny held the door open as the soldier entered and stood grinning in the frame before taking a few steps inside. Over his shoulder, Benny mouthed, "Just outside," then pulled the door to, leaving it slightly ajar, no doubt so he could listen and jump in should Shelby need him.

Shelby took a breath as she steeled herself for another performance. "Come, sit. We have much to talk about," she said trying to keep some air of formality between them.

"I seem to remember you needing proof about how Chinese men handle their women. There are better ways to get you the proof you seek than conversation," he replied settling on a large red cushion. His fingers played in the silk threads of a tassel sewn into a seam on the corner. Dark eyes twinkled up at her as the lamplight threw shadows across the small room. "But we can start with that, if you wish." His hand gestured to the pillow next to him.

Shelby intentionally sat on a different one slightly farther away. It was mere inches, but a statement to him about who was in charge. His lips curled into the crooked grin again as her message hit home. Once more, her strength seemed to turn him on. "Now, tell me, soldier, why do the men on your side of the Wall fear their women so much?"

He laughed. "Fear them? No, we aren't afraid of them. What is there to fear? They are merely women."

Shelby's expression darkened some as her feminist side reared. "*Merely* women?" she asked. "I've known many women who are stronger than men. And not just physically. Clever, cunning, and ruthless. Some who were great leaders. Revolutionaries. History is full of them. These *mere* women have challenged and beaten armies of men. Tell me the truth, *that's* what the men fear, isn't it?"

He looked steadily at her for a moment, his jaw tight and lips set in thin lines, before softening again. "Some, perhaps. But not all of us. Some of us prefer to see women as beautiful as precious stones and delicate as the flowers. To be appreciated and taken care of."

"And if they can take care of themselves?"

"Then we just appreciate them," he said with a wink. There was the Alcibiades she remembered him to be. Suave, flirtatious, and in command of the right words at the right time. "Clearly you can take care of yourself. But does Khan appreciate you?"

"To a certain extent. It's complicated."

"I'm sure it is. More for him, though. How does one keep a woman like you as a concubine?"

Shelby's brow wrinkled. "A woman like me?"

The soldier shifted to the cushion next to her and ran his finger along her cheek. "Strong, independent, beautiful. You aren't what I expected a Mongol woman to be. There's more to you than just a concubine."

Concubine. She hated that word and hated that it applied to her in this life. She was definitely going to chew Apollo out for this one. "There's more to a lot of people than meets the eye," Shelby said trying to steer the subject away from her profession, as it were, to her mission. "Like you. What if I told you there was more to you than a soldier?"

"Deserter, you mean." His face darkened as his hand fell away from her cheek to his lap. "There's nothing more to me than that as far as the men here are concerned. I will be part of Khan's army because I deserted my own. Dishonored, but alive. With only the company of a surprising woman to take my mind off my troubles."

"No," Shelby said laying her hand on his before she realized what she was doing. A shock raced through both of them, but she didn't let him pull his hand away. She wanted him to feel the electricity and connection to her.

Dark eyes widened with surprise, then narrowed again as the quick jolt of pain eased. "What was that?" he whispered.

"Maybe it's just energy in the air," she said, her eyes holding his gaze as she spoke. "Or, maybe the night is trying to get your attention so you will see that you are more than a soldier. There's much more to your life than that." Shelby let his hand go as he relaxed again. "Sometimes," she said steering the conversation carefully, "I feel like I don't belong in certain places. Certain times. Like I shouldn't be there. Do you ever feel that way?"

The soldier's face studied hers for a moment before answering, "Sometimes, yes. But don't all people wish they could be somewhere else sometimes? Who would really wish to be here, in the middle of a battlefield?"

"But more than that. As though you don't belong where you are. *When* you are."

Once more his eyes settled on hers as Alcibiades determined if she was earnest or playing him for a fool. Slowly, he nodded. "On the Wall. In the battle. It felt strange. Hollow." He leaned back against the pillows and sighed. "Truthfully, I think that's why I did what I did." His eyes closed as he talked. "There was a moment when I was fighting against the horde with everything I had, then, it changed. Hopelessness washed over me, as though I knew, even though we were pushing them back, that we were going to lose everything. Like a message from another time. Something deep inside moved me to save my life, whatever the cost, and before I really knew what was happening..." He trailed off as his eyes slowly opened again but didn't focus on her.

"You were coming down the ladder to join Khan," Shelby finished for him.

Glazed eyes became clearly focused again. "Yes," he said simply. Muscles flexed in his arm as he pushed himself up from the ground and paced for a moment. "I don't know why I told you that."

"Because you know I'm right. This isn't where you belong. Not just with Khan, but here in this time and place."

"So what if it feels strange? So what if there is some other time that would feel right? This is where I am and the life I have now. Serving the will and whim of Genghis Khan," he said, turning to face her, "just like you." He sat next to her again and reached for her hand. Knowing it would shock him again if he touched it, Shelby put it behind her as if she was trying to steady herself. All that did was open the front of the robe slightly as her back arched. Instead of taking her hand, he slid his arm around her back. "This doesn't feel strange. You feel comfortable somehow. Familiar."

"I can help you find where you belong," Shelby said softly as the soldier moved closer to her.

"I think I've found it all by myself," Alcibiades answered, letting his lips find hers.

As Shelby put up her hand to stop him, sparks flew around her wrist and leapt toward the door. "Shelby!" Benny shouted from outside as the door burst open. There, filling the small opening, was the rage-filled figure of Genghis Khan.

With a roar, the Mongol tore the soldier off of her and threw him to the ground. Panicked, Alcibiades began scrambling backwards toward the open door, but he was no match for Khan. In a flash, the soldier's neck was being crushed by the furious leader. The ger walls shuddered as he slammed Alcibiades against the center post. "I spare your miserable life, and *this* is how you repay that mercy? She belongs to me!" the Mongol spat in the soldier's face.

Purple and sputtering, the soldier hissed, "She belongs to no man!"

Khan roared again and tightened his grip on the soldier's throat as Shelby screamed. Benny flew to her side and shielded her from the blind fury of the Mongol leader. The Watchers could only hope that his rage didn't turn on them once he was finished with Alcibiades.

"Your head will be on a spike by dawn," Khan snarled.

Benny turned Shelby's head away a split second before the sickening crack of the soldier's neck being broken by the mighty Genghis Khan. "Now!" he shouted.

Through her tears and searing pain of the bond between Watcher and Traveler being severed again, trembling fingers found the delicate silver snake on her finger and turned it. "The Traveler follows the serpent."

"The Watcher follows the Traveler."

CHAPTER 22

White light shimmered around the Watchers as they waited on the next jump location to solidify around them. And waited. Nothing. Whiteness and nothing. No sound. No shadows of some other time. No new life. Just whiteness. "What's happening?" Shelby asked. "Something's wrong." As she hovered on the verge of panic, that they had been thrown into some weird dimension and abandoned, massive colorful columns began to emerge from the whiteness like a fog clearing in the sunshine. The huge things held up a tremendous slab of stone roof creating a cavern of color and shadow as the blinding light vanished.

Benny's Roman eyes drank in the sight around him. "It can't be. It doesn't make sense."

"Has *any* of this made sense?" Shelby asked. Something wasn't right about their clothes. No ancient togas or Mongol pants. No, she was in cutoffs and a Rolling Stones tank. Benny was in a t-shirt and chinos. Modern clothes. The ones they were most comfortable in. Blinking her eyes, Shelby focused on where she was. "I've been here before. Right here. This is Karnak. But not really Karnak."

As she said the name, soft chuckling came from the shadow of one of the tremendous columns. "Good girl," a woman's voice said as she emerged into the light. Red lips curled into a grin as slender fingers pushed a shining black braid out of her caramel face. "Nice to see you again, Shelby."

"Seshat?" Benny asked as if his breath had been sucked out of his lungs. Shelby nodded. "How? Why?"

"How the hell do I know? Ask *her*," Shelby said grinning at him. She couldn't remember seeing Benny star-struck before, not even over Apollo. Not that Shelby could really blame him. The Egyptian goddess was stunning and exotic standing ramrod straight, but still feminine and seductive. The leopard skin she wore hugged every curve it barely covered. Her red full lips and kohl lined eyes were framed by hundreds of tiny shining ebony braids that brushed her exposed shoulder. Tiny turquoise stones were threaded in rows around her ankles and wrists. Larger ones formed a wide flat band that draped her collarbone. Bare feet padded softly across the polished floor as Seshat held slender hands out to Shelby.

Before placing hers in the palms of the goddess, Shelby put a finger under Benny's chin and closed his gawking mouth for him. "Forgive his stare. He's never seen a goddess before. He's a good guy, really."

"The best," Seshat agreed leading Shelby to the base of one of the large columns to sit. Realizing Benny hadn't followed, she leaned around Shelby and smiled at him. "You can come, too, Benny," she said with a warm smile.

"Sorry, I- I mean, I- Sorry," Benny stammered not sure if she should bow or kneel, so he did some weird combination of the two before blushing to the roots of his dark hair completely disarmed by the ethereal vision grinning at him.

"Benny, I feel like we're old friends," the goddess said. "Please, don't stand on ceremony."

"Or ever do whatever that was again," Shelby said giggling at him. "Come, sit down." Benny did as he was told but was clearly struggling with his machismo and awe doing battle with one another and both sides losing. "Why did you bring us here?" Shelby asked Seshat, coming right to the point even though it felt good to not be chasing anyone or dodging arrows and swords for a while.

"You needed rest, first of all," Seshat replied following Shelby's thoughts. "And reassurance."

Shelby leaned back against the column and closed her eyes. "We aren't very good at this Watcher thing. I mean, our failure rate is staggering. How many times can one Traveler *die*? Don't you and Apollo want someone else to do this? I think there's been some mistake about our destiny. Pretty sure snarky travel writer was all I was really meant for."

"See what I mean?" Seshat asked. "Reassurance. In large amounts."

Benny finally got over some of his starstruck muteness. "Shelby has a point. We've lost him four times. Not just lost him. He's died. Spectacularly."

Shelby shrugged and picked at a thread on the frayed edge of her shorts. "That's got to be some sort of record, right? At least we can hold the record for the worst Watcher job ever done."

Seshat shook her head, shining braids moving like liquid ebony as she did. "I wouldn't say that. You haven't died on the job, yet."

"Well, there *is* that," Shelby conceded.

"Wait, that can *happen*?" Benny asked.

The goddess nodded. "Can and has. Tricky stuff when it happens. Hard to get the Watchers and Travelers back in the same place. The universe doesn't like tangled life threads in the first place and that makes some nasty knots."

"So, we could have been killed in any of those battles?" Shelby asked, still trying to wrap her head around the weaknesses of the universe.

"Yes."

"Apollo threw us, a couple of city kids from the future, into ancient sword fights and archery battles to fend for ourselves while we try to do the gods' dirty work for them, and he wasn't even protecting us?" Shelby was on her feet pacing the temple floor fuming. In her mind, flashes of all of the ways she wanted to let Apollo have it played out in rapid fire.

"Calm down, Shelby," the goddess said standing up and putting a hand on her arm to stop Shelby's pacing. "Although that third idea of yours wasn't half bad," she said with a smirk having read her thoughts. "Look, I know you may not realize it now, but you have weapons stronger than the swords and arrows. You have knowledge."

"Sure, you'd say that," Shelby spat. "You're the Goddess of Knowledge."

"I'm serious, Shelby. Stop pouting like a petulant child for a minute and listen." There was no way the pouting was going to stop, but she did at least stop griping as she crossed her arms over The Rolling Stones logo on her chest and stared defiantly back at Seshat. "Only a slight improvement," the goddess said rolling her eyes, "but I'll take it. Now, listen to me. You know what's going to happen, and that's a powerful weapon. Benny knows his history to navigate the time periods, and you know Alcibiades and how he works. At least, if you'd let yourself get over being unhappy about the roles you have to play, you would."

"It's insulting," Shelby grumbled through set teeth.

"As a woman, I can't disagree with you there, but you need to change your perspective. No matter what role you have to play, you're in control. Always. You also have one more weapon."

Benny spoke up. "The diary."

"Right."

"Hang on." Shelby held up a hand. "Are you telling me that he managed to touch something from all of his former lives, and we have the diary as some sort of guidebook to them?"

Seshat narrowed her ebony eyes. "Mostly."

"This is where the reassurance part comes in, isn't it?" Benny asked, picking up the pacing where Shelby left off as he thought out loud. "You needed us to trust ourselves to figure out what the book can't tell us. We realized Eli and Alcibiades are the same person, but you don't want us dependent on the journal alone. We need to be able to trust ourselves to fill the gaps in Eli's visions, especially at the end."

"Right." Seshat said again. Her crimson lips parted in a smile at the handsome Roman who stopped pacing and grinned back at her.

Shelby wrinkled her brow. "Tell me again why this is my destiny and not Benny's. He's way better at this shit than I am."

Seshat chuckled. "Shelby, it has to be you. For one, I don't think Benny is going to be able to get as close to Alcibiades as a woman could. There's only one man who was really able to do that, and it was long ago."

Benny's eyes got huge. "So that bit about Socrates is *true*? Al and the old philosopher were a thing?"

Seshat's eyes danced as she nodded, ripples of tiny braids swaying.

"Huh," Shelby said.

The goddess laughed. "At least when Alcibiades was young. It was a different time. Sexuality was looser and probably pretty strange to your era, especially when it came to men and boys, but there you have it. Of course, Alcibiades grew to enjoy the hell out of women as he aged, as Shelby can attest to. Enough to have his death blamed on an affair with a woman in one of the legends."

Shelby began pacing again. "So, I get recruited to chase after this guy because he's horny all the time and that lets me get close enough to get him to do whatever I want, like talking him into going on a random trip to Delphi?"

"Partly. No matter what life he's living, his nature is not going to be much different, except for Elijah Faircloth. That one was odd, and I still don't know what happened there. It was as though, by that time, his soul was getting tired of the womanizing and was settled more into maturity. Of course, maturity doesn't always stop people from making horrific decisions." The goddess trailed off as though she was revealing more than she planned to and got back to her point. "You know him for the man he is, Shelby, and can play on that weakness to do what needs to be done. That's why it has to be you and why you have to trust what you know about his character when you're dealing with him. And," Seshat paused again, "there's more to this whole thing than you know."

"Then, maybe you should start talking about *that*," Shelby said planting her feet. "I could use a little motivation."

Seshat's shoulders dropped slightly as she sighed. "I can't, Shelby. There's nothing I'd like more than to tell you everything, but I can't. Some things have to play out on their own, and the full extent of your destiny is one of them. If you know too much, you lose focus and things can change. You'll know everything in time. Please, I need you to trust me and let this go. Just know you're the one who has to do this, and we have a very good reason as to why."

Shelby and Seshat fell into a silent standoff. Two very different beauties staring at one another in the silent spectacle of the temple of Karnak. One with pleading eyes and the other with waning defiance. As much as Shelby wanted to beat the goddess at her own game of tug of war with the powers of free will and destiny, she knew the goddess would never relent. And she needed Seshat's help. Besides, Shelby liked her, even if she was keeping secrets. "Alright," Shelby relented. "I'll let it go, and we'll keep trying to get Al back to Apollo, but I can't guarantee he won't die again. He seems hell bent on doing that shit."

"He does, doesn't he?" Seshat laughed, her snark returning.

"Will you keep helping us?" Benny asked. "We appreciate it more than you know."

"Of course, Benny. You'll always have whatever help I can give without shifting the balance." Seshat led them back to the large base of the column where they had been sitting before all the pacing. "But now, you need rest. Chasing horny Greeks can be exhausting."

CHAPTER 23

Pulses of dull sound threaded through muted shouts as the earthy smell of smoke danced with salty sea air. Haze hung over the battered masts of war vessels clinging to the sea walls. Strips of canvas fluttered where artillery fire had ripped through the sails. One ship burst into flame with the explosion of a powder keg sending sailors into the sea under a hailstorm of arrow fire. Bodies scrambled beneath the waves to safety or bobbed limply to the surface in trailing pools of crimson. Letting the time and space around them solidify, the Watchers stood on a tiled rooftop as the city's soldiers scratched out a hopeless defense against the attacking force on their shores.

"Another battle. It's always a battle," Shelby moaned, her words hollow, then tightening as time settled around them.

"But one we know." Benny said scanning the scene. "Remarkable," he said after a moment.

"What is?"

"Look out there. Where the ships are. The invaders seem to know exactly where to fire to do the most damage. The defenders are just aiming at anything they can hit. No plan. No strategy. But the Ottomans are firing with precision. How do they know what they're aiming at in all that chaos?" Benny shook his head in wonder, then broke his own mesmerized stare and glanced around at the rooftops. "Come, bella. We're exposed here." Pointing to a more sheltered part of the roof, he took Shelby's hand and helped her over the uneven tiles. A loose one skittered down the steep pitch and clattered to the cobbled street below. There was no one in the streets to see them or care, but Benny wasn't taking any chances. Out of the sightline of anyone below, he said, "This should be safe enough to check the book."

Shelby's hands sizzled as she reached into the ever-present pouch at her waist with the diary of Elijah Faircloth. "This *is* familiar," she said as she laid the book on the tiles. "He wrote about this, too. Constantinople?"

Benny nodded, a strand of dark hair falling into his face. As he pushed it back, Shelby's heart skipped a beat. He had always been sexy, but now, there was even more that pulled her into the Roman's orbit. Strength, loyalty, and dedication. In all of the madness of chasing a nut job through space and time, Shelby was aching more and more for those long-ago nights in Benny's arms. Eons were racing by them, and there was no time for each other. A sense of urgency in Benny's words broke the spell of her thoughts. "We need to find Alcibiades fast. The city can't take much more of this and we don't want to be here when it falls," Benny said as Shelby held her hands over the tattered leather book.

Pages fluttered then settled on Eli's description of Constantinople. Much of it was centered on the town as it was in 1871. Not helpful. Then, there was his episode at the top of the tower.

From my post atop the tower, I could see Byzantine soldiers firing crossbows and guns from the sea walls at the invaders, but the numbers were sadly lopsided. In the village below me, buildings were closed tightly, except for once in a while when someone would emerge in hysteria and attempt to flee the city. Distance could be seen better than details concealed in the narrow streets between the buildings, so I have no idea if the attempts to flee were successful. I would be given no time to find out, either. As I stood staring into the distance, a small whimpering sound came from behind me. Turning to see what had made the noise, I saw in the haze the frightened dirty face of a child huddled against the cold stone wall. He was frail, almost sickly, and seemed to plead with me without saying a word. Clearly, he had come to the tower to hide from the horde. My heart broke for him and his plight, knowing that his fate was not likely to be good if he stayed in the city during the fighting. I didn't know what I could do for him, but I had to try. No human with a heart would leave the frightened child there like that. I knelt down to his level. At first, he drew back in fear, but seemed to slowly trust me as I smiled. Hoping to encourage him further, I leaned forward extending my hand to him. As I did, my other hand came away from the post and the blinding light once more covered me.

"You're right," Shelby said. "This is the battle he described. The screaming, the smoke rising from all over the city, and the ships losing their fight along the sea walls. It's all here. But where's the tower? He's at the tower. We have to find it!" Shelby shoved the book back into the pouch and scrambled up the pitch of the roof sending more tiles smashing to the street below. Nothing about her climb was graceful as her feet tangled up in the long medieval dress.

"Bella! Wait!" Benny called after Shelby as he followed. Climbing better in his pants, he caught up to her and yanked the sleeve of her dress. "Get down before the soldiers see you!"

Shelby flattened herself on the roof and scowled at him. "Fine. But I can't find the tower if I can't see the city!"

Crouching next to her, Benny said, "Apollo put us up here so we could tell where and when we are. I don't think he meant us to stay. Eli said it was hard to tell what was happening in the streets because the buildings were close together. We'll be better off down there where the soldiers can't see us."

"But we have to find the tower -"

"And we *will*, bella, but we won't live long enough to do it if we're a pair of moving targets on a rooftop!"

Damn if he didn't have a point, so Shelby reluctantly nodded as she stood to make the climb back to street level. "Fine. How?"

"I think we start by tying your dress up," Benny suggested, helping her to her feet.

Shelby looked down at the draping fabric. "I'd kill for some pants," she grumbled as she tied the sides up at her knees. By the time she managed to shimmy down from the roof after getting hung up more than once, the dress was torn and filthy.

Standing at street level, Constantinople was a winding maze of cobblestone and stucco. Buildings were set right up against the street and so close together they seemed to be leaning on each other for support like drunks after the last call. "I can't see anything from here, either. We need to be out in the open!"

"Death is out in the open. Keep moving and stay in the shadows. We'll find the tower." Benny's curt instructions were eerily similar to the ones he gave her in Athens lifetimes ago. Now that she knew they could actually die doing this, she was a little less inclined to argue with the former Italian soldier about what she should do in a battle situation, even if her stubbornness wanted to be in charge.

Homes and shops were shut tight against the advancing threat in the water. Only the screams and shouts of the soldiers filled the streets. Citizens that couldn't fight either fled the city or hid from their inevitable fate. The Watchers wove through the abandoned streets searching the skyline for the tower that should rise from the city center.

Hearing their footsteps echoing on the cobbled street must have proven too much for a terrified villager who burst through a door shrieking as she raced hysterically down the center of the road away from them. Shelby slapped her hand across her mouth to stifle her own surprised cry, flattening herself against a wall as the terrified woman tore past. Catching her breath, Shelby's chest heaved as she turned to Benny. "What the hell was that about?"

"She must have heard us and thought we were the enemy coming for her."

"But we could've just gone right past her house and done nothing. Or been on her side. Why would she just run like that?"

Benny shook his dark head and shrugged. "Fear can be a powerful thing." His eyes searched the street where the woman vanished below the hill line. "I hope she makes it," he said softly. He held out a hand to Shelby who put her stinging one in his once more and continued the search for the tower.

"What's that?" Shelby asked as they rounded a corner. The sun streaked through the spaces between the buildings, hiding the skyline in glare, but something glinted in the sky. It was a pulse of light, then gone.

Benny shaded his eyes, but it didn't do any good against the blazing light. "I don't know. Maybe if we get on the other side of it, we can see better."

Shelby nodded and followed him to the other end of the block, keeping her squinting eyes focused on where the light had come from. As they moved and the light shifted, a huge shadow emerged. "The tower!" she cried.

"And the light is coming from the top."

Shelby made a move for the tower, but Benny caught her arm. "Wait, bella. Something isn't right here. That light is no accident. Look."

Light flickered in a quick pulse from the tower, then stopped. Then again. A pause, then once more. "It's like Morse code," Shelby whispered.

Benny nodded. "We need to get back up on the roof. If that's Alcibiades, we need to see if he's signaling who I think he is."

"What? Who?" Shelby asked.

"I'll tell you when we get up there. Hurry, before he stops, and we can't track him." Benny led Shelby through the deserted streets, carefully skirting the tower so they wouldn't be seen by whoever was on the balcony above them. Behind it, he searched for a way up where he could see the tower and the coastline at the same time. "If you can reach that window there," he said, pointing at a frame well above Shelby's head, "you should be able to pull up on that low part of the building next to it."

"Except there's no way I can reach that." Shelby squinted up at the windowsill just out of their reach, then a thought occurred to her. "Crates! There were boxes in that alley around the corner."

Benny grinned at her. "Good thinking! Come on."

Between the two of them, they managed to carry a large empty crate, which would have been easier if they weren't trying to be quiet and could have just dragged the damn thing. Panting, Shelby set her end down and dragged her sleeve across her forehead. "I'm getting sick of this shit. This isn't what I thought being a Watcher was like at all. Naomi and Gael just did tours and drank wine all the time." Dusting her hands on her skirt that was just as filthy, she plopped down on the crate.

"Shelby," Benny said gently taking her face in his hands, "I'd love to argue the finer points of being a Watcher, but we don't have time right now. Come, bella. You can pout later, I promise." He kissed her on the corner of her mouth and her heart fluttered.

"I miss you," she whispered.

Grinning, he replied, "I miss you, too. Come on. Let's get this guy back where he belongs so we can get back to us." Kissing her again, he held her hand as she scrambled up on the crate and began the climb to the roof.

* * *

After a pointless climb to the rooftops to find their view of the Ottoman ships blocked by buildings, the Watchers shimmied back down and sped to the top of the Galata tower. Benny and Shelby paused at the top of the winding tower stairs to catch their breath. As anxious as they were to catch up with the wayward Greek, they weren't stupid enough to go charging onto the balcony. Shelby's stinging hand pressed against the heavy wooden door at the top of the dark staircase lit only by torches on the verge of burning themselves out. As she did, the old iron hinges creaked. "Damn it," she cursed.

"We have to get through that door." Benny groaned and leaned against the curved stone of the staircase wall.

"But we can't make a squealing announcement as we do." Shelby paused as she thought. "Spit on the hinges," Shelby said.

"What?"

"Spit on the hinges. Something I read in a book once," Benny smirked at her and shook his head, amused. "*What?*" Shelby asked, putting her hands on her hips indignantly. His eyebrow raised, but he said nothing. "I *read!*" Shelby insisted. "Occasionally. Got a better idea?"

Benny shrugged and spat on the top hinge while Shelby did the same on the middle and bottom ones. After a few disgusting moments, Shelby pressed gently on the door. It eased open with only a soft grinding sound of old rust.

Disgusted, but impressed, Benny grinned at Shelby. "I'll be damned."

"Me, too." Color rose in Shelby's cheeks as she pushed the door a little harder.

Opening the door a crack, they listened for signs of soldiers on the other side of the tower door, but heard nothing. Benny stepped in front of Shelby and pushed the door open farther. The bodies of two Byzantine soldiers lay on the ground in pools of thickening blood. "This is all they put up here to protect the tower?" Benny whispered. "What were they thinking?"

"Maybe they had a little too much faith in that sea wall. But I think the real question is who did this to them?"

Benny nodded. "And where are they now?" Kneeling just outside of the blood, he pulled a dagger from the sheath at the waist of one of the dead men. "Take this, bella," he said handing it to her as he looked for the man's sword. Daylight streaming through the massive arched windows splashed across the emptiness of the round tower room. Looking for the sword of the first soldier was fruitless since whoever left the one standing straight out of his chest must have replaced theirs with his. Benny tugged at it, but the sword didn't budge. It was either wedged between bones or driven through into the cracks of the stone floor and there was no time to work it loose. Along the wall behind the dead soldier, Benny caught a glint of metal at the edge of the shadow and found the second soldier's weapon. Armed, the two Watchers made their way cautiously to the perimeter.

The stone windows went to the floor making them more like arched doorways to the outside balcony where they had seen the flashing from the ground. Each support around the room hid their presence while each arch gave them away depending on where someone on the balcony was standing. They did the same for whoever was signaling the troops below. Going up the spiral staircase, they had lost their bearings to know which opening might have led to the view of the sea. They were going to have to step out into the open if they wanted to find Alcibiades.

"There," Shelby whispered unclenching her stinging hand to point at the fabric fluttering at the edge of one of the arches where the tower curved. From their vantage point atop the tower, it was clear what Alcibiades was doing. Like their original view from the rooftops, they could see the struggle between the ships along the sea wall and the Ottoman ships in the bay. "He's playing Battleship, only with real ships!" Shelby whispered. Below, the warring vessels and soldiers were clearly defined as though they were looking at a battle map in three dimensions. What they hadn't been able to see from the rooftop below were the answering flashes from an Ottoman ship in the center of the fleet.

"We don't have much time," Benny said in her ear. "It won't be long before someone realizes what's going on and stops him. You have to get to him first."

"Jesus Christ," Shelby cursed.

"Born, but not likely to help much."

Shelby rolled her eyes. "Guess he's more of a 'big picture' guy. Come on."

Inching her way closer to Alcibiades, she saw the sword of the fallen soldier hanging in its scabbard at his side while his hands worked a polished piece of metal in the sunlight. She didn't want to attack him but knew that she may very well have to defend against him if she startled him. Keeping a safe distance, she softly cleared her throat. Wheeling around, Alcibiades' hand went to his sword as Shelby put her hands up in a show of peace. "Wait!" she said. "I'm not here to hurt you. I need to talk to you."

"You shouldn't be here," he answered tightening his grip on his sword but not drawing it. His lips pressed into a firm thin line.

"I don't want to be here any more than you want me here, but there's something important you need to know."

Eyes narrowed in suspicion, Alcibiades cautiously asked, "Who sent you?"

Shelby shifted her weight. That wasn't where she wanted to start. "Please, I'll tell you that and more, but you have to come with me. Now."

Alcibiades shook his dark head. "I've got work to do here, wench. State your business or take it elsewhere." He glanced at Benny over Shelby's shoulder and eased the sword a few inches out of its sheath, strength pressing against the fibers of his sleeve.

"She's telling you the truth," Benny said, sliding his sword into his belt and holding his hands away from it. "We don't want a fight and we don't care whose side you're on. What we have to say goes beyond all this," he said waving a dismissive hand at the fighting in the distance.

"You don't belong here," Shelby began.

A sharp laugh escaped Alcibiades. "Of course not. I'm a traitor and a spy. I damn sure don't belong here, but I doubt you're going to stop me any more than those two did," he said with a jerk of his head toward the dead soldiers.

"We aren't here to stop you. We're here to get you to come with us. To Delphi."

Alcibiades looked Shelby up and down for a moment before his eyes settled on hers. "You're beautiful, and in another time and place, I'd be tempted to take you many places. But not today and not to Delphi."

"Please," Shelby said taking a step closer to him with a glance at the hand on his sword. "Please come with me. There's so much more you're capable of. More you're supposed to be. Haven't you always felt out of place? Out of time? Like you didn't know where you belonged?" Shelby watched as his eyes lost their rigid stare. It was only an instant, but it was enough to let her know she'd hit on something. "Your destiny isn't here on this tower. Your destiny is in Delphi."

"You aren't Greek," Alcibiades said slowly. "And you aren't Byzantine. Who are you?"

"My name is Shelby Starling. I've been sent by someone very powerful who wants to show you the life you should have had all along. The life you deserve." If Shelby hadn't been terrified for her life, she would have lost it in a giggle fit over the drama queen that was oozing out of her at the moment.

Once more, Alcibiades scanned Shelby. "You seem… familiar somehow."

Finally getting somewhere, Shelby smiled at him. "I should. We've known each other before. Benny, too."

Benny nodded. "Good to see you again."

"I don't -" Soft footsteps echoed across the stone floor from the direction of the tower door drawing Alcibiades' attention away from the Watchers. "Christ, now what?" he cursed under his breath. A young boy, fear flooding his eyes, stepped through the opening, then flattened himself against the arch. It was hard to tell what frightened him more, the height of the balcony or the sight of the three of them.

"The diary!" Shelby whispered. "This is it!"

"Shadows!" Benny hissed as he tugged Shelby against the stone wall.

"Why? He's just a kid," Shelby mouthed back as Benny held a hand up to silence her. Benny's head inclined leading Shelby's eyes to the sky. Overhead, a raven circled lower and lower. "Apollo!" Benny nodded and glanced behind the stone support. Pressed against the cold stone, Shelby tightened her grip on the dagger in her hand as she saw the real threat for herself.

A whimper escaped the mouth of the small boy as his frightened eyes darted back at the blood-soaked bodies of the soldiers sprawled in the middle of the stone floor. He made a move to retreat but couldn't. There was a sword tip pressed between his shoulder blades. By his dress, the child was as Byzantine as the soldiers on the floor.

"Time to earn your keep, boy," the man at the other end of the sword hissed too quietly for Alcibiades to hear. Another Byzantine soldier. "Distract the traitor so I can kill him, then you'll get your pay."

"Shit!" Shelby said. "Not again!"

"Not this time," Benny whispered. "We've got him outnumbered." With a nod to Shelby, he stepped out of the shadows and over to the child. Alcibiades was kneeling in front of the boy trying to convince him to go back down to the town. He couldn't see the soldier behind the child just out of sight behind the arch. All the child could do was shake his head violently as tears streamed down his face. Benny knelt beside Alcibiades and whispered in his ear, "Let Shelby take him then draw your sword. He's bait." Then to the boy, "Come, child. She can take you down and help you find your parents."

Shelby stepped over to the boy with one hand clutching the dagger. "It's alright. I can help you, but you must come with me. Now!" she cried as she yanked the boy away from the wall and shoved him behind her. Dagger drawn, she braced for the assassin to charge as she backed toward the balcony railing. The sobbing boy clutched her tattered skirts as fear of the struggle and the dizzying height consumed him.

Lunging from the shadows, the assassin's sword barely missed Alcibiades who only dodged it in time because of Benny's warning. Blades clanged as Benny and Alcibiades took on the trained killer who met them blow for blow. Shelby shielded the child until she got him to the door at the tower staircase. "Run," she said, "and don't look back. Get as far away as you can. The city's going to fall." A frightened nod then he vanished into the shadows down the steps.

Benny and Alcibiades were locked in an even match with the assassin as Shelby raced back over to the balcony. Her dagger wasn't likely to do much good against the sword, so she stayed out of sight looking for another way to turn the tables in their favor. Taking a savage hit, Benny lost his balance and stumbled backwards. As he did, Alcibiades clashed with the Byzantine soldier. Shelby's breath caught in her chest and sparks flew around her wrist as the soldier's sword plunged into Alcibiades' chest.

"Not this time!" she snarled as the assassin stepped back to pull his blade free. Diving at his feet, Shelby grabbed his ankles and took the stunned soldier by surprise. Swinging wildly at the air with his blade coated in slick crimson, the soldier toppled over the edge of the balcony to the stone pavers two hundred feet below.

Benny rushed to her side as Shelby turned her back on the sickening sound of the soldier's body hitting the ground. A muted crunch of flesh and armor then the distant clatter of a sword on stone. "Bella! Are you okay?" he asked, grabbing her hands.

"I- I killed him," she said as a tremor raced through her whole body.

"You had no choice. Bella, look at me." Benny took her face in his hands. "You had *no choice*."

Tears streamed down her face as she nodded, but there was nothing he could say that would stop the convulsing and nausea. The sound of the body hitting the ground echoed in her ears. A groan from Alcibiades pulled her from her own misery back to the mission at hand and the reason she'd killed the assassin. "Alcibiades! He's alive!"

Benny knelt beside the wounded Alcibiades and felt his pulse. "Barely."

Ripping at her skirts, Shelby pressed cloth against the wound in his chest frantically trying to stop the gushing. Each heartbeat pushed more blood into her hands, but each was weaker than the one before. "No!" she said as hot tears splashed on his face. "You have to live! You have to listen to me!" Alcibiades' eyes fluttered open for a moment as he looked up at the stranger trying to save his life. "Please!" Shelby begged pushing on his wound. "You don't belong here. You're a Traveler, born in the wrong place and time. You have a destiny greater than dying on this tower, but you have to get to Delphi to find it. Don't die on me again, goddamn it!" She screamed. Benny knelt beside her and held Alcibiades' head. "Apollo!" she shrieked over the din of the battle on the sea that was bleeding into the city streets. "Where the hell are you when I need you?" Gliding down from the slow circle it had been keeping above the tower, the raven swept onto the balcony and settled on the railing. Shelby cut her eyes at the creature but knew from the bird's lowered head that there was nothing to be done for Alcibiades. She looked at Benny in a panic. "He said we were familiar somehow. Maybe things can carry from one life to the next."

"It's worth a try," Benny said with a shrug. "What are you going to do?"

Shelby looked down at the whitening face of the man with the gentle lisp and traitor's heart. "Your name was Alcibiades when you told me to come find you. I've found you over and over again and you never know me. Never listen. Never live long enough to know who you really are. You left me with this in a vision, so I'm leaving you with the same thing hoping you'll remember me next time we meet." Taking his strong jaw in her hands, Shelby pressed her lips to Alcibiades' trembling ones. Feverish as the life bled out of him, he shivered, then slowly raised his hand to hers on his cheek. As he touched her fingers, a shock went through them both. Eyes that were clouded in death focused sharply on her face as Shelby pulled away from him. "You know me, don't you?" she breathed. A nod, almost imperceptible, was her answer as his eyes closed and the familiar pain of being severed from her Traveler brought an anguished scream from deep in the Watcher's core.

Taking her hands in his, Benny gathered Shelby close to him and held her as she sobbed on his shoulder. "He knew you, bella," Benny whispered in her ear as he stroked her dark hair. "He knew you when he died. We're getting closer." For a moment, Benny held her, letting the pain and grief pour out, but soon, the sounds of fighting drew closer as the city began to fall. "Bella," he began gently, "it's time."

Never raising her head from Benny's shoulder, Shelby's fingers found the silver snake and turned it. "The Traveler follows the serpent."

"The Watcher follows the Traveler."

CHAPTER 24

The twilight sky settled into a deep sapphire as shadows of the island's hills gave vague borders to the land, sea, and heavens. Stars had yet to break through the atmosphere, but twinkling began in pinpricks among the gentle curves of the settlement nestled against the fort dominating the curve of the coast. Larger fires shimmered to life in iron braziers placed along measured distances of the battlements as soldiers readied for the night watch. Drifting offshore, an armada transformed from war-worn battleships to spectral shadows as the tattered remnants of sunlight frayed away to blackness.

"Malta," Shelby whispered. Her voice echoed in the thickening of time and space around the Watchers.

"We seem to be following Eli through his journal exactly as he experienced it," Benny said nodding.

Shelby looked at the quiet night surrounding them. "It's nice to have a break from the constant string of battles, but the change of atmosphere makes it seem eerie somehow." There was energy in a battle. Vibrance. Rawness. In the quiet of the Mediterranean night, there was anticipation. Not the night before Christmas kind, either. More like a snake coiled and still. Waiting. Watching.

The shadowed fleet bobbed in the distance; faint flickers of ship lanterns the only things giving them away now. Shelby and Benny stood watching from the stone wall at the water's edge. "They've backed out of the range of the cannons. Taking the night to rest and repair before the battle begins again at first light," Benny explained.

"Why not fight through the night and get it over with? We can see where the fort and ships are. Can't they?"

"Yes, they could keep going, but you lose accuracy at night. That's a lot of ammunition wasted on missed targets. Winners of wars are usually the ones with supplies when the other side has run out."

"So, what do we do now?"

"We know where he'll be once the fighting gets going again. Until then, he'll be deep inside the fort with the other soldiers. I say we take Seshat's advice and get some rest."

Shelby glanced toward the settlement behind the fort. "There?"

Benny grinned down at her. "It's a nice night. How about a little camping? That looks like a good spot," he said pointing up the hill to an outcropping in the rock. Sheltered enough to keep them hidden from the fort and settlement, but in a good position to keep an eye on the ships at dawn.

"I'm not usually one for being outdoorsy, but I've had to get past some things over the eons, like my need for indoor plumbing. Camping it is." It really didn't matter to Shelby where they slept or if they slept at all. Nothing mattered except knowing she'd have until sunrise in Benny's arms.

The space under the outcropping was mercifully free of other creatures large enough to see in the faint sliver of moon, but Benny tossed a rock inside that skittered around in hopes it would scare away anything they couldn't see before they crept inside. "Well, it's not the Plaza," Shelby said as she settled on the cool grittiness of the stone floor, "but I'll take it." Curled in Benny's arms, blue sparks swirled delicately and slowly around her wrist. Shelby took that as Seshat's blessing over their night of peace together before hell broke loose in the morning. Slowly, gently, they made the most of it. Not the impatient burning of their first night together, or the electric passion of the other ones in their own time. There was something deeper about this night. Trusting and tender. Longing without the urgency.

* * *

Night's trance was shattered by the first rays of the sun that streaked over the horizon, bringing with them shouts and cannon fire as Benny predicted. Once more, Shelby fought against her destiny and the desire to stay in Benny's arms forever. Destiny would always come for her. She knew better than to try to skip out on it like a truant child, so she got to her feet and shook the peace of the night from her along with the dust on her clothes.

Sunrise bathed the fort walls in a ruddy glow as soldiers poured forth from the protected depths of the battlements. Cannons lumbered toward the sea walls on wooden wheels that groaned with every rut and bump in the path. Always, eyes of the soldiers flitted toward the armada bobbing in the distance.

Dawn also illuminated the battering the fort and sea walls had taken at the hands of the cannons from the enemy ships. Fort St. Angelo wore the scars of battle; gashes and deep pocks in the stone where cannons had grazed or slammed into their marks. The sea wall was fragile in places, tumbling haphazardly into the water that sloshed over the gaping wounds.

Shouts and calls the English-speaking soldiers couldn't understand wafted over on the sea breeze. Orders barked in the native tongue of the Ottoman attackers gave a sense of wary expectation to the Knights of St. John. The Watchers, however, understood every word.

"What do they mean by, 'load the prisoners'?" Shelby asked, straining to hear more. Only words spoken with the wind made it across the sea. "Or did I hear that wrong?"

Tiny lines creased the edges of Benny's dark Roman eyes as he squinted toward the ship, as though that would help him hear better. It reminded Shelby of someone turning down the car radio as they look for a street sign to make a turn as if the lack of sound would make it easier to see. "No, bella," he said, "you heard it right. They said, 'load the prisoners.'"

A moment passed while both Watchers stared wide-eyed remembering the story in Eli's journal. "They're going to float the bodies back!" Shelby felt a knot forming in her chest as the thoughts of headless knights flashed through her mind.

Benny nodded and glanced around. "Eli got here in the middle of the retaliation for that. We're early."

"But, why?" Shelby asked. "Why do we need to see what led up to the events that Eli wrote about?"

"Apollo must need us to see something before the heads started flying back over the sea."

Shelby groaned. The mental picture of headless corpses floating across the water to the fort was bad enough, but now she had flashes of heads being cut off Ottoman soldiers and shot back at the ships. Nauseating. "Then where do we start? I don't want to be here when the bodies get pushed over. I've seen enough corpses for a while."

"The journal. We need to know exactly what Alcibiades' role was. Knight, or common soldier. That way we narrow the search."

Casting a furtive glance around them, the Watchers retreated back into the shelter of the outcropping, not from fear of the cannons that were still out of range, but to prevent the sparks that would inevitably appear from drawing attention. The dull stinging that had been in Shelby's hands since they arrived became searing pain as she pulled the book out of the insulating pouch and threw it on the stone floor. A moment of habitual and useless rubbing of her hands, then she held them over the book as the cover flew open and pages fluttered. The sparks made their expected appearance as the aged pages stopped at the entry on the battle of Fort St. Angelo.

Benny bent over the book and read:

"Realizing the Turks were across the harbour for the time being, I rose up some to get my bearings. In the distance, smoke hung in a haze over fires that had been burning for some time. In the midst of the fighting, I could see the Turks vastly outnumbered the local forces. Flashes of red tunics were more scarce but seemed to be the most skilled. They barked orders and organized the others. The Knights of St. John. Under the red tunics bearing the iconic white cross was chainmail more common for professional soldiers. Proper helmets, shields, and swords in addition to superior training put the knights at the head of the charge."

His dark eyes scanned the rest of the entry. "He describes the knights and the killing of the Turks, but never mentions how he was dressed. Damn it." Benny leaned back against the stone and closed his eyes in frustration.

"So, we know where he ends up, but we don't know whether he's a knight or a common soldier. How are we going to head him off if we don't know how to find the needle in the haystack?"

Before Benny had a chance to answer, shouts different from the orders being barked and echoed across the battlefield erupted from the direction of the fort. Shelby's hands began to burn savagely, and sparks flew from her fingertips. "I guess Seshat's found him for us. Leave it to Al to be in the middle of chaos."

"Let's go, bella. There's a reason we're here early and this could be it."

Shelby took a deep breath and picked up the book that seared her hands before it went harmlessly back into the pouch. "Great," she groaned. "Let's go see what the maniac has gotten himself into this time."

CHAPTER 25

Knights pushed through the crowd of common soldiers to the center of the throng as the Watchers arrived at the base of the fort. In the middle of it all, was a man with dark hair and wild frightened eyes. His hands clutched at his chest as though he'd been scared out of his wits.

"Go on, men!" one of the Knights of St. John shouted to the other solders gawking at the man. "There's a battle on and you've work to do. Now!" Reluctantly, but obediently, the soldiers tore themselves away from the strange man and went back to their posts.

"What's happening?" Shelby whispered as she and Benny watched hidden by a curve in the fort wall. "What happened to that guy?"

"Not sure, bella, but we can't go asking questions. The Knights won't be as easy to fool as some of the others. Best to see if we can find something out by staying hidden."

Shelby nodded and flexed her burning fingers. "Look at him trembling. It's like he's seen a ghost."

"I saw her!" the man shouted, his voice shaking in his fear. "You can't tell me I didn't! I know what I saw! The Gray Lady! It was her; I swear it!" Weaving through the panicked words was a gentle softness on the 'r' sounds.

"It's him!" she whispered.

"You're right about two things, bella," Benny said turning from the pathetic scene to face her. "It's Al, and he's seen a ghost."

"What?"

"The Gray Lady," Benny explained, "is the ghost of Fort St. Angelo. Poor fool thinks he's seen her."

The Knight was getting irritated with Alcibiades' blubbering about the ghost and was threatening to have him put in the dungeon if he didn't shut up. Shelby had to admit this blubbering mess was an unattractive side of the great Greek commander and was starting to endorse the Knight's plan.

"No! Don't put me down there! That's where *she* is!" Alcibiades cowered against the fort wall, digging his nails into the stone as though he could hold onto it and keep himself from being hauled down to the cells.

"No one is down there but prisoners," the Knight spat at him. "Soon to be joined by one hysterical Maltese soldier."

If Alcibiades pressed himself any closer to the wall, he would have been part of it. "She's down there, I tell you! I saw her! *I saw her.*"

Another Knight who had stopped to see what the ruckus was all about spoke up. "I'll bite. What did you see?"

For a moment, gratitude flashed in Alcibiades' eyes before the maniacal look returned. "I – I went to take water to the prisoners, like I was told to. They were huddled in the corners of their cells, scared out of their wits. Not being able to speak Turkish, I had no idea what they were going on about. There was no use in trying to tell them to be quiet. They don't speak English anyway. So, I tried to give them the water. None of them wanted to come close enough to the door to get any. 'Let them die of thirst, then,' I thought, then I turned to go." His eyes grew huge as he finished his story. "That's when I *saw her*! With my own eyes, I did! Beautiful and fearsome, floating just above the stone floor."

"Then what?" the newly-arrived Knight asked as the first one grew more impatient.

"Who cares?" the first one snapped. "It's all nonsense. Get back to your post."

As the second Knight turned to obey the order, Alcibiades' hand shot out and grabbed his arm. "No! You can't go out there and fight them! She said England has worn out her welcome and her soldiers will die! Don't you see?" he pleaded, clutching at the Knight's red tunic. "It's a warning! If we flee now, we could save our skins!"

"Run? And leave Malta to the Turks?" the first Knight snarled as the second peeled the white-knuckled fingers of Alcibiades from his cloak. "Never. I'd rather die here than live a coward knowing Fort. St. Angelo was in the hands of the infidels." Then, the Knight drew his sword and held the tip against Alcibiades' throat. "One more word and my blade finds a new sheath. Now, make yourself useful or scarce. I don't care which." With a jerk of his head, the first Knight signaled the second to follow back to the sea wall where the cannons were being loaded.

For a moment, Alcibiades watched them go looking like a scolded child. Once they were further away, however, his expression shifted to a sly grin.

"Holy shit!" Shelby whispered. "It was all an act! But why?"

"What's the one thing we know about Al?" Benny asked sarcastically.

"The common denominator of all these lives has been the fact that he's a traitor. But what does a ghost story have to do with being a traitor?"

"Hard to say just yet, but if he can convince enough of the common soldiers, it might just be enough to sway the odds against the Knights." His eyes scanned the bay and settled on the shore across the water. "Look, there. St. Elmo. The Turks outnumber the Knights considerably. The Knights need the Maltese soldiers to win this. Even with them, it's almost impossible odds. Mutiny would leave the fort as an easy prize for the Ottomans."

"Convince enough to run from the ghost, and turn the fort over to the Turks," Shelby said shaking her dark head. "What an ass. Why would he do that? He's English in this life."

Benny shrugged. "Perhaps the British weren't the highest bidders."

"Sounds about right," Shelby grumbled. "So, now what do we do? Go talk to him?"

"Not just yet. We're Watchers. Let's watch for a while."

* * *

Rumblings of the Gray Lady's appearance had spread through the ranks like gossip at a beauty parlor by the time the first of the headless Knights were being floated across the bay to the furious Valetta. The leader of the Knights of St. John vowed revenge while others whispered of the curse of the mysterious ghost. Valetta condemned the superstitious nonsense and anyone who spoke of it, but nothing could stop the murmurings of the soldiers out of his earshot. As the first of the bloated bodies of once noble knights were being scooped out of the water like game fish, the sight brought the rumblings of mutiny to a fever pitch. Swollen headless corpses have that effect on people.

After spending some time blending in amongst the soldiers as servants, Benny and Shelby found one another at the edge of the village beyond the fort. "His story is growing roots," Shelby said shaking her head and pacing. "It's hard to believe anyone could take that seriously."

"Desperate men will hang on to anything that serves their purpose. If they want out of the battle, this is as good a thread to cling to as any other."

Alcibiades' whisper campaign to raise a mutiny seemed to be working as well as he planned from the amount of grumbling and furtive glances toward the hills away from the fort. Still, it was a pointless plan. Certainly not one of the great commander's epic betrayals of eons gone by. "The thing I don't get is what these people think they are going to do?" Shelby said stopping her pacing and sitting cross-legged on the ground, her long skirt puddling around her. They keep talking about running and letting the Knights take the fall, but run to where? This is a freaking *island*. They can only go so far without a fleet. It's idiotic. Surely, they can't all be that stupid."

"Not stupid," Benny said sitting next to her and threading his fingers through her stinging ones. "Just afraid. Very afraid. Remember, we know something they don't. We know who wins."

"Valetta."

"Right. They see themselves outnumbered and at the mercy of the Turks. Any other option looks good at this point."

Shelby's dark eyes met his. "So, how do we stop Alcibiades from taking the army with him and making liars out of the history books? Expose him for the fraud he is and risk getting him killed again in the process?"

Benny sighed heavily. "I don't see any other way around it. Of course, he's not likely to come with us to Delphi if we betray him to Valetta."

The two Watchers sat in silence for a few moments, each trying to untangle the threads of Alcibiades' latest life and traitorous endeavor without tightening the knots in the process. Shelby turned the problem over and over in her mind playing through one scenario after another, but each ended in Alcibiades being killed as a traitor as soon as he was revealed to Valetta. Except for one. "Benny, what if we let the mutiny happen?"

Benny blinked at her a few times before asking, "What? Why?"

"They can't go anywhere, and Valetta will squash any uprising. If he can defeat the Turks who outnumber him, he can handle a few mutineers, right?"

"Yes, but I don't see how this gets Al to Delphi."

"What if we don't give him a choice?"

Benny stared dumbstruck at Shelby. "*Kidnap* him? Bella, he has to go by choice. *His* choice."

Shelby crossed her arms over her chest defiantly. "I'm pretty sure once he's not being executed for treason and safely on board a ship to Greece, he'll be easier to convince." She paused for a moment, letting the Roman process her words. "Unless you have a better idea," Shelby added flatly.

"God, Shelby," Benny said pushing his hands through his dark hair. "How the hell do we get a ship?" Shelby's face tightened into a pained smile. "Steal one? And just which side do we steal from? The Turks or the British?"

Shelby got to her feet and stared out to the coastline. "The Maltese. We don't need a fleet ship. Just something big enough to get us to Greece. Look," she said pointing toward a bend in the coastline on the far side of the fort. There, in cove, bobbed smaller fishing vessels that had been largely ignored by the Ottoman onslaught as they focused their attack on the fort and soldiers on the sea wall along the bay.

"The armada will never let us through," Benny said shaking his head. "It's suicide."

Shelby chuckled. "You forget whose side our dear Alcibiades is on."

CHAPTER 26

Valetta stood on the sea wall with a hard gaze fixed on the armada across the bay. The Watchers kept their distance as history and diary entries unfolded in front of them. "Bring the prisoners," the Knight said through set teeth. In his helmet, eyes blazed with fury. Orders to fetch the Turks from the dungeons of the fort were barked back in the ranks escorted by whispers of the rage of the Gray Lady if the prisoners were executed. No one stepped up to carry out the orders and instead they were thrust on three young men that couldn't have been much out of their teens. Shaking with fear of the dungeon haunting, they resigned themselves to their fate and descended into the prison cells. Long moments passed as Valetta continued watching the armada while others threw furtive glances in the direction of the dungeon stairs. Long moments later, a chain of shackled prisoners was dragged into the fresh sea air to their deaths. Iron cuffs on the doomed men's ankles and wrists clanked as they dragged their feet toward Valetta who stood rigid and resolute. Leading them were three ashen-faced young men.

"They look like they saw the ghost," Shelby said.

Benny nodded. "Maybe they did. Fear and suggestion can make even the most logical person see things that aren't there."

Shelby's burning hands began to spark as Alcibiades was led to the Knight of St. John at sword point. His dark eyes darted over to her, and his brow furrowed. A flicker of confusion flashed over his features. "No," Shelby whispered. "Not confusion. Recognition."

Benny followed her gaze as the look flickered away as Alcibiades turned to face Valetta. "Odd."

Shelby nodded but said nothing. Instead, she held her breath and waited for Valetta to speak.

The red tunic and white cross shone in the sun streaking through the smoke curls of cannon fire floating in the sea breeze. Valetta was indeed a commanding figure, but Alcibiades stared at him with a defiance-drenched smirk. The men were more on his side than Valetta's and he seemed comfortable with his impending mutiny. Slowly Valetta circled Alcibiades as though attempting to determine his worth or worthlessness, as the case may be. For a moment, Shelby's mind flashed back to Palmyra and Queen Zenobia sizing him up in the doomed war camp. "You defy not only my orders but our Lord God with your ghost stories, soldier," Valetta snarled.

"I haven't seen God," Alcibiades answered steadily, "but I *have* seen the Gray Lady. Perhaps God needs to show himself to the people. They are more inclined to heed her warnings than His death sentence."

"It is the infidel enemy who will suffer the death sentence, not the Knights of St. John. God's men."

Alcibiades snorted in derision. "God's men? Where is this God now? Where was He when His soldiers were being beheaded and floated back to you? The Gray Lady offers warning and life. God has given you only death. It seems the enemy has proven themselves powerful and ruthless, yet you depend on prayer and an absent heavenly protector." Murmurs erupted in support of the traitor's statements. Prickles of mutiny began to stand on end throughout the camp as Alcibiades' words rang true. The grin dancing at the edges of Alcibiades' mouth began to spread across his face.

Valetta's eyes narrowed as he fought to control his rage. Straightening his shoulders, the Knight collected himself and turned to face the grumbling crowd. As he did, cannons fired in thunderous staccato from the sea wall. Valetta's eyes cut over to them, then back to the crowd. "I think it's time our enemies saw the might and vengeance of our Lord God! Shall we show them?" he shouted with his chain mailed fist held high. The tide of the crowd shifted on Alcibiades, turning instead back to their leader. "Take the prisoners to the cannons!"

This time, soldiers eagerly rushed to escort the prisoners to their deaths as Alcibiades shouted protests about the anger of the Gray Lady in their wake.

"Looks like his mutiny is losing traction," Shelby whispered as she and Benny fell in with the crowd heading to the sea wall. Cannons on the fort continued to bombard the armada, distracting the ships from Valetta's movements to the other cannons. For now, the ships seemed to be held at bay. Taking the men on shore would accomplish nothing if the Turks couldn't breech the fort, so the armada kept its focus on trying to bring the walls down.

At the sea wall, Valetta directed the soldiers to line the captives up behind the cannons instead of in front of them. Momentary confusion ensued, but orders were followed even if they weren't understood. Once more Valetta circled Alcibiades as he explained the fate of the prisoners. "It seems our enemy finds it amusing to collect the heads of fallen soldiers. Perhaps they need a few more to add to their collection." Then, leaning closer to the would-be mutineer, he hissed, "Fear the vengeance of God, not ghosts of jilted whores." In one fluid movement, Valetta turned, unsheathed his sword and sliced through the neck of the nearest Ottoman prisoner. Shelby vomited as the head hit the ground and rolled to a stop at Alcibiades' feet. "Load it into the cannon and send it back to the infidels," Valetta ordered, his voice strained and tight.

Benny clutched her face to his chest as the Knight of St. John swung his sword again and again, taking the heads off of one prisoner after the other. Sickening sounds filled the air as flesh was cut and bodies dropped to the ground, punctuated by the explosions of cannons firing heads across the sea to the Turkish ships. Shelby didn't need to see what was happening to feel every bit of it. She'd read it already in Eli's journal and could put each sound to his words. Benny held her tighter and whispered in her ear, "We have to get Alcibiades out of here before Valetta turns his sword on him out of spite."

"How?" Shelby asked. "We can't just go take him from Valetta and walk away."

"We need a distraction."

Shelby nodded but was out of ideas. Around them, a rumble of hushed comments about the wrath of the Gray Lady let them know the mutiny wasn't as dead as they thought. "Mutiny. We need a mutiny."

"I don't think Al's in any position to start one, bella."

"No, but we are," Shelby said pushing back from him. "Fear and suggestion, remember? Follow my lead. Like Athens." Benny's face twisted in confusion, but before he had a chance to ask anything, Shelby pointed at the fort and shrieked. Her dark eyes grew huge and maniacal as she backed away, still screaming at the top of her lungs pointing with a shaking hand at the walls of St. Angelo. "It's *her*. I can see her! It's the Gray Lady!"

Shelby's words took on unintelligible babbling in between the shrieks as Benny whirled around and screamed. "God have mercy on us!" he shouted, crossing himself wildly. "She's angry! Stop this! Stop the killing! She's coming for us!"

Soldiers turned to the fort in disbelief at first, but then their own fear began to play with their thoughts as more and more of them 'saw' the ghost for themselves. Terror rippled through the camp and chaos began to take hold. Shelby's incoherence became clear and strong as she screamed, "*She's coming! Run!*"

Soldiers began to scatter despite the shouts of the Knights to hold their positions. The Maltese recruits weren't taking any chances with the ghost that had been legend as far as they could remember. As the Knights broke rank to chase down the deserters, Shelby and Benny grabbed Alcibiades, who was stunned by the sudden turn of events.

"Come on, you idiot," Shelby spat at him. "You wanted a mutiny; you got it."

"We're on your side," Benny said. "Now, go!" Benny drew his sword and slashed at the soldiers in their way as they broke into a dead run toward the fishing boats on the other side of the fort village.

"Where are we going?" Alcibiades asked.

"Does it matter? You're getting your mutiny and getting to keep your head in the process. I suggest you shut up and follow our lead!" Shelby snapped.

"No! I didn't do all this just to run!" Alcibiades said stopping and drawing his sword on them. "Who are you?"

Benny squared off with him and answered, "It doesn't matter who we are. We know who you are. Who you really are."

"You recognize me, don't you?" Shelby asked, gripping the dagger in her belt.

Alcibiades looked closely at her then answered, "Yes, but I don't know why."

"We've met before. Many times now. Your destiny isn't here. Not with the Maltese or the Turks. You know that, don't you?" she said watching a flicker of understanding play across his features. Slowly, he nodded. "I know where you belong. You have to trust me."

Alcibiades stared at her for a long moment, then glanced over his shoulder as sounds of battle rose over the hillside. "It's too late for me. I've already traded my soul to the Turks. My fate is here. And so are they."

"What?" Shelby asked.

"The Turks!" Benny shouted turning his sword from Alcibiades to the wave of soldiers pushing back the mass of fleeing Maltese. "It was a trap! The whole mutiny was a trap!" The Maltese soldiers had no choice but to abandon their retreat that was now cut off by the Ottomans and fight back instead. Swords clashed and bodies fell as more soldiers and Knights poured out of the fort to take down the Ottomans invading their shore.

Shelby grabbed Alcibiades by the shoulders and held him to face her. "Listen to me! Your name is Alcibiades, and you were a great Greek general. You have been chosen for a different fate than that of a traitor and mutineer. Your destiny awaits, but you have to get out of here alive." He shook his head at her, but Shelby grabbed his face and held it still. "Look at me, Alcibiades. You know who I am! Say it! Say my name!" Confusion clouded his eyes and before he could protest anymore, she kissed him hard. Electricity shot through them both, but Shelby kept her grip. Finally, as the electric shock eased, she released him. "Say it," she said softly.

Alcibiades blinked at her for a moment, then whispered, "Shelby?"

Tears gathered on Shelby's lashes. "Yes!"

"Come on, bella," Benny urged. "We don't have much time. We have to get out of here. Now."

Shelby nodded. "Come on. We have to get you back to Greece. To Delphi. If you stay here, Valetta will kill you if the Turks don't. We know who wins, so you really don't want to be here."

"The Turks won't kill me. I'm on their side. Traitor, remember?"

Shelby nodded. "Right. That may be just the thing we need to get through that armada. You've gotten them on the island with the mutiny distraction. Think they'll let you sail through to return the favor?" Alcibiades nodded. "Good. There are some fishing boats in the harbor around the bend, but we've got to get to them first. That means going through that shit," she said pointing at the battle being fought on the hillside. "Stay close and don't get yourself killed."

The three set off through the throng of bodies slashing at anyone who got in their way, English or Turks; it didn't' matter. All that mattered was getting to the boats. Benny led the way with Alcibiades between him and Shelby. Blades flashed and blood spattered on their clothes and faces as they cut their way through the fighting and climbed over fallen bodies from both sides. Finally, through gaps in the press of flesh, they could see the harbor.

"We're almost there!" Benny shouted as they shoved through the last of the clashing soldiers.

"Coward!" shouted a familiar voice. "Running from your own mutiny?" Valetta said as he lunged at Alcibiades.

"No!" Shelby screamed, pushing Alcibiades out of the way just in time to save him, but not fast enough to keep from ending up on the end of Valetta's sword herself. Searing pain rushed through her chest as stinging fingers clawed at the wound. The pain brought her to the ground.

Sparks flew from her fingertips as Valetta drew back and cursed. "Witchcraft! May God have mercy!" Crossing himself, he drew back from her rather than help.

Benny dropped to his knees at her side on the ground where she collapsed. "Shelby! Bella!" Tears flowed down his face and dropped onto her cheeks as he held her face in his hands. She was deathly pale as every heartbeat pushed more blood through the hole in her chest. Tear-stained eyes looked up at the Knight of St. John. "God damn you for what you've done!" he roared.

Alcibiades knelt beside Shelby and stroked her cheek. "I'm sorry, Shelby. This is my fault. It's all my fault."

"Yes, it is," Valetta snarled. "And you'll die for it, traitor!" With a swift stroke of his strong arm, the Knight drove his sword still dripping with Shelby's blood through the heart of Alcibiades.

Shelby roared in pain as she was ripped from her Traveler once more. As his limp body fell on top of hers, with her last breaths, she turned the silver snake on her finger and said, "The Traveler follows the serpent."

Benny turned his ring and said through his own tears praying it was fast enough to save her, "The Watcher follows the Traveler."

CHAPTER 27

Familiar surroundings dusted in white, shimmered around the Watchers. Squared stone buildings with arched windows nestled in layers against the flattened hilltop protecting their inhabitants from the biting wind coming from the sea. Ruins shivered alongside the newer structures. Above them all, standing sentry against the gray cold of winter was the crumbling magnificence of the Parthenon.

"Athens," Shelby whispered, her voice hollow and weak as the pain in her chest still throbbed where the sword ran her through in the last life. Putting her hand on the wound, her memory drifted to the first jump into Athens and the throbbing in her chest from Apollo's arrow. It seemed forever ago. Lifetimes. Yet, it had been only weeks. "We've failed again. He's brought us back."

"No, bella," Benny said wrapping his arms around the love he thought he'd lost, "we haven't failed. If that was the case, we'd be in Delphi. You know why we're here."

"Eli. The end of the diary."

Benny nodded. "We get to see why he stopped writing."

"He was hurt. Badly. We have to find him before that happens. But how?" Shelby's voice echoed then became thick as time and space settled around her. The wind swirled around her, and she pulled the shawl around her shoulders tighter. Looking down at her dress, she grumbled, "Women's clothes are irritating. How am I supposed to move in this get-up?" Shelby yanked impatiently at the half-train and bustle, twisting around to try to see the back of her dress. "I guess no one ever told Victorian women that their butts looked huge in these things."

Benny chuckled. "Glad to see you're feeling well enough to be snarky, bella. You look beautiful, big butt and all. Not tank top and shorts hot, but I think that's the point of the Victorian dresses. Feminine but demure."

"Yeah, well they can have it. I'd rather have your pants." Shelby eyed Benny's gray trousers jealously as she squirmed in the tight bodice of her dress. He looked damn good. Like something out of a romance novel. A black jacket and tails, a blue velvet vest over a white shirt, and a dark devilish grin above the high starched collar completed the image of the dashing European traveler. "You look pretty good yourself. Not shirtless and jeans hot, but it'll do." Shelby winked a dark eye at the blushing Roman and kissed him. "Let's get Al to Apollo so we can get out of these clothes."

Benny pulled her a little tighter and kissed her again for a long moment before letting her go and taking a step back to survey their position. "Apollo let us off a little far from the target. Isn't he coming by sea?"

"Yes. Unless he's already here. Seems like he's always here before us."

"Do you have the diary tucked somewhere in all that skirt?" Benny asked, the corner of his mouth twitching in its struggle not to grin at her.

Shelby rolled her eyes. "Hell, I could have Eli *and* his diary hidden in all this freaking fabric. But, yes, I have the book. Can we get out of this wind first?" A chill raced up her spine and her lips quivered in the cold.

"Think your gloves can keep the sparks hidden?"

Shelby spread her fingers out in the black kid gloves that stretched halfway up her arms. "I think so. Why?"

"Because I'm starving and could use a drink. You?"

"The drink, definitely. As far as getting food in this damn tight dress, well, we'll see about that."

Benny shook his dark head and laughed. "Then, come, bella. There has to be a café around here somewhere. We can take care of food, drink, and the diary at one time."

"Good, because time isn't something we have much of."

"All the more reason to go after him with a plan."

* * *

Tucked into a corner of a small café with Shelby's back to the rest of the tables, the Watchers poured over the last sections of Elijah Faircloth's diary for clues to Alcibiades' whereabouts in Athens. While the gloves seemed to tame the dancing blue sparks somewhat, they didn't hide them completely as she turned the pages.

"At least we know we're on the right track," Shelby said tucking her sparking hands under the table as the waiter approached with their drinks.

"But there's nothing here that we haven't already read. No clues to where he's staying. No name for the inn. Nothing." Benny nodded at the waiter. "Thank you." Once more, the Watchers were grateful for Apollo's gift of understanding and speaking the language of the time and place they found themselves in.

As the man left to go check on their food, Shelby pulled her hands back out and held one over the book flicking her finger to turn the pages. Across the yellowed pages, Eli's elegant script deteriorated with his health until it disappeared completely in the cliffhanger. "It just stops," she said shaking her head and sighing. "We've missed something, but what?" The Watchers settled into the silence of their own thoughts among the hum of the café. Absently, Shelby flicked the pages back and forth as she thought. First one or two pages, then several. After a moment, she flicked through the empty pages at the end of the journal as her thoughts wandered.

"Stop!" Benny said sharply, startling her out of her reverie.

"What?" she asked with her heart pounding in her ears from the scare.

"The last page. He scribbled something there."

Shelby flipped the pages to the end of the book and held her hand over the page to keep it flat. There, in the bottom corner of the page, was a number and a word in Greek. "What does it mean? What is it?"

Benny's dark eyes danced. "The answer! An address!"

Sparks swirled around Shelby's gloves and dove relentlessly onto the page in front of her. With a flick of her wrist, she closed the book and shoved her hands under the table. "You'd think Seshat would know better than to show off in the middle of a crowd."

Benny chuckled. "She's not one for subtleties. Put the book back in that pouch and have a drink. We're close, bella. Very close."

* * *

Neighborhoods surrounding the Acropolis seemed to cluster in haphazard jumbles of buildings like boulders in a rockslide. They seemed stacked against one another unless you were walking the narrow streets and buckling sidewalks that threaded through them. Horse-drawn carts and carriages picked their way along the dirt roads, made slick or muddy by the snow depending on whether the cart was in the shade or sunshine. Shelby did valiant battle with her skirts in an effort to keep the excess fabric out of the dirt, but eventually gave up on the whole ordeal. By the time they reached the address scribbled in the book, water and dirt were seeping up the half-train and smeared across the bottom of the front of her skirt weighing the whole thing down. Even Benny's trousers were showing their own run-ins with the muck in splatters along the well-tailored hems.

Another reason for giving up on the war with her skirt was the blue sparks that insisted on swirling around her hands the closer they got to the address for the inn. Keeping her hands wrapped in the shawl and tucked under her crossed arms was the only way to keep passersby from noticing the strange phenomenon. "We have to be close," she said as the stinging in her fingertips became almost unbearable.

"We are. Just up ahead," Benny answered pointing to a three-story building in need of paint but looked respectable otherwise. The exterior of the inn had very little in the way of ornamentation to set it apart from the apartments and shops that surrounded it other than the small wooden sign on the front. It was simple, verging on austere, except for the yellowing lace curtains in the windows. Only those gave a sense of welcoming at all. "That's it. Let's hope they have a room available."

Inside, behind a worn wooden counter, the innkeeper was startled from reading his newspaper as the front door opened letting in the Watchers and a gust of cold wind. "Come in, come in!" The portly older man glanced at their soiled clothes. "Terrible weather," he said genially. "Makes a mess of the roads. What can I do for you?"

"We were hoping you could help us. A mutual friend suggested we meet someone that is staying here. An Elijah Faircloth. English fellow?" Benny asked hopefully.

Mercifully, the interior of the inn was cozy with dark wood and stuccoed walls painted in a buttery yellow. Colorful handmade rugs adorned the wide planked wooden floor giving the small lobby the feeling of someone's personal parlor. In the corner, a small coal burning heater glowed with warmth against the damp chill of the day.

"Nice man," the innkeeper answered nodding. "Arrived yesterday. He's staying with us, but I think he's gone out at the moment. Would you like to leave a message for him?" the man asked pulling a scrap of paper and a fountain pen from under the counter.

"Actually," Shelby said stepping in, "we were hoping you'd also have a room for us. We could meet up with Mr. Faircloth later. You see, we had written ahead to book a room at another inn and there was a mistake. Somehow our reservation was given away and now we're without a place to stay."

The innkeeper was clearly taken with Shelby's dazzling smile but eyed the pair curiously. "But you've no luggage."

"It's still at the port." Benny lied. "We hope, anyway. There was some confusion about where it ended up. Hopefully, they will locate it."

Shelby's smile faded some as she added, "So far, our grand adventure hasn't begun well."

The old Greek patted her hand in reassurance. "Now, now. Let's see what we can do about changing that. We have a warm comfortable room available on the second floor. It has a view of the bell tower, too!"

The old man seemed quite proud of that fact, so Shelby rewarded his generosity with another beautiful smile. "I'm sure it will be just perfect. Thank you."

The tight stairs to the second floor were lit only by a single flickering sconce by the landing halfway up. Down the hallway with a shared bathroom was a small but cozy room. Simply appointed, there was a bed, side table with an oil lamp, and a small dressing table with a wash basin and oval mirror. True to the innkeeper's word, the bell tower in the distance was perfectly framed in the window.

"I hope you'll be comfortable here," the old man said as he turned to go.

"I'm certain we will," Shelby answered gracefully. She was beginning to impress herself with her own ability to keep up with the politeness of the Victorian Age.

The innkeeper nodded and pulled the door closed behind him as he went back downstairs.

Shelby flopped down on the bed and dangled her muddy shoes off the side. "Well, now what do we do? We have no idea where he could have gone. Do we just wait on him to come back like some galactic stalkers?" she asked as her modern snark found release at last.

"It's not a great day for touring ruins. Maybe he's nearby. Shops, cafés. Something."

"Worth a shot. We need clothes anyway, though I'd rather just lay in this bed for a while. Think we'll ever be able to just rest, or are we going to spend eternity chasing this guy until we collapse?"

"Rest will come. Make the most of the day looking for him, then, I promise, we'll make the most of the night." Benny took her hands in his and pulled her back to her feet then wrapped his arms around her, kissing her neck.

"Better stop that or I won't be as willing to go out in the cold," Shelby teased but did nothing to stop him. She was sick of chasing the elusive Greek all over kingdom come and was more interested in a warm bed and a hot Italian. Against all her longing, she let Benny lead her back out into the biting Athenian wind in search of Elijah Faircloth.

CHAPTER 28

Mercifully, the wind was dying down some as the Watchers made their way back out into the neighborhoods of Athens in search of a solitary Victorian Traveler. Narrow streets were lined with homes and businesses interspersed with restaurants or small bars. Occasionally in something not much bigger than a window, there was a street food vendor turning meats and flat breads on a charcoal grill. All around them were locals and the occasional tourist clustering along the sunny side of the narrow sidewalks where the warmth kept the chill at bay. Most of the people were Greeks with dark hair and the usual Mediterranean olive complexions. Tourists were few and far between, but none drew any reaction from Shelby's hands to let them know that somewhere under the scarves and hats was the elusive Alcibiades in the form of Elijah Faircloth.

"This is pointless," Shelby grumbled as she side-stepped a puddle for what seemed like the millionth time. "I mean, what the hell are we supposed to say when we find him? 'Hey, you don't know us, but we have your book and you're going to die if we don't get you to the god Apollo in Delphi.'"

"Something will present itself, bella. At least we aren't running from murderous hordes this time. We might be able to strike up an actual conversation with him for once."

"Good point." Shelby trudged on with her arm tucked in Benny's for warmth as much as stability as she tried not to trip over her skirt on the uneven pavement. "You know," she began after a moment in her own thoughts, "I don't understand this life of his. He's been in wars or in the confidence of some ruling power controlling things from the sidelines in every life we've seen. In this one, he's just some rich Englishman with a mild addiction to international travel. Hardly the traitorous power-hungry schemer of lives past. How much trouble could he possibly be as the mild-mannered Elijah Faircloth?"

Benny shrugged. "You're right. It doesn't make sense. Why bring us into a life that seems harmless? Unless…" His words trailed off as though he wasn't sure of them himself.

"Unless what" Shelby urged.

Benny stopped and turned to face her as he thought out loud. "Unless the diary didn't end because he died. Maybe he survived, but the diary was abandoned for some reason or another. Maybe he did go on to do something heinous in this life."

Shelby shook her head. "I don't know. It just doesn't sound like Eli. But maybe. We won't ever find out if we don't ever find *him*."

As they continued in silence for another block, they were distracted from their own thoughts by a frustrated conversation between a local and a British tourist who seemed to be having trouble understanding each other's accents. Shelby's hands burned fiercely in her kid gloves.

"Acropolis," said the Greek pointing up at the ruins on the hill. "There, yes."

"Yes, yes, I know where it *is*," the Englishman said. "How do I get someone to take me there? To tell me about it? History?" Even with the distinguished British accent, the soft lisping 'r' sounds were there.

Shelby squeezed Benny's arm. "We've got him!" she whispered. "Come on!"

"Very old. Much history," the Greek said smiling.

"Yes, but I need a guide to take me there. To tell me history." Clearly Elijah Faircloth was getting nowhere but frustrated with the local man and was bowing to take his leave with a frustrated 'thank you' as Shelby stepped in.

"Excuse me," she said sweetly with her newly acquired Victorian charm. "I didn't mean to eavesdrop, but it seems you could use some assistance. Maybe we can help."

Benny quickly followed her lead. "I'm a historian and tour guide in Rome. I happen to know a bit about the Acropolis if you'd like to join us. Benito Moretti, and this is my companion, Miss Shelby Starling," Benny said extending a gloved hand.

"Elijah Faircloth," the Victorian diarist answered shaking Benny's outstretched hand. Shelby kept hers bundled in her shawl to keep any sparks out of sight, so Eli nodded gracefully to her in greeting. "And I'm grateful but couldn't impose."

"Nonsense!" Shelby said, beaming at him. "We'd be glad for the company. Please join us. If you'll be seen with us. We're a bit of a mess. Our baggage was lost, and the weather hasn't been kind to our clothes." She laughed, her dark eyes dancing. Shelby was laying the charm on thick, but it seemed to work.

After a moment's hesitation, Eli answered, "Alright, if you're certain it's not an imposition."

"Not at all," Benny said. "We'll hire a carriage, if it's alright with you. We've had enough dodging puddles and buckled sidewalks for the day."

"Only if you allow me to pay the fare in exchange for your company and knowledge of the Acropolis."

"Fair enough," Benny said with a chuckle and scanned the muddy street for a hack they could hire to take them across the city.

Shelby turned her attention to Eli. There was something surreal about standing face-to-face with the man she felt like she knew through his writing only to realize he was indeed a total stranger who had no idea who she was. "So," she began slightly awkwardly, "what brings you to Athens, E- Mister Faircloth?" She caught herself before letting the familiar 'Eli' slip out and replaced it with the more formal Victorian address.

"It's been a long and complicated journey. A strange one, really. I'm afraid you wouldn't believe me if I told you, Miss Starling."

"Oh? I may surprise you, Mister Faircloth. I've had my share of fantastical journeys. I've spent a long time as a Traveler." Shelby leveled her gaze at Eli and held it as her smile faltered. He stared back quizzically for a moment but said nothing. "You see," she went on trying to tug at what information she knew he had by his writing in the journal, "I never felt like I belonged anywhere, not truly, so I wandered around the world hoping to find a place that felt like home."

"And," he ventured, his voice dry but his blue-eyed gaze rigid, "did you find what you sought?"

"Most places held only memories for me. But, eventually, yes, I found where I belonged." Her face softened into a pleasant smile. "How rude of me, Mister

Faircloth. We were talking about your journey, not mine." She glanced over his shoulder where Benny was waving at her. "Looks like Benny found a carriage. The Acropolis awaits! Shall we?"

* * *

The jolting ride through the pocked and muddy streets of Athens to the Acropolis was not conducive to conversation given the constant need to brace themselves to prevent being slammed into the sides of the carriage. Other than a few mundane comments about the weather or landmarks passed, little was said between the Traveler and the Watchers. Shelby noticed that once in a while she would glance at Eli to find him staring thoughtfully at her only to look quickly away when he was discovered. She had grown used to the dark swarthiness of Alcibiades in previous lives. This blonde and bashful rendition was intriguing and a bit confusing to her. He seemed so genuine, so genteel. Not at all like the divisive traitor of lives past. She wasn't entirely sure she liked it. There was something exciting and sexy about the swarthy traitor. Like pirates are sexy. Other than the lisp and the name, she would never have put together that this gentleman was her target. How in the world could he be planning some vile treachery? It didn't make sense to her, but if she was ever going to have a life of peace with Benny, she had to get Eli to Apollo whether she understood why or not.

As they disembarked from the carriage at the gate entrance for the Acropolis complex, Shelby looked around at the place she had experienced in multiple incarnations already. In this life, it seemed more crumbled and less magnificent than even the ruins of her own time had. Her forehead wrinkled as she tried to put her finger on why.

"Sad, isn't it? Benny asked as Eli settled the fare with the carriage driver.

Shelby nodded. "I knew it wouldn't be packed with tourists and tour buses, but it seems smaller. More disheveled. Elderly."

"It is. Restorations have begun, but they are far from where they are in our time."

The feeling of sadness surprised Shelby who had never really cared about history, or ruins, or anything other than herself if she was honest. Something in her had changed in all of this bizarre experience. She was connected to these places and their well-being now. History had tightened its grip on her.

Without either one of the Watchers noticing, Eli had come to stand beside them. "It's incredible," he said. A shudder raced through him.

"Are you alright?" Benny asked.

"Must be the cold," Eli mumbled.

"Or the magnificence of it all," Benny suggested gently.

"Certain ruins have a similar effect on me," Shelby added. "Although, they didn't used to. It's a more recent development." Eli nodded slowly as Shelby let her words sink in. Rather than insisting to him that he was something he didn't think he was, she had a new plan of letting him come to that realization himself. From his journal, Shelby knew he was already experiencing things that his other incarnations hadn't or weren't embracing like Elijah Faircloth was. If she dropped enough hints that she understood him, maybe he would realize the truth without having to frighten him with insane declarations about his purpose.

"Come, bella," Benny said breaking the momentary silence. "We should go so we don't lose the light."

Shelby nodded and smiled at Eli as she let Benny take her arm for the walk through the gate. "The view from the Parthenon is breathtaking. It would be a shame to miss it in the darkness." As Benny walked on one side of her and Eli on the other, the diary in the pouch at her waist seemed to hum with excitement, practically trembling to be so near its author. Shelby wondered if the duplicate in Eli's coat pocket was doing the same thing. Could Eli sense it? If he did, he was damn good at hiding it under that flat British expression.

Even though the number of tourists in the late nineteenth century were far fewer than the twenty-first, there were still many who made the city a destination stop on their tour of the Mediterranean. On this dreary cold day though, there were mercifully few. "Well, bella," Benny asked quietly as Eli stopped to examine crumbled temple stones, "do you have a plan to convince him? He seems too sensible for historical fairy tales."

"I'm sure he'd like to think so, but you've forgotten something. He's already had experiences with monuments in this life. We just have to show him he's been here before, too."

"As Alcibiades."

"Right. The Parthenon. Surely Alcibiades would have been there." Shelby glanced over at Eli in time to see him reach out as though he would let his fingers trace the carving on one of the fallen pillars. Holding her breath to see what would happen, she waited as his hand stopped a hair's breadth from the stone before he pulled it back. Getting him to touch the Parthenon wasn't going to be easy, but she had to find a way. Otherwise, it was back to being a raving lunatic about destiny and past lives that would surely scare off the English gentleman.

"So many have passed this way," Eli said as much to himself as anyone else. He shoved his hands into his coat pockets and continued the trek along the hilltop as his blue eyes scanned the crumbling ghosts of a decadent past. "It seems so strange that a city with such civilized ways when it came to governing its people could hold so tightly to such mysticism and nonsense like these pagan gods."

"Oh, I don't know, Mister Faircloth," Shelby countered. "One could say the same thing of Europe or America today. Such advancements in science and civility, yet we cling to our religion based entirely on something we can't see. Faith can take many forms and flow through the veins of even the most logical of people."

"That's true," Benny added. "Shelby is one of the most cynical and stubborn women I've ever had the good fortune and *mis*fortune to know." Shelby rolled her eyes, but grinned at him as he went on, "But even she can't deny that destiny has a way of reaching out and grabbing you whether you like it or not."

Elijah Faircloth stopped his trudging through the ruins and stared at the two Watchers. His jaw set as if he was struggling with something, then his mouth opened and closed again. Whatever it was he had been tempted to say to them, he thought better of. As he turned away and continued on, Shelby winked at Benny with a satisfied grin. Her plan was working. Maybe she wouldn't have to sound like a psychopath this time around.

As they wandered through the temples of the Acropolis, Benny's tour guide side couldn't resist making an unscheduled appearance as he narrated the history he knew of the site that seemed woefully decrepit since the last time they'd seen it. Even more decrepit than the first time. Eli and Shelby followed him over stray stones and mucky paths trying to find the parts that would be the least destructive to their shoes and Shelby's nearly unsalvageable skirt. All the while, Eli kept a safe distance from the stones and pillars. Once in a while, he would put a hand out as if testing the air for the surge of electricity that accompanied the time warping. It was as though he was curious about what would happen if he made contact, but simultaneously terrified.

Furtive glances exchanged between the Watchers became impatient as Shelby waited for a natural way to get him to touch the stones. Even Benny's suggestions about tracing the craftmanship of some scrollwork with his fingers didn't entice the Traveler to touch anything.

"What are we going to do if he won't touch it?" Benny whispered as Shelby looped her arm through his pretending to take a romantic moment with the view.

"We make him."

"I've seen that look in your eye before. Makes me nervous. Like when you face off against obstinate immortals."

"Eli is hardly the power Apollo is. Don't worry. Women faint a lot in this time period, don't they?" she asked, swapping the determined look for a twinkle.

Benny grinned. "The romance novels seem to think so."

A very unladylike snort escaped Shelby. "*You* read Victorian romance novels?" she asked incredulously between giggles.

Benny blushed making his handsome face even more irresistible than it usually was. "No. That would be Carmelita. She loved them and when Nonna wasn't around to tell on her about them, I was a captive audience."

Shelby smiled at the thought of the 60s glam psychic who once told her what she was. One day, she hoped to see her again. "That sounds just like her," Shelby said kissing Benny on the cheek. "Time to see if those novelists knew what they were talking about."

"Careful, bella. You've been here before, too. Getting him to see his past is going to do the same thing to you if you touch it."

"I'm counting on it."

The Watchers made their way casually back to where Eli was slowly walking the perimeter of the Parthenon examining every fallen stone and skeletal column. "It's breathtaking," he whispered as though not to disturb the spirits of the past.

"That it is, Mister Faircloth." Shelby answered.

"Please, call me Eli. You've both been so kind; I'd prefer not to stand on formalities."

"I agree. It feels as though we've known each other for ages, Eli. Please, call me Shelby."

Shelby held her gloved hand out thinking it might protect her from the shock she knew would come when Alcibiades or Eli touched her hand, but it didn't work. A bolt of electricity shot up her arm as soon as he touched her. While it wasn't enough to do anything more than hurt, she used it as her opportunity to follow the lead of many a romance novel heroine and pretend to faint.

"Shelby!" Benny and Eli said in unison as both lunged to catch her.

"Set her down against the column," Benny said as they eased her limply against the huge stone pillar. Taking off one of her gloves, he began patting her hand, knowing it was doing nothing at all but exposing it to the stone she would need to touch if the plan was going to work. As he moved her, she slumped a little forward. "Here, help me brace her a little more," Benny instructed.

Eli, focused on his concern for Shelby's wellbeing, completely forgot about the power of the monuments over him and put one hand on the column to brace Shelby just as her hand dropped to the stones next to her. Electricity shot through each of them, then from one to the other as blinding white light surrounded them both. As the light faded, memories began to flash like machine gun fire before their eyes. Some of just Alcibiades. Some of just Shelby. Alcibiades as a young man paying homage to the goddess. Facing off with senators and men of power in heated debates. Laughter among his friends. An embrace with an older man Shelby could only assume was Socrates. Then, flashes of Shelby in the Peloponnesian War with Sparta closing in as she raced from the steps of the temple with Benny shielding her and warning her to keep the pointy end of her dagger out. Touring the temple in her own time period with Apollo's portlier form. Then memories of the two of them that weren't in the Parthenon at all. The bathhouse blunder. Dinner at his house in Persia. Flirtation in the garden. And, finally, a dreamlike kiss on the patio of the temple in Delphi. Eli turned slowly to Shelby and put his fingers to his lips. Shelby nodded. She could feel the ghost of that kiss on her lips, too.

"It's true," Eli said, his eyes wide with realization of the impossible. His voice echoed slightly in the space between time.

"You're a Traveler, Eli. Your name is Alcibiades. And it's time to go home."

"Who are you? Who are you really?"

"My name is really Shelby Starling. And Benny is really Benny Moretti. But we are not just here by accident. We're Watchers. *Your* Watchers. We're here to lead you back where you belong. To your destiny." The glimmering splendor of the Parthenon in all its glory began to fade as the light surrounded them once more, forcing them back into the gloom of the Athenian afternoon and the strangeness of their new reality.

CHAPTER 29

As the trio made their way back to the entrance to the Acropolis, the Watchers gave Elijah Faircloth the time and space in silence to process the information the Parthenon forced on him. Securing a carriage, Benny gave the driver the address of the inn and helped Shelby and her encumbrance of skirts inside. Eli once more took his place on the seat across from them but was largely engrossed in his own thoughts. After some time, he asked barely above a whisper, "How did you find me?"

Shelby's hand instinctively went to the journal, but she glanced at Benny for reassurance. He nodded and said, "Now is as good a time as any."

"We had some help," Shelby said as she reached into the pouch, "from you."

"Me?" Eli asked incredulously. "How could that possibly be?" Shelby pulled the diary out in a shower of blue sparks as its author recoiled and plastered himself against the back of the seat. "How in the *hell*?"

"The sparks won't hurt you," Shelby insisted trying to reassure him. "They're just light. No heat. They're a message from someone who is helping us to bring you home."

"How in the hell did you get my diary?" Eli asked, still not comprehending the sparks. His hands went to his coat pocket and fumbled around for the book he knew he had put there. Ashen, he pulled it from the pocket and laid it on his lap. "You don't have mine. What's going on here?"

Benny nodded more encouragement at Shelby. "Show him. Open it."

"This *is* yours, Eli." Laying the book on her lap to relieve some of the pain from holding it, Shelby held a hand over the journal and flicked her finger to open the cover revealing the name and date that matched his. Page by page, she slowly went through the book as Elijah Faircloth sat across from her dumbstruck, clutching his own leather diary in his hands. His words curved delicately or scrawled hurriedly across the pages depending on what was happening around him at the time they were written. Stories of past and present weaved across pages yellowed with time in ink turned brown with age. A nameless map, sketches of the Nile banks, and other markings that were identical to the ones in the book he held. Up to a point.

"Wait," Eli said as Shelby turned a page to reveal the end of the story he had not yet written. "That's different. Why?"

"This part of your journey," Shelby began slowly, "hasn't been written yet." She paused for a moment to let that sink in. All traces of snark and sass had vanished in her as she watched her Traveler try to come to grips with his true reality. She thought when she was finally able to convince him of his destiny, she would feel relief and giddiness at knowing her life would soon be her own again. Instead, she felt pained for his inner struggle between knowing who he really was and knowing his life would never be the same. Now, she had more crushing news for him. His own future.

"I don't understand," he whispered. "If I haven't written it, how are the words there?"

"You haven't lived it yet in this life, but Shelby found this book over a century later in a library in Rome," Benny explained.

"A century later," Eli echoed mechanically. His face was colorless, his blue eyes distant. Comprehension was hovering just out of reach.

Shelby gently continued to explain. "What Toth told you in the temple is true. You're a Traveler. Born out of time. Hurtling through lives until you find your destiny. But no Traveler travels alone. Watchers guide you. Keep you on the path as much as we can."

"'We'?" he asked, blue eyes coming into focus on her dark ones.

Shelby nodded. "I was a Traveler, too. Watchers helped me find this book and my destiny. But my destiny didn't end where I thought it did. My destiny is you. To be your Watcher. Both of us, actually," Shelby said with a nod toward Benny who smiled sheepishly at Eli. "You don't belong here. This isn't your time or place. I've tried to tell you so many times in so many lives."

The carriage lurched to a stop in front of the inn and Shelby had to catch the journal to keep it from sliding to the floor. "I don't find my destiny in your book, do I?" Eli asked. "If I did, you wouldn't be here. What happens?"

"We- we aren't exactly sure," Shelby admitted. "But we know you are badly hurt and seriously ill. Then, the story stops."

"I die?"

Benny shrugged. "Honestly, that's what we thought, too, but there is no way to know for certain. It could be abandoned for many reasons."

"Cautiously optimistic," Eli said sourly. "How am I hurt? When?"

"Tonight," Shelby answered.

Before she could explain further, the carriage driver opened the door for them. Benny paid for the fare as Eli and Shelby put the books away and climbed out. As the carriage lunged down the rutted street, the Traveler and his Watcher stared at one another. Benny cleared his throat and said, "The sidewalk is probably not the best place for this conversation. Bella, maybe he needs to read it for himself." Shelby nodded and the three of them went inside with passing polite smiles to the innkeeper reading his paper at the front desk.

"I see you found your friend," the Greek said cheerily.

"We did," Shelby answered trying to force a smile even though her heart was thundering in her chest. With a nod, the man went back to his paper as the three ascended the creaking steps to their rooms.

* * *

Shelby stood motionless staring out the window across the Athenian rooftops at the bell tower as Eli read his own diary entries depicting his attack, injury, and deteriorating condition. Her stinging hands swarmed with sparks now that her gloves lay on the foot of the bed. Benny sat on the other end of the bed leaning against the headboard with his eyes closed. Fingers picking at a loose thread on the well-worn bedspread was the only indication that he hadn't drifted off. Every quarter hour, the clock in the distance would toll. While she wasn't consciously counting, Shelby knew she'd heard it three times as she waited for Eli to come to grips with his fate. Pages seemed to whisper as the Traveler turned them back and forth. Finally, a different sound. The closing of the book.

"It's simple, really," Elijah Faircloth said at long last.

"What is?" Benny asked without opening his eyes. Time and exhaustion seemed to have settled heavily on his shoulders and eyelids.

"The answer to changing this story. I simply don't go to dinner. If I don't go, I don't get attacked."

"Eli," Shelby said turning slowly away from the window, "the universe is rarely that straightforward. Besides, everything in that journal is only an instant of larger moments in time. Everything you wrote there is but a blink in your history. What we've seen of your pasts has been far more frightening, more deadly, but exactly accurate to what you wrote about those glimpses. Time hasn't changed your words, even when we tried to pull you out of it all and get you to Delphi."

Eli stared at Shelby with his mouth unattractively agape. "What did you say?"

"No matter what we tried to do to get you out of there, each of those things you wrote about played out anyway. Even a couple of Watchers interfering didn't change the outcome."

"Not that," he said waving a dismissive hand at her. "Did you say Delphi?"

"Yes."

"But that sailor Apollo wanted me to see his hometown. Delphi."

Benny's dark Roman eyes eased open. "That was no sailor."

"Of course, he was. He was on a ship. I was there. You know that. You read it yourself."

Benny's eyes closed again. "He was on a ship, and he was acting like a sailor, but he's not. He's a god. That is Apollo."

"*The* Apollo," Shelby added. "And it wasn't his hometown he wants you to see. It's his temple."

Any credibility Shelby and Benny had built deteriorated with the mention of an actual Greek god and his temple. "That's ridiculous," Eli said dropping into a small chair with worn upholstery. "It's *all* ridiculous. And I almost fell for it." His fingers pinched the bridge of his nose as his eyes shut tightly.

"Eli," Shelby said putting her hand on his. As she did, electricity shot through them both. Eli jumped up and away from her, nearly knocking the chair over as he did. "I'm sorry! I forgot!" Shelby said holding both hands up and away from him.

"What the hell was that? What do you mean, you forgot?" Eli shouted.

Benny, now wide-awake, jumped up from the bed. "It's her connection to you. It happens every time she touches your hand. Always has. Every single life."

"I'm so sorry, Eli. I didn't mean to hurt you. I was trying-"

Eli cut her off. "I don't care what you were trying to do. I don't care about any of this nonsense. I need some air." Despite the protests of the Watchers, the Traveler strode out of the room stopping just sort of slamming the door behind him.

As his footsteps retreated down the creaking staircase, Shelby collapsed on the bed in defeat. "Goddamn it!" she cursed into her folded arms across her face. Tears burned hotly in her eyes as exhaustion washed over her. "We were so close this time!"

Benny lay next to her and wrapped her in his arms. "Bella," he whispered into her hair, "you don't know it's over. He knows the truth; he just can't accept it yet. Victorians are very-"

"Stubborn."

He chuckled softly. "I was going to say logical. He's trying to make all of this fit into his rational reality. Throwing a Greek god into the mix was more than he could handle. Give him time."

"Time," Shelby snorted as her Victorian gentility gave way to modern snark. "He either has tons of that or none. Who the hell knows anymore?"

* * *

The gray twilight had faded into a dull blackness as night fell over Athens. Clouds shrouded the moon and stars as the only light was the golden glow from windows and gas lamps dotted in the cluttered hillside. The Acropolis stood in inky blackness instead of the rich glow of the modern lights that illuminated it the first night Shelby saw it. Exhaustion had finally become more than the Watchers could ward off. Still dressed in mud-splattered clothes laying on top of the bedspread, they slept through the tapping against the window. It wasn't until the rapping became insistent that either one stirred.

"What the hell is that noise?" Shelby asked thickly as sleep slid slowly off her.

"Sounds like it's coming from the window," Benny said turning the small brass key at the base of the oil lamp on the side table. The low golden flame illuminated a vague shape at the window that came sharply into focus as Benny brought the lamp closer.

"Holy shit!" Shelby cursed. "It's a raven! It's like Edgar Allan Poe!" The huge black bird beat its wings against the glass as its tapping became almost crazed.

"What's wrong with it? Apollo's messengers have never acted like that before," Benny said as he unclasped the latch between the hinged panes of glass.

As the latch released, the raven threw itself at the window, pushed it open, and darted wildly around the room. Shelby's hands began swarming with sparks as the bird dove for her. Ducking, she covered her head with her hands and stifled a scream. It dove again and talons pulled at her hair, dragging her to the window. "What the hell, you freaking *psycho chicken*?"

"This isn't just a message, bella. It's a warning!"

The raven cawed and shrieked, still pulling her hair toward the window. "*Eli*! Something must've happened to him!" As the words left her mouth, the raven released its grip and soared back out the window making circles just outside. "Let's go!" Shelby said jerking the door to their room open and racing down the creaking stairs, nearly tumbling down them in her tangle of skirt and petticoat. "God damn this dress. I'd kill for some fucking pants!"

Outside, the Watchers scanned the sky for the bird that was almost invisible against the starless sky. Frantic cawing echoed dully off the small close-set buildings making the raven seem like it was everywhere at once. "I can't see it!" Shelby cried into the night. As if in answer to her, the bird dove once more and caught a long loose tendril of her hair in its black beak. Instead of yanking at it like before, the raven held her hair as it flew forcing Shelby to follow. "I don't need a leash, you nut," she snapped at Apollo's messenger. "Just stay where we can see you."

Releasing her hair, the huge bird looped lower so it could be seen in the scattered dim lights of the sleeping city. Golden light glinted on the wings of the bird making them shimmer like an oil slick. Winding through the narrow streets, Shelby and Benny raced on. Hearts pounded in their chests from panic more than exertion. "How far could Eli have gone?" Benny asked, squinting ahead of them into the night.

"I don't know," Shelby answered, "but this is all my fault. I scared him off. Damn it. If we'd only stayed awake and gone after him!"

"The damage is done. Nothing can change it. I just hope we aren't too late."

Shelby shook her head. "We aren't. I would have felt him being torn away from me. And the raven wouldn't be panicking."

The bird banked around a tight corner and fluttered to the ground beside a crumpled heap of battered flesh and filthy clothes. Sparks poured from Shelby's hands onto the barely breathing body of Elijah Faircloth. Swollen blackening eyes barely opened to look up at the Watchers who knelt over him. Words were elusive and only a groan escaped his bloody mouth.

"Eli!" Shelby gasped as she put her hand under his head. "I'm so sorry, Eli! This is all my fault. We're going to help you. Hang on! We've got you." Her words tumbled from her lips and splashed over him like her tears. Another groan punctuated the slightest nod before his eyes rolled back and closed. "No! You aren't dying on me again!" Shelby ripped at her petticoat and wadded the fabric in her hands then pressed it tightly to his stab wounds to stem some of the bleeding. "Hold that. I'm going to get him breathing again," Shelby barked at Benny.

The former Roman soldier took the material and field dressed the wounds to the Traveler while Shelby began CPR. As her mouth touched Eli's, a shock went through them both, jumpstarting his heart and breathing. It was weak and shallow, but it was life and that's all that mattered at the moment.

"Stay with him, bella. I'll get help." Benny looked at the raven who remained almost motionless at Eli's head while the Watchers worked to save his life. "Don't leave her alone," he told the bird as he turned to go. The raven bowed its head as though it understood the order.

As Benny searched frantically for someone who could get a carriage to help them, Shelby held the wadding on Eli's wounds hoping to stop some of the bleeding as his heart pumped blood weakly through the cuts. From the diary, she knew his most serious wound was somewhere inside his core. She hoped her chest compressions to get him breathing hadn't made it worse. Exhausted and frightened, Shelby lay gently across his chest listening to his heart beat. Tears streamed from her eyes and over the bridge of her nose as she listened for any change to the faint rhythm of his heartbeat and breaths. One of her burning hands rested on his side and began to pulse with sparks. The change from their normal behavior, if showers of blue sparks could ever be called that, caught her attention. The pulse kept time with his heartbeat. "I wonder," Shelby whispered. Pulling his shirt away so she could see his injury better, she saw a massive bruise spreading under Eli's skin giving away the location of far worse internal bleeding. The raven, who had been largely disinterested since Benny's departure, seemed to focus on the Watcher's movements. Black eyes shone in the glints of blue from the pulsing sparks of her hands as the bird watched Shelby hold one hand over the bruise then lower it gently down. Eli whimpered slightly at her touch, and she pulled back. The pulsing sparks and stinging in her fingers grew worse until she lowered them back onto his skin. Slowly, the sparks began to settle into the bruise, working their way into the Traveler's body. Gentle warmth spread through her fingertips as she concentrated on stemming the bleeding deep inside. By the time carriage wheels were heard coming down the rough street, the bruise was largely gone, along with Shelby's strength.

CHAPTER 30

Dust motes in the streaks of twilight through the window followed Shelby's footsteps as she paced the small room where Eli lay perilously close to the edge of death two nights after his brutal beating. With his internal bleeding and multiple injuries, the visiting doctors were hesitant to move him again, knowing whatever they opened him up to find was going to be largely beyond their ability to repair. Fever set in overnight signaling an infection from the other open wounds making them more firm on not further risking his already fragile state through surgery. In the periods between doctors, nurses, and a nervous innkeeper hovering over the Traveler, Shelby attempted to use whatever worked for her on the street in the night. Time and again, the only result was the sapping of her own strength. Whatever good it had done the first time was all there was.

"Bella," Benny said gently from the chair in the corner, "you're wearing a path in the rug. Please sit down. You need the rest."

Shelby stopped her pacing next to Eli's bed and looked down at him. His face was ashen and sweat plastered his blond hair across his forehead. "I don't know what's worse," Shelby whispered, "losing him quickly or watching him fade away like this. He was always so strong. There seems to be something horribly unfair about this life. He's done nothing wrong, yet he suffers on the edge of death." She sat next to his still frame and sighed. "It's not fair, Apollo," she said to the space between the Watcher and Traveler, hoping the god could hear her.

White weak fingers twitched then slowly groped across the bedspread in search of her hand. Knowing touching hands would cause the electric shock, Shelby hesitated letting Eli find hers. His dry lips parted as he struggled to open his eyes and focus on her. Reluctantly, Shelby gave him her hand. She felt the shock, but in his weakened state, it didn't seem to surge through him like it normally did. The Watcher was both relieved and saddened by that. "I believe you." The words were barely audible and, at first, Shelby wasn't certain she'd heard them at all. As though they were words she wanted to hear so badly she'd imagined them. "All of it." Eli's fingers that had weakly curled around hers went limp once more with the word, "Delphi."

"Eli?" Shelby asked in a panic, cupping his face in her hands. Sparks washed over his whole body as panic seized her. He was dying. Just as he believed her, he was dying. She turned blazing dark eyes on Benny who was out of his chair and by her side in two long strides. "Alcibiades!" Shelby choked on her tears. "No! This isn't fair! He's willing!" She shook Benny's hands from her shoulders and screamed to the space around her, aiming her fury at the Greek god who was absent as usual when he was needed most. "*Damn* you, Apollo! He believes and he's willing! Don't do this, Apollo, you *bastard*! You can save him!" Shelby's rage consumed her as she slammed her palms down flat on Eli's chest as though she could hold the very soul inside of him by force of will alone. She was done with the pointless quest to find someone who, like her, was perfectly fine with their lives before fate and destiny got involved. Done with coming close only to have the rug pulled out from under her at the last minute. Done with doing the Universe's dirty work. Done with Apollo. "Self-centered asshole and pathetic excuse for a god! You're *useless*, Apollo, you know that?" she sobbed. Burning hands tore the diary out of the pouch at her waist and threw it across the room. It slammed into the wall and clumsily to the floor as the Watcher sank defeated to her knees next to the Traveler's bedside.

Eli's body shuddered as though death was having a hard time claiming the defiant Greek general. As the battle for Alcibiades' soul raged on the small bed, the cover of the diary flung open. Pages turned rapid-fire like cards being shuffled until they lay flat and still on the final pages. Aged brown ink in Eli's dying scrawl faded as though being absorbed into the paper itself until the page was completely blank.

"What's happening?" Shelby asked breathlessly as she scrambled to her feet.

"The ending. *His* ending. It's been rewritten. Or, *un*written," Benny answered in quiet amazement.

Fingers curled around Shelby's hand that hung limply at her side. No longer clammy and cold, they were warm and stronger. "Thank you, Shelby," Eli whispered with tears glistening in his blue eyes. The Watcher brought Eli's hand to her cheek, tears of relief splashing onto their laced fingers.

"Bella?" Benny whispered as if his words would shatter the air around him. "Look."

Shelby tore herself away from her Traveler and stared at the diary on the floor. New words in a different handwriting were forming on the page. *Get him to Delphi. Now.*

* * *

Even with the improving weather, the roads outside Athens were rough and barely passable as the cart lumbered over ruts and holes. Provisions for the journey were piled into the cart along with Eli who protested weakly over Shelby's insistence that he lay down and rest on the way. Benny took the driver's seat while Shelby sat bundled up next to her Traveler like a nervous nanny keeping an eye on her charge. Apollo may have brought Eli out of the worst of his injuries, but he was far from miraculously healed. It was clear the healing was more for Shelby's sake than any pity Apollo may have felt for his traitorous nemesis Alcibiades. Whether Eli remembered his past or not, Apollo had certainly not forgotten and was leaving him in just enough pain to make a point.

What would have taken a little over two hours by car took them as many days in the horse-drawn cart. The only advantage to the long and grueling trip was the time for Eli to regain more of his health and strength before he would face his destiny with Apollo. The Watchers were hesitant to answer any of the Traveler's questions about what he was in store for when they arrived at Delphi. It was less about maintaining a sense of mystery and more that they had no idea. Who really knew what stunt Apollo would pull? He could be merciful, or he could be an ass. It was hard to say, and so they didn't. After a day of only vague answers and avoidance by the Watchers, Eli eventually gave up his inquisition.

There was another reason for the quietness of the Watchers as they made the trip to Delphi. Dexios wasn't with them this time. "Strange, isn't it?" Shelby asked not lifting her head from Benny's shoulder as the horse tugged the cart up the mountain side toward the temple city.

"What is, bella?"

"Coming here without Dex. I know we'll see Dina again, and Apollo, but it's strange to think that Dex hasn't been here for thousands of years."

"Technically, neither have we."

"And now it's even weirder. Thanks." Shelby slipped back into silence for the last few miles wondering what had become of the Athenian soldier who risked so much to help them. Had he lived in peace under Apollo's protection? Had he lived to see the city he loved so much rise again after the Spartans conquered it? Had he fallen in love? Had children? One day, when she wasn't so pissed at him anymore, Shelby would make Apollo answer her questions.

Delphi, like the Acropolis, was a far cry from the splendor they had seen last. No temples, no shrines, nothing but a cluster of small, weathered homes with an incredible view of the valley below. A large section of the town was rubble. A modern and recent ruin. The result of frequent earthquakes in the area. Only here and there among the remining buildings were remnants of stone walls that marked where the ancient temple city once stood in the place where Kastri now huddled, small and afraid of the very ground it occupied that threatened to demolish it in another quake. Not only was Delphi unrecognizable, it wasn't there at all.

"I don't understand," Shelby said as the cart rocked to a halt at the edge of the village. Smoke curled from chimneys and candlelight glowed in dingy windows in an effort to keep out the damp cold. Most of the inhabitants were tucked in their homes except for a few stray pedestrians who walked with heads down and faces tucked into bundled scarves. "Where are we? Where's Delphi?"

"This," Benny said, "is Kastri. Delphi is buried under the houses. It'll be another twenty years before the town is relocated and the ancient site excavated by the French."

"You're a walking textbook, aren't you?" Shelby sighed. "Now what?"

"We do what we came to do. The temple wasn't here the first time, either. Just ruins. Apollo wouldn't tell us to come all this way and not get his Traveler back."

Climbing slowly out of the cart, Eli absently rubbed his hands and scanned the looming hills. Shelby's hands were burning harshly too, the closer they got to their destination. "Come on," she said to Eli. "There's something we need to do first:

stop the burning in our hands or we won't be able to stand it inside the temple. If we can find the damn thing."

"Why don't Benny's hands burn?" Eli asked.

Benny shrugged as he tied the horse and cart to a tree. "I've wondered that, too. Maybe it has to do with how many lives you've lived. I only had the one before all this started with you. We didn't know I was anything but a tour guide until Shelby saw I was a Traveler in a vision at the temple. Even Apollo missed that one."

"But he's a god," Eli said wrinkling his brow. "Shouldn't he know something like that?"

"You'd think," Shelby answered rolling her eyes. "Turns out the gods aren't all they've been made out to be. Apollo's no exception."

"I've always thought of a god as all-powerful and all-knowing," Eli said as they descended the valley path to the spring.

"More like somewhat-powerful, and knowing just enough to be arrogant," Shelby snorted and pulled a few blankets from the cart then tugged them around her shoulders.

"She doesn't like Apollo much, does she?" Eli asked Benny.

Benny laughed. "They have a complicated relationship. Apollo wants Shelby to be all she's capable of, and she wants him to go screw himself." Another chuckle rippled through the Roman. "Come to think of it, that's how she's felt about *you* most of the time."

Eli glanced at Shelby who tossed a sheepish look back at him. "Should I be worried?" he asked.

"No," she answered with a grin. "You haven't tried to kill me or sleep with me this time, so, we're good."

The Traveler nodded. "Apparently I deserved your derision."

"You didn't keep your scoundrel behavior contained to just Shelby," Benny said as the trio reached the Kastilian Spring. "You deserved the derision of entire nations. And got it. You were a traitor in every life we've encountered you, so far."

"Except this one," Shelby added. "At least, as far as we know." She cut a sideways glance at the very different incarnation of Alcibiades. Only the soft lilting 'r's gave him away as the rogue they chased through the centuries. "You've put on one hell of an act if you are."

"Don't pick fights, bella," Benny said stepping in before Shelby's mouth ran away with her attitude. "Here, Eli, put your hands in the water. Let it run over them for a while. It insulates them from the magic surrounding the temple."

"It's a temporary fix," Shelby said putting budding suspicion aside as she eased her own hands into the icy spring, "but it'll hopefully last long enough for whatever Apollo has in mind."

Eli winced as the freezing water hit his skin, then relaxed as it cooled the stinging in his fingers. "I just wish I knew what that was."

"You and me, both, Al," Shelby said with a sigh.

"Who?"

"Never mind. Just wash your hands."

CHAPTER 31

Clouds clung to the summit of Mount Parnassos, shriveling the giant. Lower clouds draped themselves in the valley between the Phaedriades making the bases of Phleboukos and Rhodini seem as though they just vanished softly into mist. Only the town of Kastri stood out clearly as the three made the trek up the road that lay on top of what was once the Sacred Way. Eons of dirt and vegetation sealed the crumbled buildings and temples hiding their splendor or purpose. Other than legends and the fact that they had seen Delphi for themselves, the Watchers would never have guessed what lay beneath the mountain village.

Shelby's head began to swim as she walked over places where the temples and shrines slept deep underground, but the nausea would fade as she continued on. Her palms, no longer burning thanks to the insulating power of the Kastilian Spring, seemed to pull at her to touch the earth connecting her to the ruins beneath. Knowing what that would mean, she tucked them firmly into her thick wraps keeping out the mountain cold. So much of who she was destined to be lay hidden in the stones below. They called to her, like a jilted lover begging to be taken back. *No*, Shelby thought, *not today. There's work to be done. I don't have time for memories.*

"Are you sure?" a familiar voice said behind her.

Shelby spun around and stared into the dancing eyes of the Roman emperor Hadrian.

"Bella?" Benny asked. "You okay?"

"What is Shelby looking at?" Eli whispered. "She looks like she's seen a ghost."

Benny shook his dark head. "I can't see anything, but whatever *she* sees, she wasn't expecting. Bella?" Benny asked again.

"Hadrian?" Shelby asked the specter in front of her.

Benny's face contorted somewhere between shock and jealousy. "*Hadrian*?"

If Shelby heard Benny, she didn't let on. Instead, she kept her focus rivetted on the other Roman in her lives. "How? Why? I didn't touch anything."

The emperor shook his head and smiled at her. "You have more control over these things than you realize. Especially here. We share something in this place, like so many other places."

"What's that?"

"We both want it to be what it was meant to be. Culturally, artistically, magically. Your heartbreak at seeing it this way brought me here. You feel things more than you allow yourself to," Hadrian said laying a hand on her cheek. "Shelby, this place wasn't always forgotten, and it won't always be. You know that. But you also know it calls to you. Can't you feel it?" Shelby's eyes flickered down at her hands then back to the dark eyes of the emperor. "Ah," he said as a smile crept over his lips. "You do."

For reasons she didn't want to accept, Shelby's heart pounded in her chest as she stood inches from the emperor. Like Alcibiades, there was something sensual in the connection to him. Years of intimacy in another life, even though Hadrian's heart would always be with the young man he loved and lost. There was more to it, though. She knew that now, standing together in this place. An understanding. A connection to something and someplace bigger than both of them. "It's pulling me, but I have a job to do. I have to get Eli home so I can have my own life back."

Hadrian's smile drifted away, and a hint of sadness took its place. "Our lives are never our own, my darling one. Do your job but let yourself find your home. Don't fight what you've always searched for." Holding her face in his hands, Hadrian kissed the corner of her mouth then stepped back into the gathering mist and was gone.

Shelby stared at the empty space where Hadrian had been a moment before and flexed her fingers. Her palms tugged with a gentle pressure as though reaching desperately for the ruins. "What the hell did he mean by that? Why can't ghosts ever say what they mean?" Shelby said shaking the trance out of her head.

Benny gently touched her arm and turned her to face him. "Bella," he asked taking her hands in his, "are you okay?"

Shelby nodded. "Hadrian. He said my sadness about Delphi brought him here. He loved this place and wanted me to remember that it won't always be forgotten."

"He came back here to tell you not to be sad? That's it?"

Shelby shrugged. "Something about doing my job and our lives are never our own." It wasn't a lie, but it wasn't the truth. The truth scared her if Hadrian was right, and she didn't want to say that part out loud. Not to Benny. Not to anyone. Maybe not saying it would make it go away, but if her lives had taught her anything, it was that there was no running away from destiny. It would reach out and drag you where it wanted you.

"Hadrian?" Eli asked, thoroughly confused.

"Still hung up on that?" Shelby snapped. Instantly, she regretted her stinging words with the hurt look on Eli's face. "Sorry. This place is just a bit...much for me."

Benny took over the explanation as Shelby turned to keep walking up the Sacred Way. She was saying no more about the incident with the emperor. "Shelby has memories like you do when she touches things. Several of them had to do with Hadrian in Rome and in Athens. Historically, Hadrian protected Delphi instead of looting it like other conquering Roman emperors did. Maybe all of those connections stirred up something in time and space between them."

"I'm starting to see why you wouldn't answer my questions. There are no straight answers, are there? Nothing is the same for any of us in all of this."

Benny nodded. "Now you're getting it."

* * *

Shelby pulled the wraps tighter around her shoulders and kept her hands well buried in them to hide the increasing swarm of blue sparks from the occasional passing local as the three of them wandered the streets of Kastri. The houses were huddled together as if they were afraid to get too close to the edge of the mountain. Maybe something innate in their builders remembered the fates of their ancestors who had been tossed from the heights on either side. Maybe it was fear of the earthquakes that plagued the village. Whatever the reason the buildings were so close together, it was making the search for the site of Apollo's temple hell on the Watchers. Eli was, of course, useless, having no memory of ever being in Delphi before. All he could do was follow behind them. Once in a while, he would wince, and a hand would drift to the half-healed wound in his side that Apollo had apparently left him with out of spite.

"How are we going to find the temple?" Shelby asked Benny as they walked slowly through the streets. "Sure, there's a few walls jutting out of the ground here and there, but it's hard to tell what they used to be. There's no outline of the place, much less the spectacular temple from eons ago. Or last week, depending on who you are."

"Couldn't we just ask someone?" Eli asked.

Shelby shrugged. "And what would we ask? 'Excuse me, could you tell us where Apollo's temple is? He's invited us over, but we can't find the door.'"

"We could say we just want to see the site of the famous temple," he suggested.

Shelby looked around. "This isn't exactly a tourist destination. That might raise more questions than we need to be answering."

"Shelby's right. Probably best not to draw attention to ourselves." Benny's gaze went from searching the ground as though he could pull the ruins through the ground to give him a clue to the topography of the land around them. "If you look up at the mountains and not the buildings, everything looks the same. It's the town that makes it difficult to tell where we are."

Shelby scanned the landscape of the mountains around them. "You're right. If the town wasn't here, I could almost see the ruins from our first trip in my head. The town throws my bearings off. Damn it. I wish the temple would just show up like Hadrian did." Shelby's mind spun for a second. Surely, it couldn't be that easy. Nothing was easy with the gods. "Stop for a minute," she said quietly. "Let me try something. Hadrian said I had more control over things than I realized. Maybe there's a way for me to see where we should be going."

"What are you going to do, bella?" Benny asked. His dark eyes held traces of his jealousy over Hadrian in them.

"Nothing. Just let everything fade away."

Eli still had no idea what had happened with Hadrian and took her words entirely the wrong way. "You're giving up? We came all this way, I almost *died*, and now you're just going to do nothing?"

"No, not like that," she said rolling her eyes at him. He may be less slimy as the genteel Brit, but he was less sharp, too. She missed the old Alcibiades, wandering hands and all. "The land is the same. The town is in the way of us knowing where the temple is. If I can clear the town out of my head, I may be able to see the temple."

"I don't see how," Benny said, "but it's worth a try. We can't just keep wandering around like this."

Shelby nodded and turned slowly in a circle taking in the details of the rise and fall of the massive hills and deep valley before closing her eyes and standing completely still. Darkness. Just the inside of her eyelids. Nothing helpful at all. Then, her mind walked back through the landscape she had just seen, town and all. Frustration began to build as she struggled to remove the buildings from the landscape in the mental image. *Damn you, Apollo. You could've made this a little easier. 'Bring him to Delphi' you said. Well, here we are, asshole. Now what?* Shelby's thoughts swirled as she cursed the god imagining his smirking face as if this was all a game to him.

"You're almost there, Shelby," Apollo's rich voice said from the recesses of her mind. "If you'd stop pouting for a minute, you'd see it."

Mentally eye-rolling the god, Shelby thought, *You could just make the damn thing appear. Or is that, like so many other things, beyond your ability?*

Apollo chuckled. "That's not the point and you know it. The question is not if it's beyond *my* ability but is it beyond *yours*. Can you see what you need to see? Can you find your destiny?"

Enigmatic prick.

"Shelby." Apollo seemed to be losing his patience as much as Shelby was. "Grow up for a minute and clear your mind. Find the temple."

Shelby would much prefer petulant pouting to doing anything Apollo wanted, but since she had a life to get back to, she reluctantly relented. Letting her mind settle, she focused on the landscape again. After a moment, Kastri began to fade, and Delphi took its place. Not the splendor of the temple city as they'd seen it last, but the ruins of their original visit. As the houses and shops shimmered out of view, the scattered stones of fallen treasuries and altars once again littered the paths as though an image of Delphi on vellum had been laid over the barren landscape. A few stray columns rose in clumps to mark the prominent buildings, including the one she was searching for. Not more than a hundred yards away from where she stood was the temple entrance. Now that she had her bearings, the houses once more appeared to overlap the ruins as landmarks.

"I know where to go," Shelby said aloud at last. Without waiting for the others, she set out in the direction of the columns before the mental image frayed too badly to be useful.

Benny glanced back at Eli. "Come on. It's time to get you to Apollo."

"How are we going to do that? There's no temple. There's no entrance."

"Shut him up, will you?" Shelby shot over her shoulder to Benny. "I need to think. I can't be bothered with details right now. First things first. Find the temple."

Benny gave Eli a warning look and picked up the pace in following Shelby who wove between the buildings with determined speed. All through the town were bits of walls or stones that could have been significant if there was only a way to tell what they were. It was as though the village of Kastri enveloped whatever was left of Delphi, both concealing and preserving the place.

Several turns through town later, she finally slowed her pace and came to a stop alongside a stretch of worn stones that resembled the ruins of a wall. Shelby's hands tugged ruthlessly toward the ground at her feet and the wall next to her. "It's here. I can feel it."

Eli looked pale and sweat beaded on his forehead. "I can, too." His voice was dry and barely above a whisper. "I can't do this." His wide pale blue eyes glistened in the fading light as tears threatened to splash down his drawn cheeks. "I can't, Shelby. I can't do this."

"You don't have a choice." Her words were harsh, but she tried to say them in the nicest way she could, which at this point was a weak effort. She'd been through too much and given up too many lives to let this pansy man wimp out on her now. "Look, I know this is scary. I get it. But you need to understand something. When the Universe has a bone to pick with you, it doesn't stop 'til it gets what it wants. You can turn around and run away, or you can face your destiny like a man. But let me make one thing very clear," Shelby said an inch away from his face, "if you run and the Universe doesn't stop you, you can be damn sure I'll be on your heels to drag your ass back here myself."

Benny cleared his throat. "Bella," he began gently, "I don't think that's really the right tactic to take. Maybe some reassurance?"

Shelby sighed and cast an exasperated look to the heavens. "Fine. Apollo's a dipshit and full of himself, but he's not a bad guy. And his Oracle Dina is a good friend of mine. You'll like her. She's gorgeous." Benny nodded in support but got a withering look from Shelby for his efforts. "I have no idea what he has in store for you, but whatever it is, you'll be fine. If he wanted you dead, he could have done that in the first life you had. There's a reason you've lived all these lives, and the answer is inside the temple. So, we can stand around here talking about the inevitable, or you can help me figure out how to get inside and get this over with."

Benny glanced over his shoulder as footsteps approached. It was just a local going about some evening business, but it was enough to raise concern. "Bella, I'm not sure we should be doing this right now. We could be seen and that could get messy. Maybe this is something best left until dark?"

Shelby struggled with wanting to punch Benny in the face for making her put off getting Eli back to Apollo and wanting to be grateful for him being the only one with a level head on his shoulders. "Alright," she conceded. "You win. It'll give us time to figure out how to get inside."

"Maybe there's somewhere we can get a drink? Do you want a drink? I feel like I need a drink," Eli said verging on babble.

"I feel like I need all the drinks," Shelby said. "Come on, then."

CHAPTER 32

An hour and a half later found the Watchers and Traveler in the corner of a small pub with a few locals who were winding down conversations peppered with curious glances at the newcomers. Since it would be decades before tourists were frequent, visitors were regarded as things to be both inquisitive about and cautious of. There was nothing fancy about the place, except for one gilt mirror that hung over the simply carved wooden bar. It seemed garish and out of place in the modest establishment until Shelby realized that it was angled to allow the pub owner to keep an eye on the door and the till while he went to whatever the back rooms were. She had to hand it to the guy, that was a pretty smart security system.

A look and a raise of her eyebrow was enough to get another glass of wine headed her way from the bartender. Benny waved him and his offer of another drink off and shot a glance at Shelby to slow down on the alcohol. The look he received in return was clearly defiant. Eli was on his third drink but was quickly being drunk under the table by Shelby who had a better handle on red wine than she had on her own life. "You're not going to be in much shape for your usual rounds with Apollo if you keep this up, bella," Benny said trying to change his approach.

"Apollo can go to hell," she snapped. "Well, maybe he can't technically. I don't know how that works." She held up a hand to stop the history lesson she could feel coming from Benny. "Nope, don't really care where he goes as long as he takes Eli with him," she said and tossed back half a glass of wine.

"What if I don't want to go?" Eli asked.

"We've been over this already, Eli," Shelby said. "That name. It just doesn't feel right. That's a name in an old book, not the man we've been chasing all this time. Can't we just call you by your Greek name?"

Benny stole a glance around him. "I wouldn't. Not in Greece. The people here aren't exactly part of Alcibiades' fan club. He was a traitor, remember?"

"Shit. I forgot." Shelby swirled the red liquid around in her class watching the candlelight from the small votive on the table dance in the ripples. "Look, Eli, Al, whatever the hell your name is. You're going to do whatever Apollo tells you to do. Whatever it is, you've earned it, like it or not. Even if you haven't earned it in this life, you've earned it plenty in the past. And I'm sick of chasing your ass all over kingdom come. I'd much rather be spending my time sleeping with him," she said with a jerk of her dark head to Benny, "than being thrown into battles with *you*."

Her words, along with her inhibition, were getting loose and Benny's concern was plastered plainly across his face. "Then let's get this over with before you pass out or end up slapping Apollo across the face."

"Hell, I'd do that straight sober," Shelby said and swigged the end of her wine. "But, fine, let's go."

Benny set some money from Shelby's pouch on the table to cover the tab and led the two weaving drunks out into the street. The air hit them like cold knives. "Maybe the night air will sober you up some before you face the god."

"Wait!" Shelby said, stopping her feet a few seconds before her body found its balance.

"What?" Benny asked.

"We have to go back in there," Shelby said, turning on her heel.

"Oh, no you don't!" Benny snapped, tugging her elbow and steering her back in the direction of the temple.

"But we didn't figure out how to open the entrance. We forgot to do that. We have to go back in there."

She was right, but definitely didn't need any more to drink. Benny shook his head. "We can talk as we walk."

"But," Eli chimed in, "it's just over there. That doesn't give us much time."

"Then, we'll walk some laps 'til we figure it out. You could use the time to sober the hell up."

Eli frowned. "I was really counting on going into this thing a couple of sheets to the wind. Liquid courage and all that."

"I'm not so worried about you. Shelby'll end up firing off at the mouth and get us all turned into something ridiculous."

"Apollo can do that?" Eli asked like a fascinated child.

Benny dropped his head in frustration. "Of all the times to be the designated driver. Now I need a drink."

Shelby grinned. "I know this great little place…"

The Roman rolled his eyes and groaned.

Eli blinked down at his hands through a fog of inebriation. He turned them over and flexed his fingers, then rubbed them together. "My hands hurt. Why do my hands hurt?"

Shelby wrinkled her nose and wiggled her fingers, too. "So do mine."

Benny snorted. "You mean all that booze didn't numb you?" Rolling his eyes, he pulled a small leather pouch from his coat. "Here, hold out your hands. I was afraid this could take longer than the first times, so I filled this with water while you were busy being bitchy to Eli at the spring."

Obediently, for the first time in probably ever, Shelby held her hands out and let Benny pour water over them. At first, it was warm from being in his coat, but soon the icy air made it almost unbearably cold. Sparks danced along her fingertips as the water threaded between them. "Take a sip of it. Seemed to help clear your head the first time." Next was Eli who first held out his hands with his gloves on. "You might want to take those off," Benny said with a grin at the tipsy Brit. "Unless your gloves are burning and not your actual hands."

"Oh," Eli said with a sheepish grin as he tugged the gloves off. "Sorry. Wasn't thinking."

"It's okay," Benny said as he dribbled water over Eli's hands then handed him to the pouch to drink. "It's a lot to take in, sober or not."

Having gotten the stinging pain under control once more, the Watchers and Traveler continued their weaving walk to the spot in the middle of the street where the temple entrance was. Given their condition, neither Shelby nor Eli were much help figuring out how to open the temple from this side of the mounds of dirt and time on top of it.

"Maybe we need a shovel," Eli suggested.

"Or a bulldozer," added Shelby.

"A what?" the confused Victorian asked.

Benny shook his head. "Hasn't been invented yet. And a shovel would take too long."

"Pickaxe?"

"Trowel?"

"Hoe?"

"Spade?"

"Now you're just naming garden tools," Benny said exasperated.

"Well," Shelby said crossing her arm over her chest. "If you don't like our ideas, we'll just stop giving you any." With a toss of her head, she turned to stomp off like a sassy toddler but tripped over her own petticoat. Before she landed on her face, Shelby's hands hit flat on the road, breaking her fall. As they made contact with the dirt, the ground around them began to tremble.

"Shit, another earthquake. That's *all* we need!" Benny grumbled.

"No," Shelby said. "It's *exactly* what we need! Look!" Her voice was hollow as time around them stood still. Candle flames in windows stood still. Nothing flickered even as the ground rumbled. No plaster cracked. No rocks fell. No locals panicked. This was no ordinary quake. "It's opening the temple!" A fissure streaked from her sparking hands and opened the ground in front of her revealing the layers of stone that formed the inner sanctum of Apollo's temple. As the first time, there were no steps to lead them down, only jutting stones and footholds.

Eli stood looking into the pit with his mouth dropped open. "I don't understand."

"Trust me, things only get weirder from here," Shelby said as she pulled her hands away from the edge of the sinkhole. "Follow Benny. Put your hands and feet where he does. It's stone at the bottom of this thing and it won't feel good to go falling a couple stories down on it." Shelby stayed behind Eli to make sure he didn't decide to double-back on them as they made the descent.

The three of them descended slowly followed by loose pebbles and drifting dirt until their feet finally found the floor in the darkness. One by one, torches on the walls sprang to life illuminating the stones surrounding them. Scraping sounds echoed as the ceiling closed over them.

Eli began to panic. "We're trapped! He's sealed us in!"

"He doesn't need the stones to keep you in here, Eli," Shelby said dryly. "He's a god, for crying out loud. Not a great one, but still a god."

"She's right," said a gentle voice from the shadows. "Although I disagree with her on her appraisal of Apollo."

"Dina!" Shelby squealed as the Pythia stepped into the light.

Eli's blue eyes traveled over her. "Shelby was right," he whispered.

Benny chuckled. "Well, I see your eye for gorgeous women hasn't changed in this lifetime."

"Will you two stop ogling the oracle, please?" snapped Shelby.

"We could always ogle *you*," Benny teased.

"Or we could get to the reason you're here," said a sonorous voice from the far corner.

Shelby turned to see Apollo leaning a shoulder against the stone wall, badly veiling his amusement with a look of irritation. "You're right," she said. "That's much better than the frat boy stare fest we've got going on over here."

The god laughed. "Finally, we agree on something, Shelby."

"Don't let it go to your gorgeous head, Apollo."

"Shit," Eli whispered as the wind went out of him in a wracking cough. Recovering himself after a moment, he asked Dina, "Do I bow or something?"

The oracle's laugh put him more at ease. "Nonsense. You two go way back. No need for formalities. Of course," she said smiling at the Traveler, "you don't remember any of that."

"But *I* do," Apollo said losing his mirth for the moment. "You've been a thorn in my side for a while now, Alcibiades."

Eli stiffened. "I don't know why, but it sounds like an insult when you say the name like that."

"Perceptive in this life, I see," Apollo said coming to the center of the room to get a good look at his nemesis. "Not sure I like this incarnation of you. I prefer the other ones."

"Me, too!" Shelby chimed in. "I said the same thing! There. That's two things we agree on."

Benny chuckled. "That's got to be some kind of record." Dina grinned at him, nearly melting the Roman where he stood.

"I'd imagine the third would be getting Alcibiades to his destiny," Apollo said.

"Yep. And us back to our lives."

"One thing at a time."

Shelby wasn't sure she liked the sound of that. Something about it smacked of dodging his promise. Rather than piss Apollo off when she needed him, she decided to follow his train of thought to its inevitable derailment about the time he had to keep his word to her. "And how do we do that?"

"You got him this far," Apollo said to his Watcher, "but the rest is up to him. He has to face his destiny, which means facing the music."

"Punishment? You brought me here to *punish* me?" Eli asked, his blue eyes torn between blazing anger and terror of the power of the god.

"Well, I can't very well let you off the hook after all you've done. You've single-handedly caused more damage over the eons than anyone else I know."

"Then, why not punish me in those lifetimes? I haven't done anything wrong in this one!" Eli insisted.

"Yet." The word fell heavy on the ears of the Traveler.

Dina walked forward to play her usual part of peacemaker between the god and mortals. "Eli, it's not that he didn't want to dole out consequences in those lifetimes. It's more that you kept dying before he could."

Eli turned a dumbstruck expression on the oracle. "Death wasn't punishment enough?"

"In the cosmic grand scheme of things, no."

Apollo's face set firmly. A muscle in his jaw tensed and relaxed. "Your measly life can hardly serve as the price paid for the hundreds slain because of you and the chaos that has ensued in your traitorous wake. No, hardly punishment enough."

"Can't you give me a chance to prove myself in *this* lifetime? There must be some way I can make things right!" Eli was clearly starting to panic. Who could blame him, really? A Greek god had just mentioned punishing him and the oracle supported it. This wasn't going well at all for the passive Victorian.

Dina's hands rested on his shoulders as she looked him in the eye. Her beautiful face softened to ease his fear. "Eli, it's a risk we can't take. What you do in this life is catastrophic. Consequences beyond anything you could imagine. Ripples of your choice will cause destruction on a global scale."

Color drained from his face as his knees gave out leaving him in a pale heap on the stone floor. Shelby knelt beside him taking his hands in hers. Eli snatched them away and scrambled backwards away from her in fear. "You! You brought me here! This is *your* doing!"

His words weren't wrong, and they cut deep, even if the Traveler had missed the point completely. "You're right," Shelby said slowly. Her eyes dropped to the floor ashamed of her own tunnel vision. "I was so intent on getting my own life back, I didn't think about what the cost was. Reading your diary on my journey, you became a friend to me. Someone who understood the strange existence of being a Traveler. A twin soul on a common path. Then, when I met you as Alcibiades, you were both irritating and almost irresistible."

"Excuse me?" Benny asked insulted.

Shelby shrugged and blushed. "*Almost*. Irritating won out in the end," she said sheepishly. While it was true, she left out the part about what would have likely happened if Benny hadn't been there. Alcibiades was magnetic. Eli, however, was easy to resist only because he seemed more like a genteel brother than a soldier radiating masculine heat. She knew his thoughts through his journal, his fears. Alcibiades had been pure shallow sexual tension.

"But you brought me here," Eli said still trying to grapple with what Shelby was trying to say. "*Me*, not the irritating one. I have done nothing to deserve this. Not in this life, yet you've brought me here to face the punishment of a god with a chip on his shoulder. How could you do this to me?"

"Eli, your lives have taught you to be strong in battle. To find the solutions in the chaos to protect yourself," Shelby said quietly. "I know you can handle this. You've been groomed for it for centuries. If there's one thing this mess has taught me, it's that you can't escape your fate. It *will* find you. It *will* get what it wants. Not coming here to face your destiny would only delay the inevitable." Eli opened his mouth to protest again, but Shelby held up a hand to stop him. "And, if what Dina says is true, and she's the freaking oracle, so I'm going to put my money on it being true, then not facing the consequences now could only make things worse. And not just for you. For the entire world. Eli. Please. You can't run from this, but you can face it like the warrior you've always been."

Eli's expression fluctuated from dismay and disgust before finally settling on resolute. "I can't be responsible for doing what Dina says I will."

"Finally, something noble from the great Alcibiades," Apollo said with a smirk.

Eli glared at the god for an instant before turning a pleading look toward the Pythia. "It can't be changed? It can't be rewritten like my death in the diary?"

Dina shook her head. "I wish it could, but, no, it can't. This is bigger than just sparing your life. This is universal orchestration on a monumental scale. The threads couldn't be untangled in time."

Eli's face sank. "Tell me."

"What?" asked Dina.

"Tell me what I was going to do. What was so terrible that you both decided I have to die. I'm a dead man, so what's the harm in telling me now?" His eyes searched the face of the oracle. He had no use for the judge and jury that was Apollo.

Dina closed her eyes as she searched the future and myriad of visions that must have swirled through her mind. Finally, she sighed and said, "There will be a meeting of world powers. The Congress of Berlin. You will sabotage it and give too much power to the Russians and Ottomans."

"Jesus, Alcibiades," Shelby said. "What *is* it with you and the freaking Turks?"

"Shit," Benny cursed from a darkened corner of the room. "Dina's right. That would be a disaster."

"But I don't have anything to do with that kind of political power. I have friends in high places, but I don't get involved," Eli said trying to plead his case to Dina.

She shook her head sadly. "I wish that remained true. It wasn't a choice that was going to be easy for you to make, but it *is* the choice you go with."

Eli turned his confusion to Benny. "I can't be the only one involved in making that decision. Why is it bad enough to execute *me*? And *only* me?"

"Look," Benny began, "I'm not saying anything about the sentence passed by the gods, but I can tell you that if you are allowed to do that, it would escalate tensions and shift power in a way that would make World War I catastrophic. A global disaster. Dina's right."

"World War I? That means there's more than one of them," Eli said focusing on entirely the wrong thing.

"Not if you are allowed to go back to your life," Apollo said. "You'd destroy everything in one shot. There would be no need for the second one."

"Why would you want there to be more than one World War? Seems like one would be better," Eli said still trying to rationalize his fate.

"Not if that one war ended humanity as we know it," Shelby said.

"Then, it's an easy fix. Just don't let me go to the conference."

Apollo laughed. "Perhaps we should let you relive a few of your lives where you managed to destroy things perfectly well without actually being anywhere near where the events themselves happened. No, you have to be stopped a bit more permanently than that." Apollo strolled casually to the center of the room with an odd thoughtful look on his face. "It's interesting that you think you're being condemned to die, though." The god smirked at the Traveler. "I never said that. In fact, I said it wouldn't do as punishment."

"Torture, then?" Eli asked apprehensively.

Shelby laughed at that. The thought of Apollo, the great lover of humans, torturing someone seemed as ridiculous as Eli being a hot Greek general. "What would you do to torment him, Apollo? Play your lute at him until he cut his own ears off?"

The god glowered at Shelby for stealing his power moment, then went on, "No." Then to Dina, "Remind me to find less bitchy Watchers from now on." Dina chuckled. "Death just gives you a new life to ruin. The only way to keep you from fucking things up is to keep you where I can see you."

Shelby was struggling between being amused at Apollo losing his cool and his refined language and putting together what it was he was actually trying to sentence Eli to. "So, not killing him, then?"

"And Watchers a little quicker on the uptake," Apollo tossed over his shoulder to the oracle. "Keep up, will you, Shelby? I'm not sentencing him to death or eternal damnation. I'm sentencing him to eternal life. Here. In the temple." He turned back to the perplexed Victorian. "You see, if I let you out of my sight, you'll screw things up. If I keep you here, I'll always know what you're doing. So, your sentence, my traitorous, womanizing friend, is to be a priest of the temple of Delphi."

CHAPTER 33

Silence enveloped Eli as the sentence settled over him. The weight of it must have been suffocating. Shelby could only imagine the warring emotions inside of Eli that his own British restraint wouldn't allow to surface. Relief at not being killed for something he did in past lives or hadn't even done yet tempered with what was essentially being condemned to solitary confinement for eternity. Was one really better than the other for a man like him, Shelby wondered.

The infamous fight of Alcibiades had gone out of him, even the faint shadow of it that he had in this prim existence as Elijah Faircloth. The fair-featured man in the center of the temple room moved mechanically as the purification rites began. He seemed mentally and emotionally far away as the blocks of stone slid back to reveal the doorway where the priests and female attendants emerged with incense burners, folded white cloth held out on the arms of one of the women, and bowls of herbed cleansing water shimmering with droplets of oil in the torchlight. The ceremony circled around him and even involved him as he was stripped and bathed before being ceremoniously dressed in the white garments of the priests. Still, he was silent.

The reverent hum of the priests' songs rose and fell. The water splashed gently back into bowls as the women washed his body. The stone floor rumbled as the crevice opened to reveal the gate between worlds. Between lives. Yet, none of these sounds brought utterance from the stalwart Brit. Dina stood at the abyss and inhaled deeply letting the vapors take her into her trance as she revealed a new future for the great traitor as a priest of the god Apollo. Everything about the ceremony made it seem like a great honor. Some gift of mercy and position. Shelby and Benny saw it for what it really was. Slavery. And, by his silence and expression, so did Eli.

Apollo was talking, even though Eli wasn't listening. "Your task is one that has been revered for eons. You will guard the temple, perform the rituals of the gods, but, most importantly, you will guard the gateway to space and time. You will be marked as my priest and will no longer traverse the great expanse of the universe. The gateway will hold nothing for you but a sense of duty."

Shelby wasn't entirely certain, but she thought she saw a flicker of Eli's eyelid. The slightest twitch at the thought of the gateway being useless. Of being trapped. It was almost imperceptible, but she could feel something miniscule change in the way Eli held the set of his jaw. She'd seen it before. Alcibiades was up to something, but what? What could he do in the presence of a god carrying out his condemnation? Benny must have noticed it, too, because his hand slid into hers. Not in a trying to make her feel better about her friend's fate or loving way, but one of expectation and warning. How had Dina and Apollo not seen it? Could it be that in thousands of years watching him, they had never truly *watched* him?

Apollo droned on oblivious, which seemed weird for someone thought to be omnipotent. "Your purification has purged you of anything from this life or past ones that could hamper your duty as a priest of the Temple of Delphi. Now, your vow will seal you to your new life and bind you to me. Come forward." Apollo motioned Alcibiades to the edge of the crevice in the floor. "Breathe deeply." Shelby knew what happened to her when she did that. Visions flooded her and reality slipped away. Like some sort of historical acid trip. Apollo must know that someone would have to be pretty strung out to commit to an eternity of temple servitude.

As Alcibiades closed his eyes and inhaled the sweet vapors rising from the opening in the earth, his face relaxed and his body seemed to loosen some. The mechanical tension was gone. Fluidity replaced it. Dina held her arms out to steady him. One of Eli's hands curled into hers for support as the vapors pulled him into the mist of the visions in his mind. As the Watchers looked on, a grin began to flicker across the Traveler's face.

"There can't be anything that amusing about visions of a future as a priest," Shelby whispered to Benny.

The Roman shook his head as Dina and Apollo remained too completely consumed with their ceremony to notice. "He's up to something, but what?"

As if in answer to the question he couldn't have heard across the room over the rising minor chords of the priests' song, Alcibiades opened his eyes and locked his on Shelby's. His grin widened as his blue eyes sparkled in the torch light. Then, in one fluid motion, he winked at her, crushed Dina's hand in his, and pushed off of the stone floor in a swan dive into the abyss. White sparks shot out of the huge crack as the surface of the expanse shimmered and absorbed the wayward Greek and the oracle. Apollo stared dumbstruck into the white light, then turned and roared in anger. The priests silenced their song and motioned for the women to go back through the door out of the path of the raging immortal.

Shelby covered her mouth with trembling hands to stifle the shriek that fought to escape the prison of her lips. Benny's eyes flashed from Shelby to Apollo waiting on one of them to explain what happened or do something about it.

A few terrifying moments passed as Apollo cursed every cell of Alcibiades' human body and every star fragment of his cosmic soul. Shelby and Benny stayed in the shadows to keep from becoming inadvertent targets of his wrath until the god's tantrum finally ebbed, but tears glistened on his perfect eyelashes. Not tears of fury but tears of loss. The loss of his oracle. His love.

"I-I don't understand what just happened," Shelby stammered in a whisper.

"Straight answer, Apollo," Benny said more firmly than he'd ever spoken to the god before.

Apollo paced and ran his fingers through dark curls as he tried to recover his composure. "I didn't need the ceremony to hold Alcibiades. Just the branding of him which I could have done at any time in all this. The ceremony was to make a point. To make Alcibiades feel insignificant in the presence of my power as the god here. While I thought it was making Alcibiades feel small and in need of my protection, all it did was give the bastard time to think. And make a decision. Alcibiades apparently decided to take his chances on time and space rather than an eternity of servitude to me. Taking Dina was just for spite."

"Or because he never could resist taking a beautiful woman. That dick move wasn't necessarily all about you." Shelby sighed with exhaustion and frustration. "So, where did he go?" Apollo shrugged. "Wait, you don't know? He's gone off half-cocked into that portal and you don't know where or when?"

Shelby's words were louder than she intended, and Apollo swung around to face her. His feet were planted, and jaw set as he said through gritted teeth. "The arrows send the Travelers where I want them to go. No arrows, no direction."

"So, he and Dina just vanished into time and space?" Shelby asked. "To some unknown place and god only knows when?"

"No, bella, I think that's entirely the point. God *doesn't* know when," Benny answered more brazenly smug than he'd ever been with Apollo before. "At least not *this* god."

Apollo slammed his fists into the temple walls. Dust rained down from the stones overhead as the god once more fought for composure. As the dust settled, the walls seemed to shimmer. Only for a moment. Apollo was too absorbed in his own fury and grief to notice. Benny glanced at Shelby and tossed a look at the stones that seemed to be becoming almost opaque.

Shelby shook off the change in the temple walls and mentally blamed it on the vapors that Dina left running. She took a few tentative steps toward the heartbroken god, not quite to the point of feeling bad for him, but not as angry now that the god had finally felt the sting of the Universe's whims. "Apollo, there's nothing to be done about it now but figure out how to fix it. How to get them back."

"And how exactly do I do that when I don't know where he went?" Apollo snapped. "It's not like I'm connected to him..." His words trailed off as his dark eyes met Shelby's. "Like his Watcher is."

Shelby didn't know what Apollo was rambling about but didn't like wherever this crazy train was headed. Pushing herself away from the shimmering stone wall that steadied her during the god's hissy fit, she crossed the floor in long confident strides. Whatever sympathy might have been building in her vanished. "No. We're done. We brought him to you. We did our job. You promised. You *owe* us!" Shelby stopped her advance inches from the god's face. "Release us from this idiotic mess. We didn't make it! You did! We did what we were sent to do!"

Apollo's gaze held steady. "Yes, you brought him to Delphi, but that doesn't mean your destiny is complete. It just means you brought him to Delphi."

"You've got to be fucking *kidding* me!" Shelby roared. Her voice echoed off the fading stone around her and hung in the dusty air.

Benny, ever the rational one, picked up where Shelby's words fell into a stream of consciousness rant with every profanity she'd ever heard peppered with a few he was sure she'd made up. "You sent us to find him and bring him to you. We did that."

"I know you did, Benny," Apollo said steadily. "And, believe me, nothing would make me happier than releasing this American harpy from her destiny, but it's not up to me. She still has more to do."

"What could that *possibly* be?" Shelby growled, breaking off from her ranting about Apollo's miniscule manhood hiding under his toga.

Apollo's head rested in his hands; fingers threaded through curls as he sat on the stool. "Connection."

"I don't follow, and if you make one more crack about a dimwitted Watcher, I'll find a way out of this stone prison even if I have to go the way Alcibiades went," Shelby snapped.

"You're connected to him. You can feel his life end. You can find him when I can't. I can't give you your life back yet. Not while he's out there somewhere. Not while he has Dina. I-" The next words were clearly difficult for Apollo's ego to utter, "I need you."

Shelby's fury raged. The skin in her cheeks burned and her hands shook as she clenched her sparking stinging fingers into fists she really wanted to lodge in the perfectly straight bridge of Apollo's nose. "You *need* me? *You*? Who cares about you? What about me? *Us*?" she shouted grabbing Benny's hand and dragging him in front of the god. If Apollo was going to have to answer for his decision, he was going to have to face both of the Watchers.

"You're the only one who can find him - who can stop him. I need you. If he finds his way back to that conference..."

"Bella," Benny began with words like feathers falling on thin ice, "We can't let that happen. I'm telling you, it's one of the things that could shake humanity to its core. To the ground. Our life together can wait a little longer. We might not have one at all if Alcibiades manages to succeed."

The thunderstorm in her eyes began to calm as Benny held her face in his hands. His eyes softened and he kissed her. Gently at first on the corner of her mouth, then wrapping her in his arms, he kissed her like he was going to lose her forever. Reluctantly giving the Watchers their moment, Apollo waited with an expression of apprehension as Shelby was finally released from Benny's embrace.

"I love you, bella," Benny whispered. "But you have a job to do that's bigger than all of us. Even Apollo. I will always love you and need you. Maybe our life together wasn't meant to be a little house and picket fence. Something tells me you'd get tired of that pretty fast. You've tasted adventure and adrenaline. It's hard to be a suburbanite after that. You're more than that. You're a Watcher."

Shelby's eyes glistened in the torchlight. Tears streamed down her face. "But I'm a tired Watcher. Tired of being thrust into the wrinkles of space and time never knowing what is coming next. Never knowing if we will survive it. I just want to be back in that hotel room in Paris curled up in your arms."

Benny chuckled. "I know you do. And so do I. But we wouldn't be there forever. Eventually, we'd have to go to work, live normal lives, go to the grocery store, clean bathrooms. Come on, bella. Does that really sound like you?"

No. No, it didn't. Not one little bit. Shelby sighed heavily as the weight of the world found its way to her shoulders along with her decision. "Fine. You win. I'm not destined to be a domestic goddess. I'm destined to do the bidding of a god."

"Not quite," Apollo said. "Not my 'bidding'. This, like everything else, has to be your choice. I can't force you into anything."

"Before I take this job, you're going to need to give me some details. Yeah, I'm connected to Alcibiades, but that doesn't tell me anything about what you want me to actually do. I've already been all over the world and through time bringing his ass back here. In case you missed it, that didn't end well. So, your Sexy Godness, now what?"

"We're going to need to know where he is and what he's doing."

"We?" Shelby asked. "Who is this 'we' you're talking about? The three of us?" Shelby asked glancing around the room at Benny and back at Apollo. The walls seemed to become more sheer as they argued, but there was no time to ask questions about fading ancient buildings while her fate was being decided.

"No. As you've so eloquently pointed out, things didn't exactly work out when I tried to contain Alcibiades alone. It's going to take more gods than me and Seshat."

"You're calling in back-up?" Shelby asked incredulously.

Apollo grinned sheepishly. "You could say that."

Benny's brow furrowed as he tried to put the puzzle together. "Where does Shelby come in?"

"Not just Shelby. As always, she works in tandem with you. Her fire needs tempering sometimes to focus her vision, and no one does that better than you. You'll be with her every step of the way again. But," Apollo said slowly, "there is one part of this only she can do. She's been given the gift of visions. Her memories. Using that gift and magnifying it, she can be a conduit between the world and the gods who will be working to untangle the life threads Alcibiades puts knots in."

"A conduit? I don't understand. This all sounds a bit more like what Dina does than what I do," Shelby said cautiously.

Apollo nodded. "Exactly."

"Come again?"

"Shelby, in order for you to be the liaison to the gods, you're going to need to change what you are once more. No longer a Watcher, but an Oracle."

Shelby shook her head violently. "No. You're not sentencing me to a lifetime in this temple like you wanted to do to Alcibiades. I'm *not* doing that."

"And I wouldn't want you to," Apollo said gently. "Dina wasn't confined here. How do you think you met her in New York if she was? Think, Shelby. She's only here when I am."

She hadn't thought about that. "Oh."

"As my oracle, you'll be able to see what Alcibiades is doing and communicate that to me. And let me know that Dina is safe. As the gods undo his treachery, time, that is history, will change. You'll have to keep us informed of the changes so we know what to do next in trying to stay one step ahead of him until we can find a way to destroy him."

"Keep you informed? Like some kind of galactic spy?"

"Spies tend to get involved. You won't be involved, just reporting back."

"So, a galactic Walter Cronkite."

Benny cleared his throat. "You've met Shelby, right? What makes you think she's not going to get involved?"

Apollo grinned. "That's why you're going with her."

Benny shook his dark head and wrapped his arm around Shelby's waist. "I might be able to persuade her once in a while, but I can't control her. I wouldn't even if I could."

"*I* can't control her," Apollo said sardonically, "so how could I expect *you* to? No, just be her level head when she wants to go messing with things that are above her pay grade."

Expectation hung in the air as Benny and Apollo waited on Shelby's answer. The bitch in her wanted to let them dangle for a while, but she couldn't do that to Benny. And time wasn't on Dina's side in the hands of Alcibiades. Apollo, sure, he deserved to be left hanging, but not the others. "Alright. I'll go after him and be your eyes and ears." Apollo looked visibly relieved, and Benny nodded at her. "Is there some elaborate ceremony again, or what? Alcibiades has a head start. Let's get this shit show on the road."

Apollo shook his head solemnly. "No," he said. "No ceremony. Wouldn't want to give you time to reconsider and go leaping into the abyss half-cocked, as you said. We'll keep it simple this time." Apollo took Shelby's hands in his and walked her to the chasm. "Breathe."

Once more visions filled her mind as the vapors filled her lungs. Chaotic and rapid-fire. Overlapping and cloudy. Apollo turned Shelby's hand over in his cupping the back of her hand in his palm, leaving her wrist up and exposed. Around her finger, the silver serpent ring seemed to wriggle for a moment at the god's touch but settled back into the solid ring. With his finger, Apollo traced the simple images of a silver bow and golden arrow on her wrist. As he pulled his hands away and let hers drop, the images swirling through her mind began to organize into things she could control. Like turning pages in a book, she could look for what she wanted to see.

"Do you see them?" Apollo asked.

Shelby turned the pages but couldn't see any sign of the Greek or the oracle. She sighed and opened her eyes, letting them flutter over her new tattoo before bringing them to face Apollo. "No. I can't."

"To see what you seek, don't look with your eyes. Look with your soul. You're connected. Pull from deeper within to bring him to the surface."

Leave it to the enigmatic god to say something mystical. Shelby was going to have to get better at sounding cool like that if she was going to be half the oracle Dina was. It was worth a shot, though. She closed her eyes again and looked inside herself rather than at the visions that played across the inside of her eyelids. She didn't know what incarnation of Alcibiades to search for. Would he be the swarthy

Greek or the fair Brit? It dawned on her that his appearance wasn't what she was supposed to be looking for. Anyone could look like that. She had to feel him. Deeper and deeper into her own soul she fell. Then, it was there. The pull. Not an image, but a feeling of being tied to something trying to tug away from her into the dark depths. "I can feel him. I can't see him, but I can feel the pull of him."

"That's a start. And enough to send you on your way." Apollo's expression softened. "I'm proud of you, Shelby."

The words took the new oracle by surprise. If it had been snark or irritation, she wouldn't have batted an eye. Pride in her was not something she expected from Apollo. "Why?" was all she could say.

"It wasn't that long ago you were drunk on a Jamaican beach. Now, look at you. Strong, brave, and loving. All the things you've made a habit of running from. You were always made for this. You just refused to embrace it. And for finally letting the walls down and doing that, I'm proud of you."

Tears gathered at her eyelashes, hot and barely contained. "Thank you."

Apollo kissed her on the forehead and smiled down at her as a tear escaped and ran down her cheek. "I'll keep you safe as best I can, but that doesn't mean this will be an easy task. The rings will still work if you find yourselves in danger. Use them if you need to. You'll be able to find your way back to him."

"How do I communicate with you?" Shelby asked. "Is there some special thing I need to do, or are you just going to hover in the back of my mind?"

The god chuckled. "That may be entertaining, but hardly appropriate. Touch the tattoo. It connects us."

"Like some sort of transdermal cell phone?"

"I suppose so." Apollo smiled at her warmer than he ever had.

Shelby blinked back the tears and looked past the god to the walls behind him. The stone was nearly sheer. Through them were the mountains of Delphi. "What's happening to the temple?"

Apollo sighed. A sadness had settled over him replacing the pride. "Alcibiades' revenge. He's trying to erase history's memory of me. Of my temple. It appears to be working."

"Dina would never let that happen," Shelby insisted.

Solemn words were hollow as the god spoke them. "She may not have a choice."

"And, if he succeeds?" Benny asked.

Apollo lowered his eyes to the stone floor. Before he could answer, Shelby took his hands in hers. "He won't."

A shadow of a smile of appreciation flitted across the god's mouth before he glanced at Benny. "Are you ready?" Shelby and Benny nodded. Benny wound his fingers through Shelby's in a flood of blue sparks that traveled from their fingers and washed over their entire bodies. A blessing from Seshat.

Apollo raised his hands out in front of him like Dina had done before. As he did, Shelby and Benny lifted off the floor hovering inches above the stone. Pushing his palms forward, Apollo moved them over the crevice in the earth. "Bring her back to me, Shelby," he said barely above a whisper. Grief at the loss of his love made the words difficult. Shelby smiled and nodded as tears gathered in her eyes. Squaring his shoulders for the task at hand, the God of Light continued with more strength, "Follow what you seek. Search with your soul." Apollo set his perfect jaw in determination, but his eyes softened as he raised his hand in blessing before letting it drop, releasing Shelby and Benny into the portal. "The gods go with you, oracle."

THE END

ACKNOWLEDGEMENTS

There are so many people to thank with every book I write. Of course, my family, who supports this journey like crazy. My publisher who continues to take a chance on my adventures. My dear friends Laura Kemp and Rebekah Stephens who help keep me sane and cry or laugh with me when I need it. Each and every reader and reviewer who have shown my work love. Without them I'd just be talking to myself on paper. The list goes on, but I can hear the exit music playing, so, you know who you are. I love you and thank you all!

ABOUT THE AUTHOR

Originally from South Louisiana, Nola Nash now makes her home in Brentwood, Tennessee. She grew up in Baton Rouge, but her biggest writing inspiration was the city of New Orleans, which gave her a love of the magic, mystery, and history at an early age. When she isn't writing, Nola is an online high school instructional coach and podcast host on Dead Folks Tales, BYOB, and The Otherworlds for Authors on the Air Global Radio Network. She is the author of five books: *Crescent City Moon*, *Crescent City Sin*, *Traveler*, *Watcher*, and *House of Mirrors*.

OTHER TITLES BY NOLA NASH

NOTE FROM NOLA NASH

Word-of-mouth is crucial for any author to succeed. If you enjoyed *Watcher*, please leave a review online—anywhere you are able. Even if it's just a sentence or two. It would make all the difference and would be very much appreciated.

Thanks!
Nola Nash

We hope you enjoyed reading this title from:

BLACK ROSE writing™

www.blackrosewriting.com

Subscribe to our mailing list – *The Rosevine* – and receive **FREE** books, daily deals, and stay current with news about upcoming releases and our hottest authors.
Scan the QR code below to sign up.

Already a subscriber? Please accept a sincere thank you for being a fan of Black Rose Writing authors.

View other Black Rose Writing titles at www.blackrosewriting.com/books and use promo code **PRINT** to receive a **20% discount** when purchasing.

www.ingramcontent.com/pod-product-compliance
Lightning Source LLC
Chambersburg PA
CBHW030820210726

48290CB00002B/685